COLETTE

WORKS

Colette

THE OTHER ONE

THE
BLUE LANTERN

Original illustrations by Penny Carey
Frontispiece by Daniel Briffaud

HERON BOOKS LONDON

THE OTHER ONE has been translated from
the French *LA SECONDE* by
Elizabeth Tait and Roger Senhouse

THE BLUE LANTERN has been translated from
the French *LE FANAL BLEU* by
Roger Senhouse

———

CONTENTS

THE OTHER ONE

ONE

"The eleven o'clock postman brought nothing. If Farou didn't write last night before going to bed, it's because he'd had a late rehearsal."

"Do you think so, Fanny?"

"I'm certain. *No Woman about the House* isn't difficult to produce, but that little Asselin's not at all the right type for Suzanne."

"She's jolly pretty, all the same," said Jane.

Fanny shrugged her shoulders.

"My poor Jane, what point is there in her being pretty? The part of Suzanne never called for a pretty woman. What's wanted is a Cinderella like Dorilys. Didn't you see the original production?"

"No."

"Of course not, what a fool I am! That was nineteen nineteen!"

"The play doesn't date," said Jane.

Fanny turned on her an eye half veiled by a band of black hair.

"But it does, my dear. Like all plays, even Farou's. It's only Farou himself who doesn't date."

"So much the better for you!" said Jane.

"And, at this present moment, for little Asselin," was Fanny's conclusion.

She laughed good-humouredly and peeled a juicy peach.

With a tilt of the chin Jane drew her attention to little

Farou, who was busy picking up grains of sugar by pressing them on to his fingers before licking them off, and showed no sign of having heard.

"You do understand," Fanny Farou went on, "that Asselin has been given the part on tour because, after all, the tour includes Deauville, seaside resorts and casinos? On a Casino Tour, it's no small advantage to have, as Asselin has, cars, lovers, dresses, and a paid publicity agent; everything, in fact, that prevents a summer tour from being a complete fiasco. You do understand that, don't you, Jane, pale little Jane?"

"Yes, I do."

She looked pale and preoccupied, as happened most days of the week. For this she hurriedly apologised.

"I didn't sleep well, and then . . ."

Little Farou raised his blue eyes to her when she was least expecting it, and it was to him she automatically addressed her next words.

". . . and then I think there is a rat in the wainscot . . ."

"And a loose shutter, and an owl in the plane-tree, not to mention the wind whistling *w-h-o-o-o* under the door and the kitchen window going *clickety-clack*," Fanny enumerated. "Well, Jean, have I left any of them out?"

She laughed, and the others joined in.

"Jane, my love, do get it into your head that you're just as entitled to be sleepless as lethargic. It's hot, one must live and let live, and while Farou sweats and swears and curses, it's Asselin who's 'catching' it."

"I do admire . . ." Jane began, but once again she encountered little Farou's blue eyes—less blue in the blaze of noon—and she broke off.

"Little Farou, pass me the red currants, *please*."

He obeyed precipitately, his hand brushing against Jane's beneath the electro-plated wire basket. His fingers

12

recoiled with a convulsive movement akin to a spasm of disgust, and he blushed so violently that Fanny burst out laughing.

"There's still the one at four o'clock," Jane said after a moment's pause.

"The one . . . what, at four o'clock?" Fanny enquired, her mouth juicy with the peach she was eating whole.

"Post."

"Oh!" said Fanny, pushing up her band of hair with one finger, "I'd forgotten all about it. That one hardly ever brings anything from Paris. Do you want a drink, little Farou?"

"Yes. Please."

"Please, who?"

"Please, Mamie."

He blushed because he was fair, and because he found his stepmother a little too blunt. Then he relapsed into one of his youthful daydreams, when his outlandish name Farou fitted him like a wattled hut or a grass skirt. His face became expressionless. With eyebrows lowered and the clear line of his mouth half open, he harboured, behind his habitual stolid appearance, a secret eagerness, a sensitiveness tortured by a word or a laugh. He was sixteen.

The shade of a veranda encouraged them, for the midday meal, to drag the big table cleared of newspapers and pieces of needlework as far as the hall entrance. On evenings when Big Farou returned to the bosom of his family, four places were squeezed round the flaking iron pedestal table, which never left the terrace.

"I've eaten too much," sighed Fanny Farou, the first to rise.

"By way of a change," said Jane.

"That cream cheese! Oh, children!"

Languidly she made her way to the broad divan and stretched herself out on it. When lying down, she looked very pretty: pink and white skin, long black hair, prominent, gentle eyes and full, rounded mouth. The only feature she was proud of was her short nose, silvery white with rounded nostrils.

"Fanny Farou, you're getting fat," said Jane in a threatening tone, as she stood over her.

They exchanged a glance full of mischievous understanding. The one knew herself to be beautiful as she lay with her charming nose tilted upward, revealing the plump chin of a woman passionate and at the same time too easy-going: the other held erect a handsome figure betraying no sign of fleshiness, a head crowned with fair hair—if "fair" can be applied to the colour of fine ash— faintly golden at the nape and silvery at the temples. Impelled by genuine solicitude for Fanny's well-being, Jane bent over and plumped up a linen cushion behind her head and covered over her long lazy arms and bare ankles with stiff tulle net.

"There! And don't move, or the flies will get in under the net. Go to sleep, Fanny, you lazy, incorrigible, greedy creature—but not for more than half an hour!"

"What are you going to do, Jane, in this heat? . . . Where's Jean? Whilst the sun is so high, he shouldn't . . . I'll tell his father . . ."

Overcome by the sudden drowsiness that besets the greedy, Fanny's voice petered out into silence. Jane looked for a moment at the relaxed features, at their shape and southern colouring, before she stole away.

To the more rapid beat of her heart Fanny dreamt a dream, commonplace, incomprehensible. She saw the hall, the terrace, the waterless valley, the familiar inhabitants of the villa; but overhead a purplish stormcloud filled

14

animals and humans, the very landscape itself, with disquiet. A dream-Jane was standing under the veranda, gazing enquiringly at the empty path below the terrace, and she was in tears. Fanny woke with a start and sat up, pressing both hands upon her overladen stomach. In front of her, under the veranda, stood a very real Jane, motionless, idle. Reassured, Fanny wanted to call out to her; but Jane, letting her head drop, pressed her forehead against the window, and this slight movement detached from her eyelashes a tear which trickled down her cheek, sparkled on the downy edge of her lip, and dropped on to her bodice, where two fingers plucked it delicately and crushed it as if it had been a breadcrumb. Fanny lay back, closed her eyes, and fell asleep again.

"Mamie! The post!"

"What, it can't be four o'clock! How long have I been asleep? And why didn't Jane . . .? Where is Jane?"

"Here, on the ladder," replied the high-pitched, muted voice which Big Farou called "the angel voice".

Confused both by sleep and her dream, Fanny looked up in the air for Jane, as though looking for a bird, and Jean Farou, surprisingly for him, broke into laughter.

"What are you laughing at, you young owl? Would you believe it, but at the very moment you woke me I was dreaming that . . ."

But at last she became aware that a large white letter was dancing in front of her, held at arm's length by Jean, and she pounced on it eagerly.

"Off you go, errand-boy! No, after all, stay, my little Jean; it's a letter from our Farou to all of us, children!"

She read with one eye, the other covered by a riband of black hair. Her white dress had rucked up and was wrinkled tight across her chest, and she allowed all and sundry to gaze upon the vaguely untidy but guileless beauty that gave her a slight look of a creole, or as Farou said "a touch of George Sand". She raised her hand to command attention.

"*Judging by the rehearsals of yesterday and the day before,*" she read, "*I have every reason to believe that the touring company will be excellent, and* No Woman about the House *better acted than it was originally. Little Asselin*—Hi there, Jane!—*Little Asselin is surprising everyone, self included. We are working like angels. We're through with our rows, hysterics, fainting fits, and all that nonsense—and high time too. Oh, my poor Fanny, if women only knew what bores a man can find them when he has no desire to be the cause either of their tears or their happiness!*"

Fanny pushed back her lock of hair with one finger and pulled a comically scandalised face.

"Oh, I say, Jane, I say (Jean, clear off!), it looks to me very much as if poor Farou has, if I dare say so, sacrificed himself."

"It looks to me remarkably like it," Jane repeated after her.

She sat down on the divan beside her friend and with a gentle hand smoothed Fanny's hair and straightened the fine, bluish parting above the left eyebrow.

"What a mess you're in . . . your skirt's all scrumpled up. . . . I'm tired of that frock. Tomorrow I'll go into the town and bring you back a nice length of yellow or pale blue material, and by the time Farou gets back on Saturday, you'll have a new frock."

"Will you?" said Fanny, in an indifferent tone. "Will that be any help?"

They looked at one another, the prominent dark eyes with their thick lashes questioning the grey eyes of the fair-haired friend. Jane shook her head.

16

"Oh, I do admire you, Fanny. You really are exceptional."

"I? If so, the news would have spread."

"Yes, exceptional. You accept without demur, without resentment, and even without a hint of your own importance, that Farou has . . . sacrificed himself."

"Needs must," said Fanny. "And if I didn't accept it, what difference would it make? None at all."

"Yes, yes, but all the same I confess—yes—I confess . . ."

"That in my place you'd be finding things far from rosy?"

"That's not what I meant," said Jane, evading the issue.

She got up and went out on to the terrace to make sure that little Farou, who could vanish like a snowflake on a warm window pane, was not within earshot.

"Merely this, Fanny, I think that a man who belonged to me, and made me his wife . . . To learn that at this very moment that man is mucking about with some stage tart or other, and to conclude philosophically that 'he has sacrificed himself', that 'the job requires it', well, no, I admire you, but I could never do it!"

"Quite so, Jane. Fortunately no one is asking you to do it."

In a flash Jane was beside Fanny again, curled up at her feet.

"Fanny, you're not vexed with me, are you? There are days when I'm no good to anyone; I'm clumsy, bad tempered, unhappy. You know me so well, Fanny."

She rubbed her cheeks and little round ears against the white frock, feeling with her forehead for her friend's hand.

17

"You have such lovely hair, my little Jane," Fanny murmured.

Jane gave an affected laugh.

"You say that as if it might serve as an excuse!"

"Up to a point, Jane, up to a point. I can't be cross with a Jane who has such lovely hair. I can't scold Jean when his eyes are so very blue. As for you, you're sprinkled all over, hair, skin and eyes, with a fine silvery ash, with moon-dust, with . . ."

Jane looked up at her with a face suffused with annoyance and sudden tears, and exclaimed, "There is nothing lovely about me. I'm worthless! I deserve to be loathed, cropped, thrashed!"

She let her head fall back into Fanny's lap once more and broke into raucous sobs, whilst the first low rumblings of a thunderstorm faintly reverberated from peak to peak through the echoing foot hills.

"This is her crisis," thought Fanny tolerantly. "It's the thundery weather."

Already Jane was growing calm again, shrugging her shoulders to make fun of herself and discreetly blowing her nose.

'Yet,' Fanny noted, 'she said "stage tart" and "mucking about with". I've never before heard her use slang or vulgar expressions. Coming from her lips, extreme language is tantamount to physical violence. Physical violence in this weather! It's too much of a good thing.'

"What shall we do till dinner-time?"

Jane, still in her suppliant attitude at Fanny's feet, raised her head. "You wouldn't like to go into the town and have tea at the confectioner's? We could walk back."

"Oh!" Fanny's expression was one of horror.

"No? You're putting on weight, Fanny."

"I always put on weight when it's hot and I've more

than ten thousand francs in the bank. You know enough of our 'method of procedure' to realise that I don't often lack opportunities for losing weight."

"That's true. Would you like me to wash your hair? No, you wouldn't? Shall we squeeze the red and black currants left over from lunch? A handful of sugar, a drop or two of Kirsch, pour the juice over the sponge cake we had the day before yesterday and let it soak in thoroughly. We'll serve a little jug of fresh cream separately, and so have an entirely new sweet for tonight, with no cost at all."

"Rather boarding-house," said Fanny with distaste. "I don't care for resuscitated sweets."

"Just as you like, Fanny dear. May the Lord continue to preserve you from boarding-houses, where I certainly learned to use up all sorts of things."

The gentle tone of reproof seemed to tire Fanny who, putting a hand on Jane's shoulder, pulled herself to her feet.

"After all," she exclaimed, "fresh cream, currant juice . . . yes, that will do nicely! On one condition, Jane."

"I mistrust you."

"That you'll attend to this culinary treat yourself. Meanwhile I shall write a line to Farou. I'm going up-stairs to splash myself with cold water, and . . ."

"And?"

"And that's all. It's more than enough!"

When on her feet, she appeared to be smaller than when lying down. She was utterly without any sort of protective coquetry and rolled her fine hips with a slightly vulgar assurance. Jane followed her with her eyes.

"Fanny, when will you make up your mind to wear a girdle?"

"It's a question of temperature, my dear. At five degrees above freezing point, I put on a girdle. You've only to look at the thermometer. And see that the fresh cream doesn't turn sour before this evening. I'm so fond of it."

Jane had made up on her, and started to pull down the hem of her skirt, after deftly pinning up a strand of her long black hair.

"Off you go, you naughty Fanny, all will be well for this evening. I'll even try to get Jean in for dinner by banging a bowl as they do on farms before feeding corn to the hens. What a life you lead your friend!"

She gave a contented laugh and set about collecting faded petals off the table-cloth in the hollow of her hand, blowing away the crumbs, and emptying an ash-tray.

'My friend? . . . Yes, she is my friend. All the same, to say my friend is to say a good deal . . .' Fanny meditated as she made her way slowly up the stairs. 'Who else has ever shown me so much friendship? No one. So she is my friend, a real friend. It's queer that in my own mind I never call Jane my friend.'

No sooner was she alone in the room with its twin beds than she threw off her clothes. The topmost branches of the trees reached as high as the balcony and at night scratched against the closed shutters. For the last two years the neglectful landlord had omitted to have them clipped and the large open bay in the foliage was closing up again little by little. Well wooded and gently undulating, the whole place was imbued with the melancholy atmosphere of a waterless countryside. No river, the sea a hundred leagues away, not a lake to redouble the expanse of the sky. By two o'clock the face of the house and its terrace, in full sun throughout the morning, had resumed their true appearance, criss-crossed with little beams, jutting eaves, and chocolate-coloured shutters, and bathed in an unnatural light, a dreary imitation of the sunlight that reverberated from the hillside opposite. Fanny, barely covered by her chemise, leaned over the balcony and gazed at a landscape which, on leaving it the previous summer, she had expected never to see again.

'It was Farou's idea,' she mused. 'Two summers running in the same district, that's something we haven't often experienced. However, since Farou likes the place . . .'

She turned round and took stock of the room behind her, as big as a barn, and looking larger still with the shadow caused by the half-closed shutters.

'Everything is too big here. With only two servants, how can one be expected to . . .? If it weren't for Jane, I couldn't stand it.'

Her ear caught the sound of brisk footsteps passing through the hall below.

'She's astounding. In this heat! And so kind, except for her attacks of touchiness. A shade too useful for a friend. That's it, a shade too useful.'

She caught sight in a mirror of her own happy-go-lucky reflection, hands on hips, her dark hair all anyhow, and scolded it. 'What a sight! And I talk about Jane being too useful for a friend! I who can't even tap out Farou's manuscripts!'

She plunged into the cold water as if it were a demonstration of domestic activity, did her hair, put on a last-summer's frock, blue with mauve flowers, and sat down. to write. She unearthed a sheet of white paper and a yellow manilla envelope, made do with them, and began her letter to Farou.

"*Dear Big Farou,*

"*Leaving the task of bringing some excitement into your life to one or two little Asselins, I can sum up our existence in a couple of words: no news. We await you. Our busy Jane is devising some choice new dishes; little Farou still looks like a prisoner languishing in the most awkward of all ages; finally, your lazy Fanny . . ."*

A little English song drifted up from the terrace.

'Ah,' thought Fanny, 'it's one of the days when Jane is thinking regretfully of Davidson.'

She was ashamed of herself for her mockery, then wallowed in her shame.

'After all, there's nothing unkind in what I was thinking. On the days when Jane remembers Davidson, she sings in English. On Meyrowicz days she calls out to Jean Farou, "Jean, come here, and I'll teach you a Polish folk-dance!" And when it's Quéméré, she digs up horsy memories, an old, melancholy wistfulness for a certain Breton mare, a roan, very saddle-backed.'

She powdered her face again and watched, on the face of the nearest hillside, the encroaching shadow of another hill.

'This place is depressing. What attraction has it for Farou? To come back two successive summers to the same district, I've never known that to happen before in twelve years of married life. But till now I hadn't noticed how dreary it was here. Next summer . . .'

But her courage failed her at the prospect of twelve months ahead.

'We'll first have to see whether Farou finishes his play and whether he can make something out of a second season at the Vaudeville. But if they revive *Atalanta* at the *Théâtre Français* in October . . . Oh, well, let's forget it: that's real wisdom.'

It was the only wisdom she had learned.

'The most urgent thing is that Farou should come

back here, to work on his third act. We're all so stupid when he's not here.'

A silent puff of wind stirred the lime branches nearest the balcony, revealing the white undersides of the leaves. Fanny finished her letter and went to lean over her balcony, hair loose, shoulders bare. Below her, with arms crossed on the low wall of the terrace, Jane too was leaning out over the Franche Comté landscape, so totally lacking in river, pond, laughter of water, upsidedown reflections, mists, and the smell of spongy marsh-flowered river-beds. From far above, Fanny sent a melodious call winging down to the round head with its short well-kept hair, ash-coloured and veined with gold, and Jane, as cats do, bent back her head without turning round.

"I bet you've been to sleep again."

"No," said Fanny, "actually not. Would you believe it, I've taken a dislike to this place."

Jane whirled round, and flattened her back against the brick wall.

"No, not really? Since when? Have you told Farou? Could you not . . .?"

"Goodness, Jane, don't run on so! Can't I so much as express a simple opinion without you twisting and turning and tying yourself up in verbal knots, before you dash your brains out against that wall?"

She laughed, still leaning out, and unfurled a banner of black hair, before tossing it back over her shoulder.

"*My long tresses fall to the foot of the tower*," sang Jean Farou, who was walking up the slope towards the terrace.

"Here comes someone," shouted Fanny, "who already sings as flat as his father!"

"But he's not got Big Farou's voice," said Jane. "Jean, just do your imitation of Big Farou when he comes home and says, 'Oh, all these women! Goodness, what a lot of women I've got in my house.' "

Jean walked on past her without answering and disappeared into the hall. Jane gave a toss of her head towards the first-floor balcony.

"My dear, what a look he gave me! His lordship doesn't like to be teased!"

"Nobody likes being teased at his age," said Fanny thoughtfully. "We spend our time flaying that child alive without meaning to."

Hearing a footfall on the stairs, she called out, "Jean!"

The boy opened the door of her room and stood there, "Mamie?"

He was wearing, with no loss of dignity, almost poverty-stricken summer clothes—frayed tennis shirt, white linen trousers, green about the knees and too short in the leg, a belt, and rope-soled espadrilles which the caretaker's son would have scorned. He waited for Fanny to speak and breathed through half open lips, patiently turning to his stepmother the sun-tanned, clear, expressive and impenetrable face of a sixteen-year-old boy.

"You are in a state! Where have you sprung from?"

He turned his head towards the window to indicate vaguely that he had come from the countryside, the countryside at large, from the violet of its shadows, from the green of its meadows. His blue eyes shone with an almost tumultuous animal life, but they gave away no secret other than their blueness, their intensity. Down below, Jane took up her little English song again and Jean Farou, slamming the door behind him, went to his room.

'What a ninny!' thought Fanny. 'Now he's in love with Jane. All would be fine, if only she were a little nicer to him.'

Penny Carey.

Dinner reunited the three of them on the terrace. In Farou's absence, Fanny and Jane kept up a flickering sparkle of gaiety and, whether his father were present or not, Jean Farou maintained an intolerant and rarely broken silence.

"It's curious," said Fanny as she looked up at the clear white sky, "how unrewarding the close of day is here. The sun sets for others, over there behind . . ."

"The aspect of the mountains is monotonous," Jane said.

"Maeterlinck," growled Jean.

The two women burst out laughing and little Farou looked daggers at them.

"I've had enough of your forced merriment!" he shouted as he left the table.

Fanny shrugged her shoulders and watched him go.

"He's becoming impossible," Jane said. "How can you allow him, Fanny . . .?"

Fanny gently raised a white hand, "Hush, Jane, you know nothing about it."

"You are really so kind."

She shook her head and that stirred the soft hair on her forehead and above her very small, almost round ears. When she wanted to convince Fanny of anything, she would open her grey eyes, flecked with gold, to their full extent and, by retracting her upper lip, reveal four small short white teeth. But Fanny paid no attention to what she called Jane's "daughterly expression". She did not enjoy smoking, and now put out her cigarette by crushing it under her thumb with hidden animosity.

"No, Jane, don't keep on telling me that I'm so kind. But let me repeat that you don't understand that child in the slightest."

"Do you?"

"Probably I don't, either. All I know is that we often make little Farou unhappy. You especially. For he is, of course, in love with you. And you sometimes treat him with a rather cruel indifference."

"A fine time to start, I must say!"

"Goodness, Jane, how easily shocked you are! You're pretty, my stepson is sixteen. I know perfectly well that Jean would never dare, perhaps would never wish to make you a 'declaration'."

"He'd better not try!"

Jane left the table and stood with her elbows propped on the low terrace wall.

'That's done it,' thought Fanny. 'She's bitten my head off, and now she'll tell me about the education given to adolescents in England. It's definitely Davidson's day.'

But Jane, when she turned round, had the smiling face of a thirty-year-old child.

"Don't you find it maddening, Fanny," she exclaimed, "that for weeks now there hasn't been a single thing within reach which is really cold, or even cool to the touch? Even after midnight the walls are hot, the silver's warm, the flagstones . . ."

"And who's to blame? That wretched Farou. He wishes to finish the play here."

"You should have stood up for yourself, Fanny, stood up for us all, even for the houseboy, who is wilting away!"

She frowned, knitting her ash-pale eyebrows accentu-ated by a pencilled line, and looked disapprovingly at the landscape which was settling down to rest in the dry evening air.

"But you said 'yes', and 'yes' again. If only your slavish 'yes-my-dear-isms' produced some results. Really, women are . . ."

"Kss . . . Kss . . ." Fanny hissed.

Jane held her tongue, and blushed after her fashion, that is to say her fawn complexion darkened a shade.

"I'm meddling in something which doesn't concern me, I know . . ."

"Oh what does it matter?"

No sooner were the words out of her mouth, than it occurred to Fanny that so ambiguous an absolution could hurt Jane, and she added, "Jane, don't be quite such a tease with little Farou. He's sixteen. It's hard on a boy of that age."

"I've been through that age myself. And no one was sorry for me."

"But you were a girl. That's altogether different. And besides," Fanny said, in response to a pathetic glance, "at that age, or thereabouts, in sheer desperation you ended by tossing a rose to a passer-by, on the other side of the wall."

"That's true, that's true," Jane agreed, suddenly softening. "You're right as usual, Fanny. I tell you, I'm bad, wicked, illogical."

She hugged Fanny's shoulders tight, resting her cheek against the loosely knotted black hair, and repeated "I'm bad, bad . . ."

"But why?" asked Fanny, who rarely bothered with polite lies.

Jane pushed back her head and looked up at the pink sky in all innocence, showing her four little teeth.

"How should I know! I'm not one of life's spoilt darlings. Old resentments have a way of poking up their ugly noses. Dearest Fanny, protect me! Don't tell Farou that I've been so . . . so impossible whilst he's been away."

There they stayed till lamp-time, shoulder against

shoulder, with few words passing, silently pointing to a bat, a star maybe, listening to the faint fresh breeze in the trees, imagining the reddening glow of the sunset they never saw unless they climbed the hill opposite.

Below, on the top terrace, there was a crunch of gravel.

"Hello, Jean Farou!" called out a docile Jane.

"Yes?" a hoarse young voice answered.

"Shall we put on a record? Or play a game of patience?"

"All right. . . . Yes. . . . Just as you like," said the sulky voice.

But he bounded up so quickly that Fanny was startled to see him close beside them, all white except for his face and arms, and illumined by the tragic halo that encircles the head of an adolescent.

Jane slipped her hand under his arm in a sisterly fashion and drew him towards the card-table, whose moth-eaten green cloth smelt of mould and stale cigars.

"Hello, boy!" she said in English.

'Decidedly,' thought Fanny, satisfied, 'it's Davidson's day.'

TWO

" A RE you listening?"

"I'm listening."

"Is it still the stolen letters scene?"

"I think so. Yesterday morning he gave me fifteen pages to type. Five minutes later he snatched them back, looking as if . . . as if . . ."

"I know," laughed Fanny, "as if you'd taken away the bone he was gnawing. What else can you expect! He can never achieve the throes of creation save to the accompaniment of thunder and lightning. What do you think of the first two acts?"

"Sublime," said Jane.

"Yes," said Fanny thoughtfully. "It's disquieting."

From the house rose a murmur as of a prayer meeting, a congregation at Mass, the initial stages of a riot. When this died down, the solemn responses of the last bees were audible in the air as they worked high among the topmost lime flowers and ivy blossom. The rasping cry of a wild animal interrupted the muttered office being celebrated behind the half-opened shutters; but neither of the two women—nor indeed Jean Farou, sprawled over the wickerwork couch, a book between his idle hands—even so much as turned a hair.

"It's always the same end-scene—Branc-Ursine caught red-handed attempting to force the locked drawer," said Fanny. "Where in the world shall we be able to take refuge when there are two Farous writing and intoning their plays?"

The blue of Jean's eyes, as he looked up, was dazzling.

"I shall never write plays, Mamie, never."

"It's far easier to give up than to try," was Jane's immediate rejoinder.

"Giving up isn't always the easiest way out," said Jean.

He blushed at the boldness of his reply, and Fanny noticed how the mounting blood spread up the boy's open neck to quicken the pulse behind his ear.

"Come, Jane, don't torment your young friend any more."

"I enjoy teasing him, it's true," said Jane good-humouredly. "It suits him so well. I forget exactly which day it was, but he looked charming with a tear poised between his lashes."

A silver thimble glinted on the finger with which she was playfully threatening him. Fanny lifted her forehead with its silky black band.

"What! He too!"

"He too?" Jane repeated. "Explain, Fanny dear, explain yourself!"

She was laughing, sewing, and darting happy glances on all around from her grey, amber-speckled eyes: over her unprotected head played a bright medallion from the last rays of the sun, and she seemed almost joyful on this unrewarding summer evening, redolent of sun-baked granite.

"The other day . . ." Fanny began. "Wait, it was the day Farou's letter came, and none of us knew—he least of all—that he'd be able to get back so soon."

"Wednesday," said Jean without looking up.

"Perhaps. . . . I had dozed off after lunch and on waking I saw you standing beneath the veranda where we are now. There was a teardrop about to fall from your eyelid; it trickled down your cheek, and you plucked it—just like that—between two fingers, as if it had been a small strawberry or a grain of rice."

As she listened, Jane's expression changed from smiles to childish sulkiness, and then to wheedling reproach. With her little cleft chin she pointed to Jean Farou.

"Fanny, Fanny, respect my little secrets, my temperamental moods, in front of a listener so . . . so . . ."

She broke off abruptly and over her face spread a look of stupefaction. Fanny turned her head to see her stepson erect, his mouth open as if to utter a cry. He threw both arms in the air and fled, taking the terrace steps two at a time.

"What's . . . what's the matter with him?"

"I don't know," said Jane. "He threw up his arms, as you saw for yourself, and rushed away."

"He frightened me . . ."

"There's no reason why he should," said Jane.

She removed the thimble from her skilled needle-woman's finger, and carefully picked the snippets of thread from her frock.

"He's behaving as one does at his age," she continued. "An exaggerated romanticism. He'll get over it."

"Do you think so?"

Fanny methodically folded up a width of natural coloured linen, a table-cloth she was decorating with red flowers embroidered with large clumsy stitches. She went out and leaned over the low wall and called, "Jean, are you there?"

A rather mocking voice rose from below, imitating her own, "Wolf, are you at home?"

"Stupid creature!" Fanny shouted. "You'll be hearing more from me! Behaving like a great tragic actor! Get

31

on with you, you third-rate comedian! You great . . ."

She straightened up without finishing her sentence, and pivoted round on her fine hips, which belonged by rights, according to Big Farou, to a happier era. She had just heard her husband's voice close at hand.

"There we are, he's finished!" she said in rapid tones to Jane.

"For today. . . ." Jane said dubiously.

Shoulder against shoulder, they watched Farou making his way towards them. He appeared to be sleep-walking, to be emerging gradually from his day's work, in the course of which, muttering, ruminating, or bellowing his third act at the top of his voice, he had unconsciously removed collar, shantung coat, tie, and waistcoat. Six feet from ground level he held a greying head with curly hair partly tumbling over his forehead, where it merged with eyebrows to shade his yellow eyes. Tall, tired, thick-set, ugly maybe, but ever certain of pleasing, his usual pace was that of a man striding into battle or to the scene of a fire: so much so that, when he went through the village to buy cigarettes, mothers would gather their children to the shelter of their petticoats.

He was nibbling a rose, and stared right through the two women. He was still in the dark and luxurious boudoir where the public prosecutor, Branc-Ursine, was demeaning himself to the extent of breaking open a writing-desk to steal the letters which would ruin beautiful Madame Houcquart, the mistress he no longer loved.

"Handsome Farou!" called Fanny tenderly.

Jane's softer voice mimicked her playfully, "Handsome Farou!"

And so faithful was the imitation that Fanny, surprised, mistook it for an echo.

Farou, struck by the double call and by the arrestingly

32

heavy scent of a Spanish honeysuckle, stopped in his tracks and intoned his ritual ditty, "Ah, all these women! All these women! What a lot of women I've got in my house!"

He yawned, then seemed to wake up and discover the world about him. He hitched up his shantung trousers which were slipping down, and scratched his head. Trustful by nature and devoid of personal vanity, he was happy most of the time and young, at forty-eight, as are men who will countenance, in the ordinary run of their lives, only the company of women.

"Who called me first?" he cried.

He did not wait for an answer but began to dance, singing in a pleasantly off-key voice an improvised line or two in which he insulted, in plain unvarnished military terms, M. Branc-Ursine, the lovely Mme Houcquart, and all their machinations. But of a sudden he caught sight of his son ascending the steep steps to the terrace, changed his tune and clowned for the benefit of the admiring Fanny and Jane, "Cheese it, the cops!"

"Finished, Farou?"

Fanny contrived to hide the measure of her anxiety. Farou before now had pulled so many third acts out of the mire with a final heave of the shoulder. . . . He was gazing at her with a wild but kindly eye.

"Finished? You do have some bright ideas!"

"Yes, but all the same, you've made some progress?"

"Progress? Yes, of course I've progressed. I've chucked out the whole bally scene."

"Oh!" said Fanny, as if he had broken a vase.

"That's good work, that is, my poppet. Jane, be ready to type the final version!"

He clapped his hands and strode to and fro like an ogre.

"Until today, it was going very badly. But today . . ."

"How, pray, did M. Branc-Ursine behave himself today? Did that rascally lawyer hide the letters in a safe place?"

Fanny, who was busy combing Big Farou's hair, folded up her cheap pocket-comb and stood to one side to avoid the blast of his reply.

"I should very much like it if Jane," said Farou casually, "could add a knowledge of graphology to her already varied and numerous accomplishments."

"But I can certainly learn," cried Jane. "There are text books. I know of an excellent manual. Why?"

"I have been told on good authority that a graphologist becomes immersed in the significance of handwriting, in the crossing of *t*s and the looping of *l*s, and is therefore incapable—in so far as the sense is concerned—of reading the manuscripts entrusted to him or to her."

Jane blushed furiously. "Is that a reproof?"

"Not a serious one."

"But one which I shall hold against you."

Farou's yellow eyes flashed.

"Don't put on your 'jobbing dressmaker's' expression, it doesn't impress me, Jane."

She bit her lip, restrained a couple of tears, and Fanny took up the cudgels with the ease of a woman accustomed to such outbursts.

"Farou, you brute! Aren't you ashamed of yourself? All this for the sake of that blackguard Branc-Ursine! Tell me, Farou, does he still steal the letters from that piece of furniture?"

"And what else should he do?"

She pulled a face and rubbed her charming nose with her finger.

"Aren't you afraid it will be rather . . . cinema, or rather . . . theatrical?"

34

"Rather theatrical? Whatever next!"

He railed at her, as from a great height, mercilessly.

"Yes, I really mean it," Fanny insisted.

He threw his great arms wide apart.

"Now what would you do yourself if you knew that in the safe, drawer, or what-have-you, were locked some letters from a man who had been the lover of—give your nose a good blow, Jane, and come and give us your advice —what would you do, Fanny?"

"Nothing."

"Nothing," echoed Jane in a similar tone.

"Oh, my poor dears, you say that, but——"

"Nothing," came the decisive voice of Jean Farou who, reassured by the shadows, had returned with the dusk.

"Nit-wit," growled Farou.

"Now that Jean considers that nothing should be done . . . Come here, psychologist, come a little closer. You're looking none too well nowadays."

"It's the heat, Mamie."

"The fact is . . . I know someone who is going to sleep on the little sofa tonight," Big Farou proclaimed, "and that's me."

"No, it's me!" said Fanny.

"And I'm going to sleep on the terrace," chimed in Jane.

"Not me," said Jean.

"Why, Jean?"

"Full moon, Mamie. Cats and young lads go on the prowl at night."

In the deepening dusk his hair, eyes, and luminous teeth gave him a phosphorescent look, and he seemed to quiver like a well-spring. His father looked him over with a brief glance that lacked both charity and paternal pride.

"At your age . . ." he began.

" 'I had already slain and begotten a man'," the youngster quoted.

Farou smiled, flattered.

"What's that! What's that!"

"That's a fine thing," Jane said in reproach.

"It's only a quotation," Farou said with condescension.

The eyes of youth were fixed on Farou in an open stare which, whether in meaningless amazement or charged with secrets, remained unfathomable.

The whistle of the evening train, as it trundled sadly along the track that encircled the nearest hill, shrilled from above the village already enveloped in blue mist. A moon the red of quenched embers left the horizon and rose into the sky.

"Where are you going, Jane?"

"I'm going down to the lower terrace, O Grand Inquisitor, and then I'm coming back, I ate too much for dinner."

"Three spoonfuls of rice and a handful of red currants," said Fanny.

"Makes no difference. Aren't you coming down too, Fanny?"

"To climb all that way up again!" Fanny was horror stricken.

The white dress and the little English song faded away into the distance. Fanny lifted her husband's heavy arm and placed it across her shoulders. He did not resist and his fingers lightly touched her breast. Bending down her head, she imprinted a kiss on his hand, a slightly hairy hand, the texture of a sage leaf, the wrist lighter in colour, softer, and green veined. Defenceless and trusting, the hand submitted to this almost timid caress.

"How sweet you are," said Farou's dreamy voice above her head.

The timid mouth pressed more firmly on his wrist and manly hand, shaped for plough or hoe, or to bear arms, but never wielding anything heavier than a fountain pen. He stood with his eyes open, seemingly asleep, resting on his wife's shoulder.

'Perhaps he's already asleep,' she mused. She dared not break their friendly embrace. She breathed in the healthy smell of warm flesh scented with lotion on the hand and arm abandoned to her care. She did not say to herself, 'This man, who lets me bear the weight of his arm was, is still, my one great love.' But there was not a line of the palm or wrinkle encircling the already ageing wrist that did not evoke some amorous memory and revive her passion for rendering service, her certainty that she belonged to one man and had never belonged to any other.

The stealthy sound of a cat parted the leaves and a slender body slid close to the trunk of a lime tree.

'It's Jean,' thought Fanny. 'He's keeping close watch on Jane below.'

She was about to laugh and draw Farou's attention, when she thought better of it. The shadows cast by the trees directly in front of the moon dappled the gravel with blue, and in a twinkling the sky had become a night sky.

"It would have been less hot in Brittany," Fanny sighed out loud.

Farou withdrew his arm and seemed aware that he was not alone.

"In Brittany! Why in Brittany? Aren't we comfortable here?"

"Oh, you . . . you're nothing but a sand lizard."

"We're not working badly here. Do you want us to leave?"

"Oh, no, not now. I was thinking of next year. We won't be coming back here next year?"

A broad pair of shoulders were raised to denote total ignorance.

"There are a number of inconveniencies here. It gets extremely hot without one having enough sun. The boy's not comfortable in his room, which is really baking. He ought to move out of it."

"Of course he should!"

"You stagger me! You know there's not another room for him."

"Nonsense. There's always another room."

"Yes, the east room."

"Which east room?"

"The room Jane is occupying."

"If Jane is occupying it, then it certainly isn't available."

"But will Jane still be with us next year?"

Farou turned ingenuously towards his wife.

"I really don't know. How should I know? Why think of it?"

"Because of Jean."

"What, is he complaining now?"

"Oh stuff, Farou! It would certainly not be like him to complain. Especially if it were to make things uncomfortable for Jane, don't you see!"

"Oh really?"

Fanny saw Farou's eyebrows meet above his yellow eyes over which a spark of moonlight played. The wind sent a few flower-heads and shrivelled leaves bowling along the ground. A light step sounded on the gravel almost indistinguishable from the sound of the leaves, and Jane's white dress reappeared at the end of the terrace. At the further end Jean landed lightly as he sprang from the main branch of one of the lime trees.

"Children," Farou declared, "I don't know whether you're like me, but I'm dropping with sleep."

"That means that everyone must go to bed," said Jean.

"Precisely. And you, Jane, may return to your east room."

"So I've got an east room, have I?" and she gave a shake of her head to flutter her hair.

"Yes, Moon Dust, east room. Cooler than the others. Fanny's just told me."

"Whatever were you talking about?" asked Jane involuntarily. "Oh, I beg your pardon! What bad manners I've got."

"Sometimes," Farou conceded. "Give us your paw. Good night, Jane. Lead the way, son!"

"Oh, Daddy, at a quarter to ten! In this weather! If it isn't a shame!"

A drooping houseboy was dragging himself round the villa, switching on here and there the low-powered, reddish electric light. Farou went straight on through the hall, gave a lion-like yawn at the foot of the stairs, and absent-mindedly shook his son's hand. Once behind the closed door of his sweltering room, Jean Farou began to follow Jane's every movement, as revealed by the creaking floorboards.

THREE

FANNY FAROU's life in Paris had flowed on more or less peacefully, despite the comings and goings of creditors, actors, draughts, and flitting servants. She carried her own peace about with her, together with that indispensable *vade mecum* of the chilly, a plaid, in her case a soft vicuna wrap, the long hairs of which collected cake crumbs. Farou's gesticulating shadow had first fallen on her during a rehearsal of *No Woman about the House*, when she was playing the piano off-stage during the Evening Party act.

"You look like a half-husked hazel-nut, between your bands of black hair," Farou had fired at her as early as their first encounter. Never one to dress well, on that occasion a broken sock-suspender trailed over one of his shoes.

"You're as white-skinned as a half-caste, come with me," he had commanded her ten days later.

"But . . . what will my parents . . .? I am . . . I'm a respectable girl," protested a horrified Fanny.

He looked indescribably bored. "Oh, what a nuisance! Since it can't be helped, we'll get married, if that's what you want!"

In Paris the Farous—three of them, counting young Jean, now legitimised—had lived on next to nothing. Then Farou's plays, rather heavily loaded with purple passages and acts of brutality he thought perfectly natural, moved down from Les Batignolles to the fashionable theatres on the boulevards, where they developed the habit of running for more than a hundred performances. The personality and character of Farou-the-Recluse were called into service for Farou-the-Author. Porto-Riche dubbed him "vulgar", for the simple reason that he was vulgar when with Porto-Riche. He refused point-blank— in barrack-room terms and as a humiliating fatigue-duty— to collaborate with a member of the Académie Française. Bataille wrote patronisingly of his "crude if disarming, easy-going absurdities"; Farou was like a certain three-act play, *The Bargee*, by Flers and Caillavet, for he took a delight in posing as a tramp or a foundling in the presence of those who did not know that for many years Old Pa Farou had taught history to twelve-year-old boys at an obscure public school.

Once they had attained notoriety, the Farous lived like princes, without ever giving it a second thought. Like princes, they lived in a glass house, thanks to reporters, gossip writers, stage fans and fellow actors; but nothing is more opaque than a shimmering glass house. After the fashion of a reigning monarch, Farou was credited with brilliant and short-lived love affairs, yet such trifling incidents in no way diminished Fanny's attractions for him. In between runs they got into debt like princes, but, in a princely fashion, continued to enjoy humble pleasures. Farou would expatiate on the excellence of a homely dish of piping hot food, and often rated idleness at its proper worth. Behind locked doors, he would sit in his shirt sleeves browsing over magazines, while Fanny, one shoe on and one shoe off, her long hair streaming down either cheek, inclined her gentle gazelle-like face over a pack of cards and would re-start a game of patience a score of times.

A young companion shared their bliss. From early childhood, Jean Farou had pressed his baby forehead, as later his boyish chin, against Fanny's elbow to give his stepmother the benefit of his advice, "You've missed your chance of a club sequence, Mamie, and you're done for."

The child, who was said to be lovable because he was pretty and gentle because his eyes were so blue, returned Fanny's absent-minded affection and took her side whenever he guessed her to be displeased with Farou, or down in the dumps. The kindliness she showed her stepson was more general than particular, for she loved and cherished in him some mysterious emanation of his father.

"You're quite sure you haven't kept a picture of his mother?" Fanny would ask her husband. "I should so much have liked to see what she really looked like."

Farou replied with a typical gesture—arms flung wide apart—one that sent flying all memories, regrets, and responsibilities.

"Damned if I can lay my hands on one! A pleasant creature, though, none too robust, poor dear."

"Intelligent?"

Farou's wandering golden glance rested on his wife in astonishment. "I knew so little of her, you know."

'That I can well believe,' thought Fanny to herself. 'Will he say the same about me, if ever . . .'

She never risked going beyond that 'if ever'; her conjecture was sheer bravado, since she was incapable of imagining a life without Farou, without his physical presence, his liturgical mutterings, his way of kicking a door shut to punish a recalcitrant third act, his insatiable craving for women, his moments of gentleness when she would whisper tender and primitive words of praise into his ear.

"You are gentle . . . gentle and soft as a sage leaf . . .

42

smooth as a finger nail. You are as gentle as a resting stag."

She was so surely established as favourite that she was never to cavil over his right, common to all reigning despots, to sow a few bastards.

"Handsome Farou! Unkind Farou! Intolerable Farou!"

In soft undertones, or in her heart, she would name him with no further comment, like a true believer for whom the litany is all sufficing. During the first years of marriage she had tried to serve her master by day as well as by night; but Farou impatiently discouraged her zeal as an untrained secretary. Restricted to her duties as a paramour, she soon became a fatalist inclined to childishness, greed, and self-indulgence, as lazy as those women who, labouring under the weight of a great passion, find themselves tired out by the middle of the day.

Once when seated at the back of the box at the *Théâtre Français*, as the dress rehearsal of *Atalanta* was coming to an end and in reply to Farou's triumphant "Well?" Fanny had taken it upon herself to say, "The scene between Piérat and Clara Cellerier is definitely too long. If you were to bring someone on in the middle with coffee or a telegram, the scene would pick up again much better afterwards, and it would give the audience a break." Since that time, Farou had never again asked for her opinion which, none the less, she never failed to express. If, peevish under criticism, he shot a "Whatever next!" at his wife, reinforced by a glance as weighty and yellow as gold, Fanny would thereupon display a strange freedom of mind and speech. She would expound her views, become insistent even, raising her broad eyebrows with a detached and casual air.

"Of course, as far as I personally am concerned, I

don't mind either way; do as you please. But you'll never make me, as a member of the audience, think it natural that a woman should wish to kill herself for so slight a reason."

"So slight a reason!" exclaimed Farou. "A woman betrayed in such a cold, calculated manner! So slight a reason! Really!"

Fanny tilted her nose and through half-closed lids gave Farou a look of unwonted impertinence.

"Perhaps it isn't so unimportant. But do you want me to tell you what your Denise's behaviour amounts to? It's a man's reaction, and nothing else. A man's reaction!"

Whatever she did, he refused to re-enter the discussion, sometimes exercising a tact vouchsafed only on such occasions. More often, he would break off the conversation with a sudden cry or exclamation.

"My collar stud, good God! And Coolus' letter? Where is that letter from Coolus? In the suit I wore yesterday? Does nobody ever empty my pockets for me? Do they?"

As she ran hither and thither, losing a bedroom slipper, scattering the tortoiseshell prongs that kept her long, unfashionable hair in place, Fanny's colour, expression and language would change; twelve years of matrimonial life had never cured her of her particular form of reverence, in which Farou's talent and fame counted for considerably less than he would have been willing to believe. Highly emotional, she was wise enough to accustom herself to the uncertainties of life. With unimaginative patience and the dignity of a faithful employee, she stood between Farou and his creditors. But once "Bloch's advance payment" had been overspent and the royalties on film rights had come to an end, she had no ideas

44

beyond getting rid of the car, selling her furs, and pawning her ring.

"It's curious how behind the times you are! By jingo, you ought to get a better grip on things!" was the advice of Clara Cellerier, of the *Théâtre Français*.

That great second-rate actress, well known to all yet with never a hope of becoming famous, pityingly shook her beautifully trimmed, green-gold hair, tightly fitted into a small hat. Daringly dressed, her slender figure sheathed in youthful black, Clara Cellerier betrayed her sixty-eight years in nothing except her use of the expression "By jingo!", by a certain military tomboyishness and her tendency to describe a man as a "dashing horseman".

"She never mentions a man who's been known to go on foot," Berthe Bovy declared.

Clara treated Fanny as a young country cousin, with the warmheartedness of a "good trouper", with a "Cheer up, child!", with beauty recipes and addresses of "clever little seamstresses round the corner". But Fanny, in her heedlessness, never bothered about her clothes and wore the same gowns two years running, although she was sometimes to be seen in furs. She had the otter-fur from *Atalanta*, the mink from *No Woman about the House*, and from *Stolen Grapes* the blue foxes, which she sold when *The Swap* was a resounding flop to teach Farou a lesson for giving a wartime setting to the story of a pair of lovers who had no idea there was a war on.

Fanny was never to forget that difficult turning-point: no money, or next to none, little Farou down with typhoid fever, and the maid taking to her heels for fear of infection. That was the moment chosen by the police to nab the Farous' manservant, in their own pantry, on a charge of indecent behaviour. Farou himself, withdrawn from the world while in the throes of the fourth act of his new play and hammering with his fists on the table and doors, bemoaned the fact that his shorthand-typist, Mme Delvaille, had allowed herself to be brought to bed before his fourth act had seen the light of day.

"It never rains but it pours," he shouted from afar, behind closed doors.

"How right you are," Fanny sobbed quietly as she squeezed lemons for feverish little Farou, her hair lustreless over her faded bed-jacket.

One morning under hospital lighting, amid layers of dust, curling carpet edges, lemon rinds, stray bedroom slippers, the smell of a badly regulated geyser, eau-de-Cologne and cold compresses, Fanny awoke on the divan bed from which she had been dragged during the night by husky calls of "Mamie, I'm hot . . . Mamie, something to drink", and felt surging within her an irritation akin to that of an animal at the end of its tether or of a woman with a pretty, rather weak chin.

'I've just about had enough. The charwoman's late. We haven't the money to pay for a nurse. Farou considers it all quite natural and thinks only of his third act. . . . I'm going to wake him up, that I am, and give him a piece of my mind, and hand him back his brat, that I will, and show him that it's jolly well his turn to . . .'

But little Farou moaned the name Mamie, and Fanny listened, as if for the first time, to this child who even when delirious looked for help to none other than to the woman who was not his mother. She went back to heating water, rinsing basins, squeezing oranges, and grinding coffee beans.

That same morning a charming young woman rang the doorbell, asked for "The Master", and informed him that Mme Delvaille had been "successfully brought to

46

bed of a fine eight-pound boy" and could scarcely resume her duties for another three months. She offered her temporary services to a fierce, silent Farou, who nodded his acceptance. During the days following, Mlle Jane Aubaret, with a comforting show of good humour, lunched with the Farous on a corner of the table, remade the sick boy's bed and doped Fanny with egg yolk beaten up in port. Little by little Jane gave evidence of her capabilities. Helped by Fanny, who was beginning to take heart again, the pair of them got through the work of four servants, each watching the other out of the corner of her eye. By their similar methods of polishing brown shoes, cleaning out the bath without using an abrasive, breaking eggs into a bowl, and lighting the stove without dirtying their hands, each recognised the other as a qualified woman about the house, in the direct line of true middle-class French housewives—those exacting workers who never give a thought to the trouble they take or to their traditional capacity for hard work. In this poor, proud, over-scrupulous bourgeois world, girls are still taught that before going to school mattresses must be turned and beds made, bicycles polished, cotton stockings and gloves washed out in the hand-basin.

Such a collaboration bore fruit. A young, stage-struck manservant replaced the satyr. The housemaid returned. A fresh, tart incense permeated the flat, created by the smell of English apple-pie and furniture polish, and little Farou's temperature went down to normal. Carried along with the rest, Big Farou laughed at dark Fanny and fair Jane, at his son, thin and transparent as a shell, heaved his third act out of the mire, snapped up the Vaudeville under Pierre Wolf's nose, collected a "handsome advance" from Bloch, and amorously tousled his wife.

47

"Fanny, if there's one piece of advice I have to give you, it's to go at once and choose yourself a fur. Don't put it off too long, Fanny."

She looked at him caressingly, with love-light in her eyes, rubbed her lips and soft velvety nose against his cheek, and her cup was full; she had, unwisely, paid the doctor's bill.

Later Farou said, "And don't forget the present for Jane, since we no longer need her. A wrist-watch, of course."

But neither Farou nor Fanny could have foreseen that when the moment came to say goodbye, Jane would fall into their arms weeping and muttering confused prayers wherein they could detect genuine grief, regrets at leaving "The Master", fear of a dangerous loneliness, the need to devote herself to a friend such as Fanny. . . . Fanny dissolved into tears, Farou's yellow, cat's eyes glistened and Jane promptly explained that a modest income freed her from the least pleasant alternative—to live on her new friends or to accept a salary from them.

The idea of a disinterested friendship is just as intoxicating to middle-class Bohemians as to any other Bohemians. When by themselves the Farous sang Jane's praises and their own pleasure in discovering, in inventing her.

"That girl is perfect," Farou would say, "really perfect!"

"I don't know about her being 'perfect'," Fanny retorted, "but she's certainly worth more than the compliments you make sound like 'references'. You wouldn't believe it, but it was she who cut out and made that *lamé* tunic, so that I could wear out my black marocain pleated skirt."

"Nice way of re-establishing the good name that I have degraded—to use her as a daily sewing woman!

For the matter of that," Farou added, with a look over-flowing with leonine gentleness, "Jane is rather like one of those refined persons who go out to sew for the rich because they cannot abide contact with the poor."

Fanny could not help laughing.

"Heaven preserve me from the 'nice' things you might say about me, Farou!"

In the process of losing her attractions as a newly discovered relative, a "nurse" not previously encountered, a novelty friend, Jane shed none of her virtues. She put up with Farou's moods, with his leg-pulling so often more hurtful than his rages, typed rapidly, did all his telephoning. She remembered the telephone numbers of theatres, the names of company secretaries, and knew how to flatter "the good ladies" of the box office. She called Quinson "my great friend", and shared, with no outward sign of astonishment, the financial ups and down of a couple who, trained to do without essentials, stringently demanded only the very best.

Blonde Jane—if the colour of the finest wood-ash, that of the poplar, can be called blonde—given her place in the Farous' box, was there accorded her due in the matter of personal sanction by the scandal-mongering members of the audience said to be in-the-know.

"Whose bed does that pretty ash-blonde share? Dark Fanny's, wouldn't you think?"

"No, no, old boy, Farou's of course, the old goat-foot! He invests her with the title of secretary and foists her on his wife."

In reply to a blunt question from Clara Cellerier, Farou settled the matter once and for all.

"Don't lose all sense of shame by letting your imagination run riot, my charming friend. I, like you, hold the classics in respect. There's nothing between Jane—who is my natural daughter—and me, but a simple little case of straightforward incest."

"Where is Jane?" Fanny would ask at all hours of the day, so thoroughly accustomed had she become to encountering a cheerful young woman wherever her eyes might roam.

Jane's ubiquitous presence could have passed for Fanny's one luxury. Her seven years' seniority permitted Fanny a certain ease and freedom in her behaviour and Jane the privileged attentions of a lady-in-waiting or a devoted niece. When Farou returned home he no more thought of greeting Jane than he would a piece of furniture; but her absence brought him up short, "Where's Jane?"

"In her room, I suppose," Fanny would reply. "She's just back from Pérugia's."

"So she buys her shoes at Pérugia's now! My word!"

"And why shouldn't she buy her shoes at Pérugia's if she wants to? As her foot is slightly smaller than mine, and I haven't much go in me today, she took along a woollen stocking and tried on my shoes for me. Do you want me to call her?"

"No, what do you want me to do with her?"

"But you were asking for her a moment ago!"

"Was I? It was for my glass of *vittel-pipérazine*."

"The houseboy's there for that. Soon you'll be making Jane wash your handkerchiefs."

"Well—what about you?"

They exchanged a smile of understanding and reproach.

"Where's Jane?" asked little Farou, tight-lipped and anxious-eyed, brought to a sudden halt as if a taut rope barred him from Jane's empty chair. And Fanny, to pull his leg, often answered him out loud before he had put the question.

In July, the Farous left Paris for a summer resort chosen out of the advertisement columns of *Life in the Country*, or recommended by Clara Cellerier.

Farou felt the need for isolation, for weeks of unorganised work without rules or regulations, and the certainty of not bumping into those whom he called "the ugly mugs". Once away from Paris, it was hard for him to hide his ineptitude for making the most of the lavish gifts of nature—sea, sun, and forest—and Fanny was infected with the uneasiness, the haughty fear of those who have sprung from humble origins.

"There's Pau! They say it's so lovely," was one of Fanny's suggestions. "And you know I've never seen Dinard! Don't you think it funny that at my age I should never have seen Dinard?"

"What I shouldn't think at all funny," growled Farou, "would be to find myself, for instance, having to rub noses with Max Maurey three times a day."

"What's he been up to? Hasn't Max Maurey been treating you well?"

"Of course he has!"

"Well then?"

"That has nothing to do with it, my poppet. You don't understand. It amuses Maurey to change his clothes three times a day during the summer. It doesn't amuse me. Once and for all, I want to spend my summers alone, without shoes and without a stiff collar."

He satisfied his authority as a nomad chieftain by organising the family departures. An ever changing domestic staff followed the Farous, who landed up, equipped with two new trunks and twenty badly tied parcels, at mouldering villas, somberely furnished châteaux, thin-walled cottages, all spots off the beaten track of modern tourists, where Clara Cellerier had once enjoyed clandestine pleasures. Room had to be found for the typewriter, the latest novels, Farou's manuscripts, the dictionary, cabin-trunks and Fanny's plaid, while Jean Farou was put out to grass.

'What will Jane do without us, and we without Jane?' Fanny asked herself in perplexity when July threatened the amicable honeymoon.

But she was reassured when she heard Farou say, "Jane, you'll take *One* and *Two* with you, and all the notes for *Three*. Give the typewriter to the houseboy to bring along by train."

"So that's settled," Fanny sighed.

She faced up cheerfully to the present again and once more settled down amongst french windows, cane arm-chairs, a new book, the angora wrap, a box of chocolates and the leather cushion. One day, however, she had to allow a past to intrude—Jane's past.

"You really ought to know all about me, Fanny," Jane began.

"Why?" asked Fanny, with whom honesty always took first place over politeness.

"But Fanny, I should die of shame if I kept it back from you. After the way you've taken me into your home! You must know what I am, the bad as well as the good, so that you may judge me."

At this preamble Fanny's eyes, blue-black as those of a thoroughbred mare, began to wander, settling fearfully now on a cloud, now on the lamp, now on a passer-by in the road, anywhere to avoid Jane and her affectionate gaze, Jane and her fluffy hair, Jane and her simple frock, so simple that it was impossible not to notice it.

'Why,' Fanny mused, 'why am I already bored, as I am by the adaptation of an American play? And also why

52

all that formality about pedigrees, branches and collaterals in a home where no one worries about anyone else. Is it really necessary? Is it really decent?'

But Jane was already relating how, as the dowerless child of a Parisian drawing master (You can see some of my father's work at the Duguay-Trouin School, and among it a first-rate charcoal sketch "Donkeys at the Drinking Trough"), she had hurt and bruised and dragged round a tiny garden in Saint-Mandé—between a leafless lilac and laurels in tubs—a haggard, desperate soul, the soul of a young girl who was poor and untrained for any job.

Jane never spoke of these things in front of Farou. She waited until the end of the meal sent him back to his work or his indolence. She waited a little longer, once the two were alone, until Fanny let her book slip from her knees or woke up with an "Anything new, Jane?", refreshed by her siesta. As Jane did not bother to begin at the beginning, Fanny never knew exactly whether Meyrowicz—a most wonderfully handsome Pole and a collectivist, to boot—had taken Jane from Davidson, or whether he had received her from the supple, dangerous hands of the said Davidson, "The" English composer.

'Is there only one composer in England?' Fanny wondered.

She did at least know by heart the story of Antoine de Quéméré, Jane's first misfortune.

"When I used to watch out for my father at the end of the little terrace," Jane would relate, "I used to wait—bent double, like this, over the wall—for such ages before he was due home, that I developed a pain right across my body—here, across the top of my stomach. Eventually, having searched in vain for something new to look at, I

53

became dizzy. I toyed with a flower between my fingers. Girls are little fiends, you know . . ."

'No, I do not know,' was Fanny's unspoken reply.

". . . and on the worst days I would say to myself, 'Suppose a man passes below and I drop my flower. . . .' In the end, I did let go the flower and it fell between the ears of a horse, but on that horse there was a rider!"

'Bravo!' shouted Fanny to herself. 'What a splendid curtain for Act One! What if I put it up to Farou?'

But the next moment she wrinkled her nose.

'Why does it still sound like an English play? Meyrowicz, at least, used to beat Jane. She swears he did, she has also shown me the place on her arm where that disgusting sadist burnt her. These misfortunes of Jane's have about as much effect on me—no, not as much—as *Broken Blossoms* at the cinema.'

"Farou," she said one day to her husband, "can you explain to me why it is that a spinster, when speaking of her former lovers, usually refers to them as her 'misfortunes'? Whereas the self-same gentlemen are called 'Good Fortune No. I', 'Good Fortune No. II' if the good lady is married?"

"Shut up, can't you!" answered the deep, dreamy voice. "And you might also stop plaguing me."

"Farou, I'll end by believing you know nothing about anything. Haven't you the slightest notion why Jane speaks with scorn and contumely of the men who have shared her bed?"

Farou appeared to be thinking.

"Yes, of course I have. It's natural."

"Oh!"

"It's the survival, an honourable one, of a sense of decency in the female. It's contrition. It's aspiration towards something better."

"Farou, you make me laugh."

He enveloped her in the light of his critical yellow eyes, as if she were his flock, his walled vegetable garden.

"It's you who don't begin to understand. You're much too ingenuous. You're a monster. And besides, you're in love with me, and that robs you of all discernment."

She put her arms round his neck and rubbed her little white nose against him.

"You're making me too hot," said Farou, unwinding her arms. "You are as logical and consistent as a third act. Let me work. Send Jane to me, and a glass of orange-ade, a grape or two, something light."

"Nice little second act? The bedroom scene?" Fanny suggested maliciously.

"Let me be, Fanny, let me be. No more jokes! You're the only ordinary woman I know. Mind you guard your prerogatives."

With a heavy yet gentle hand, he smoothed his wife's dark hair, and she asked him softly, with no insistence, whether he loved her.

"I really don't know, my dear."

"What do you mean?"

"No, I don't always notice that I love you. But if I stopped loving you, I would notice it at once. And I'd be very unhappy."

She looked up at him from below, deliberately insistent, knowing that an imploring look emphasised the whites of her dark eyes.

"Oh ho! very unhappy! Can you be very unhappy? You?"

"I trust not," he said with some anxiety." I never have been, have you?"

She lifted her shoulders in a gesture of uncertainty and shook her head.

"No. . . . No. . . ."

'No,' she repeated to herself. 'Worries, heaps of worries. The tricks you play me oftener than I deserve, probably. . . . Your filthy Farou temper, and my feeling of uselessness. But all that hardly counts. No. . . . No.'

"Handsome Farou! Unkind Farou! Unmannerly Farou!"

Deeply moved, she hummed the words in an undertone, so that he should not hear that the thread of her voice was wavering, like a fountain in the wind.

FOUR

'VERY unhappy. . . . Can he ever be very unhappy? Or even sad? In any case, he's not unkind. But nobody has ever had cause to say, or to hear it said of him, that he is kind. Or cheerful, either. How little he resembles a man of the theatre! Yet he loves the theatre. . . . No, he doesn't love the theatre, he loves writing plays. Why am I so made that I associate his profession, his art, with a capricious female occupation? Not quite a female occupation, but a facile way of earning one's living. But if it were facile, a great many others would make a success of it. If Farou is successful, it must be because he is very gifted. Is he very gifted?'

Having arrived at the furthest limit of her conjectures, Fanny experienced much the same discomfort as she might from imagining too vividly a bullfight, say, or a haemorrhage, or a sudden fall. She extricated herself from a kind of magnetic vacuum, one which fascinated her, by resorting to her familiar calls.

"Jean, where are you? Jane! I've lost my lipstick again! Jane! Where is the big blue vase? I've brought some flowers up from down below."

Nobody answered her. She yawned, fatigued by an early rise that morning. She leaned over the brick parapet and gazed admiringly at the slope, then at the field path, then at the roadway lined with young plane-trees.

'All that long way! What a walk I've had! They'll be amazed.'

57

The scents of daybreak still hung in the air. The north-west wind was freshening the whole countryside, gathering up all the resinous scents, mingled with wild thyme from the little chain of grassy foothills and the bitter tang of a stunted oak coppice, to spill them over the slope on which stood the "Villa Déan".

"This house is deserted! Where are they all?"

A faint clinking of china sounded from the kitchen on the far side of the villa, where the outer wall was greenish and almost porous. Fanny saw herself alone among all the hideous, gaping, yellow-painted iron furniture, suddenly alone in this little known and little loved district. . . . She threw the large, already wilting bunch of pink flax and campanulas on to the table.

"Farou!" she called.

"Present, on his behalf!" answered Farou, so close to her that she shuddered.

"You're here? How did you get here?"

"What's wrong? Are the sheep in the corn again?"

He knew well enough that "Farou" is a name often given to sheepdogs, and deigned to make a joke of it.

He filled the hall doorway, standing there in his light clothes, informal but spruce, bare-headed, with a knotty stick in his hand. He started to laugh because Fanny, in her surprise, was gaping like a fish. She grew cross.

"Why are you laughing? A moment ago you weren't in the hall, because I've just fetched the big red vase from there! You've been for a walk. . . . No, you haven't, because I've just come up from the meadows below; where could you have been? You're not a needle, or a sylph. Are you listening, Farou? And—what wide nostrils you've got. I never noticed before how broad your nose was! Why are you making fun of me? Why can't you say something?"

He was laughing at her, showing the widely spaced teeth of a man predestined to be happy. On seeing the double row of his blood-red gums, Fanny lowered her voice and prepared to assume her "favoured retainer" expression.

"Have you finished?" asked Farou.

"Of course I've finished. You're not worth more!"

She saw fine weather signs in the depths of his eyes and in a low voice began one of those *Litanies Farouches*, the words and music of which she used to compose in days gone by, during the hours of satisfied love. "Colour of old amber. . . . Colour of angry gold. . . . Of the Moret nun's barley-sugar. . . ."

A cloud passed over the eyes she was praising and Farou blinked his tired eyelids.

"Ah, Farou . . ." sighed Fanny, flattered.

But she at once took hold of herself and cloaked her pleasure under an awkward, conventional modesty. Farou followed the direction of her glance, and saw his son, disguised and smartened by tightly belted blue overalls. He fell back on his stock joke. "Cheese it, the Cops!"

"Oh, and there is one! Where have you come from, *Vergissmeinnicht*? Where have you come from, kingfisher? Where is Jane?"

"I don't know," Jean Farou replied politely.

"I hope you haven't been down to the village like that!"

"Blue jeans are all the rage," Jean replied in the same tone of voice.

Outwardly calm, he seemed to be shaking with a static impatience; the blue linen garment intensified the blue of his eyes, and the breeze raised a flame of golden hair along his forehead.

"You must admit he's becoming very good looking," Fanny whispered softly to her husband.

"Very," Farou curtly agreed. "But what a get-up!"

"Now, listen, you! Funds are low. I'm waiting until the last moment before renewing the boy's wardrobe. You know he won't really have a shirt to his back by the end of the holidays."

"Then wait no longer, Fanny. That bitch of an *Atalanta* is sold at last. Buy him silk pants—in moderation."

He held out a cheque and a letter which she could not read.

"Is it in English?"

"American, Madame. Fifty."

"Thousand?"

"*Yep*. And as for *Stolen Grapes*, that will be settled any time now. Touch wood!"

"Jean! Jean, come here!"

"I heard," said little Farou from afar. "Well done, Daddy! Thank you, Daddy!"

"Did it come this morning, my Farou? While I was down in the meadows? Blessed be the hand whence comes my bounty!"

Flushed with joy, she pushed back the black band from her right eye and bent to print a quick kiss on the strong, scented hand which still held the cheque and letter from America. On the dry knuckles she caught sight of greasy, purple stains and cried out, laughing like a child.

"Oh, you were with Jane, and got her to translate the letter. That's the ink from the typewriter she had in her room! I've caught you out!"

"Well!" said Farou, looking at his stained hands. "Well! My word, what an eye!"

"You can put that in your next play. I make you a present of it for your Branc-Ursine!"

She was convulsed with laughter as she lightly struck

Big Farou again and again with a long stalk of pink flax. She pirouetted round him, nimble and plump, and slightly out of breath. She stopped only when she caught little Farou's steely eye, filled with ascetic scorn.

'Jane is right,' she thought, offended. 'That boy's becoming impossible.'

"Jane!" she shouted in a piercing voice. "J-a-n-e!"

"Now what do you want her for?" grumbled Farou.

"I want her to come to the village with me, of course! Sign that cheque of yours, Farou, I shall be passing the little branch office of King's. And we'll bring back some nice sweet grocer's champagne and warm shortbread: in other words, we'll carry out a raid. J-a-n-e!"

Jane appeared, her hands over her ears. She was wearing a mauve linen dress, shrunk by frequent washing but kind to her tanned complexion and to her hair, lighter in colour than her forehead. She was doing her best to get a word in edgeways between Fanny's cries.

"How money . . . How money does affect you, Fanny! How you can . . . The butcher will hear you."

"I'll give him socks!" squealed Fanny. "I'll chuck his bundle of francs at him! Smack in his face, like that! Jean, just skip down to the garage and tell Fraisier to get the car out. Oh, my dears, it does me good! You're a trump, Big Farou! Jane, what would you like?"

"Me? Why, nothing . . . nothing. . . ."

"Do you hear her, Farou? Make her, Farou, do make her want something!"

She whirled round suddenly to call him to witness. Untouched by her overflowing joy, he had inclined his curly head with its thick, silver-threaded brown locks and seemed to be listening to some gentler sound, to have his mind on a less animated scene.

"What is it?" Fanny asked in a small voice.

61

Farou raised his eyes, which still held a faraway look.

"Off you go, off you go! And come back quickly. I'm already beginning to feel ravenous."

A large white rush hat and a big yellow linen hat were snatched from the pegs, and the two women ran off down the slope. Fanny pulled Jane by the hand, and Jane, ever responsive but rather detached, let her arm go limp, offering no resistance, and skilfully avoided stumbling or throwing her weight on Fanny. Farou watched them go down, his face still holding the gentle expression which, with him, denoted the most primitive innocence. He sensed that his son was approaching and his expression changed.

"Aren't you going with them?"

"No, daddy." And he added, "If you don't mind."

The pause before the respectful phrase was sufficiently long for Farou to interpret it as veiled insolence. He turned to look at his son, who was sitting sideways on the wall juggling with a pebble or two, and was about to speak gruffly to him as to a woman. He restrained himself as he looked more closely at the stranger born of his own loins, not yet fully grown, whose shape and careless attitude as he bent over the void were unquestionably virile, endowed with the overabundant virility that often emanates from a frail body and dominates its grace. Farou repressed his animosity and wisely put it behind him.

"What are you going to do?"

Jean Farou misinterpreted the question.

"Why, wait for them. They won't be long."

Farou pulled his hand from his pocket with an effort to brush that answer aside, then significantly changed the tone of his voice.

"No. What I mean is—what are you going to do?"

62

"Oh, I see."

As a gambit, he tried out a timid request.

"Would you let me go away—right away? You might find me something, say, with your friends the Secrestats, in the Argentine?"

Farou turned his head towards the steep path where a moment ago the yellow and mauve frocks were twirling like two flowerheads on the same stem as they floated downhill, and his handsome, mature, manly, countenance softened.

"It depends," he answered without enthusiasm. "It depends, of course, on the conditions under which I could . . . we could organise, arrange a visit abroad for you."

Jean was quick to seize upon this semi-acquiescence.

"Exactly! Besides, there's no hurry. If I may, as soon as we get back to Paris, I'll make an appointment to see the French Secrestats. There's the matter of my call-up, but by that time I should have managed to get in almost three years in South America of commercial life."

He was forcing his young voice, exaggerating the precision and speed of his words in order to show up a certain weakness which had dulled and slowed down his father's utterance. Each of them, looking at the other, felt loathing for an aspect of humanity different from his own. Farou was offended by this blue, metallic son, adorned with gold, piercingly sharp, studded with hard facets and mysterious refractions; while Jean blushed if he so much as touched the thick-skinned flabbiness of Big Farou, pliable as elastic, capricious, and as completely lacking in a sense of the future as any pleasure-loving woman.

Farou found no difficulty in remaining silent but a great deal in making the gesture of raising his heavy arm to his son's shoulder.

63

"Let's go a little way down to meet them."

'No. . . . No. . . .' Jean Farou protested inwardly, in revulsion from the muscular burden. 'No. . . . No. . . .'

Yet he bore the weight of the arm with painfully mixed feeling: the slightly hairy finger-joints hanging beside his cheek, with their mixed smell of tanned skin, tobacco, and scented lotion, undid his proud little boy's heart and tormented him with a terrible longing to cry, to kiss the dangling hand.

He triumphed over this, already bitterly aware that what is permissible in a child does not outrun childhood. He kept in step with his father and fell behind whenever the path became too narrow for the two of them to walk abreast.

FIVE

' "Impossible" is putting it too strongly. I was un-
nerved by that cheque. I exaggerated far too much
the other day. He's a poor little boy with nothing to do,
and we none of us look after him as we should. He's not
impossible at all. He's even very sweet.'

"Jean, do you hear me?" Fanny said aloud. "You're
very sweet."

He turned his head in a vivacious manner, to give her
a fleeting smile and a nod as though she were some tire-
some acquaintance, and returned to his alert immobility.

"Jean, you won't be doing badly with four . . . no,
with three suits from Brennan's. I say three, because it's
better to have three suits and an overcoat than . . . Be
an angel, Jean Farou, and pick up my scissors."

He sprang up, pounced on the scissors, handed them
to Fanny, and with another leap was back in his seat.

"Don't you agree that it's better to have an overcoat?
You know I'm not flattering you, but Clara Cellerier is
sure to refer to you as a 'dashing horseman'. I don't
imitate her badly, eh? Eh, Jean Farou! What are you
staring at? What on earth are you looking at?"

"At a brown caterpillar," said Jean.

It was a lie. His burning blue eyes were fixed, unseeing,
on the yellow lichen of the wall. He was all ears, listening
intently to the expression—since the wind carried away
the actual words—of two voices conversing fifteen feet
below on the first terrace. Fanny, who sat sewing in her

usual place by the front door, could not even catch the murmur of voices. Jean was mentally measuring the distance—two to three paces—which separated him from the brick parapet, and the width of the coarse, scrunchy gravel. He also reckoned that an old hibiscus bush that spreadeagled the parapet at the end of the upper terrace would permit his head, invisible among its foliage, to peer down on to the terrace below. The concentrated effort of his calculations sharpened his tanned features, rosy and dusted with freckles over the cheek-bones: he kept his mouth tight shut and never batted an eyelash. At length he took a deep breath, as if about to leap forward, and shouted in a childish voice, "I'm quite willing to hold your skein of thread, Mamie, but it will cost you an extra tie!" Then he bounded towards the hibiscus, slid his head and shoulders noiselessly under the leaves, allowing his forehead and eyes only to protrude over the wall.

Dumbfounded, needle in the air, Fanny stared at him. Eyes popping and mouth agape, she gave expression to her astonishment with the ingenuousness Farou found so amusing.

A moment later she left her seat and Jean, hearing her move, motioned her to keep quiet with an imperious wave of the arm behind his back. Whereupon she carefully stuck her needle into the linen she was embroidering, tiptoed noiselessly forward, and joined her stepson under the hibiscus.

Down below Farou stood talking to Jane. His loose-fitting white garment was faintly tinged an acid, satirical pink by reflection from a stray sunset cloud. He was conversing in short sentences as he sat side-saddle on the wall, while looking out over the parched valley. He pushed back his thick curly hair with one hand and let out a

Penny Carey

"Phew" of exhaustion. Fanny thought that he must be saying, "This infernal heat!", or else, "I'll never be quit of that fourth act!" She found him much the same as usual, tired, handsome, and very dear to look upon. Jane, in her mauve dress, was holding some typed sheets of paper. She went up to Farou and held out a page to him, which he pushed away, laughing, and no doubt protesting, "Oh, no, that's enough!" But Jane persisted and Farou, who had risen to his feet, pushed her aside with a turn of the shoulder at once so familiar and so lacking in consideration that Fanny recognised the gesture, a bargee's gesture, used by Farou to reject a tie, a comb, a caress offered by a loving and conjugal hand. To her great surprise, Jane was not in the least put out as she leant laughingly against a ladder propped up against the wall. She was laughing wholeheartedly, arching her neck, raising her hands, and fluttering her fingers in the air; the sound of her laughter reached the upper terrace and, in the exclamation which brought it to an end, "Goodness gracious, what a lot of fuss about nothing!", Fanny recognised an intonation alien to Jane's manner of speaking.

'She's imitating me, my very words. . . .'

She turned to the young boy on the watch beside her. He was gripping the top of the wall with both hands to make sure he did not slip, testifying to his prowess and his experienced skill in watching, keeping silent, and taking in the situation. He seemed neither surprised, nor pained, and he held Fanny back merely by a masterful glance which prescribed silence, and dignity in attitude if not in action.

Below them Farou was not taking Jane's merriment at all well. She stopped laughing and her features resumed a look of unconcealed, unbridled hostility. She snatched at a twig, snapped it off and nibbled it while Farou was speaking in deep, measured tones, vibrating with threats, insolence, and carefully chosen insults. Then she interrupted him, yapped out a few brief words, twisted the twig she was nibbling, threw it in Farou's face and made off, with a somewhat theatrical leisureliness, in the direction of the steps.

"Quick, quick, back to your place!" was Jean Farou's hastily whispered order in Fanny's ear.

Hard boyish fingers propelled Fanny back as far as her basket *chaise longue*. When Farou, the first to appear, arrived at the top of the steps, Fanny sat holding the loose end of a skein of coarse thread, which Jean Farou, seated at her feet, was mischievously tangling like a cat.

"'Touching family scene," scoffed Farou.

His yellow eyes were shining, clear and hard.

'He's in a bad mood,' thought Fanny.

She shivered and with difficulty shook herself free of her habitual feeling of security, still confused at having left behind under the foliage of the hibiscus all the facial and emotional accoutrements of a spy. At her feet Jean Farou, holding his hands out as a winder, began to sing in a piercing voice. 'He's going too far,' thought Fanny, and it was on him, in her indignation, that she almost vented a rebuking 'How dare you!'; but she caught in the boy's watchful eye as he glanced up at her 'We're not through yet', and she said nothing.

"Fanny," Big Farou continued in a gentler tone, "what I just said was stupid. Pay no attention to it."

By giving a slight twist to her lips, she contrived to check the tears which had no more than moistened her fine prominent eyes, and was disconcerted to find that her feelings for Farou were only those of unchanging adoration and gratitude, mingled with a desire to apologise and own up.

'No, no . . .' she protested, despite the kneeling boy, whose eyes never left her.

Then Jane in her turn appeared on the terrace, and Fanny's unease suddenly gave place to an attentiveness that imposed silence on the depths of her being. She recovered her ease of movement and speech, and secretly congratulated herself.

"Ah, there you are!" she exclaimed.

"What have I done now?" Jane asked. "Were you waiting for me? I wasn't far away."

"Yes . . . yes . . ." said Fanny lightly, shaking her head and her black band of hair.

She looked at Jane with curiosity.

'She too? With Farou? But how? Since when? Can it be true? I'm not hurt. It matters so little. It's true that I'm accustomed to it. There was that pretty Vivica, who danced in the third act of *Stolen Grapes*. And, just recently, little Asselin. Oh, it doesn't last long with Farou.'

But she remembered a certain pallor about Jane, her absent-minded and melancholy moods, the violence of her tears, so many things; but when?

'Oh, yes—the day when I read out that letter from which it appeared that Farou had "sacrificed himself" with little Asselin.'

Jane sat down, opened a book which happened to be lying on the scaly iron table, pretended to read, then raised her head to the grey sky which held a promise of rain.

"My dears, how quickly summer comes to an end! It would be very sweet of you, Jean, if you would fetch me my little sleeveless jacket which I left . . . er . . . which I left . . ."

"I know," said Jean, who dropped the skein and bolted.

69

Fanny, ever on the alert, still tingling from recent shocks, listened to Jane with amazement.

'But it's *my* book she's picked up! . . . But it's *my* stepson she's ordering about! It's in *my* house that . . .

She felt the blood pulsing gently, then more rapidly behind her ears till it constricted her throat, and she called to mind a time when she was jealous and moved to violence. Anxiously, she turned to look at Farou.

'Isn't he going to, oughtn't he to say something?'

But he was dreaming, his stomach pressed against the brick wall—huge, heavy, simple and preoccupied. He inclined his head and shoulders in Jane's direction.

"Is that a good book you're reading?"

"So so," she answered without moving.

Jean Farou brought the little sleeveless jacket, placed it over Jane's shoulders as if he were terrified of burning himself, and disappeared. The sound of cupboards being opened and spoons moved about announced dinnertime. No one spoke, and Fanny could have almost cried out for help, almost prayed that a state of deception and ignorance might return to her, or else fury, screams, some sort of free fight. . . . Farou yawned and announced, "I'm going to wash my hands", and Jane, rising suddenly, assumed her most girlish expression.

"Oh, the hot-house peaches in the refrigerator! They'll be frozen!"

She rushed away, overwhelming Fanny as she passed with a light emphatic kiss, which landed haphazardly and was received by Fanny without horror or displeasure.

*   *   *

She slept little, but did not toss and turn. With first light she could make out Farou asleep in the larger of the two beds. Still weary, she looked him over and then gave no further thought to him, or to herself. She noticed that he had indeed a broad nose dividing his wide spaced eyes. 'They say it's a sign of a good memory.' A fresh breeze was enough to make her shiver, for she had already extended a fine bathing-beauty's leg from the bedclothes before going to nestle in the other bed against a big, motionless, unconscious warm body. She controlled the automatic impulse, tucked up her leg again, and settled down once more in bed.

'How absurd I am. Really one might think that Farou was being unfaithful to me for the first time. He's had any number of mistresses since he married me. Any number!'

She began to count them over to herself in an undertone, and naming them left her unmoved and almost in high spirits. Faint footsteps overhead, a woman's stifled cough, told her that someone else was not sleeping well or had awakened with the dawn.

'It's her. I'm certain it's her. She's not sleeping either. She's waiting for daylight, she's waiting . . . What's more, she's a young woman admirably suited to waiting, despite her short-lived outbursts. What is she waiting for? After all, we're a sensible young woman. We know perfectly well that Farou . . .'

But at that very moment, her docile mood underwent a disruptive change which, by telescoping a short period of time, caused her to relive that August afternoon, with its nap after a heavy meal and the dream of storm and expectation in the midst of which she caught sight of Jane furtively weeping. As she came out of the dream, reality—as in the dream—had shown her Jane weeping where she stood, hiding a tear. A tear, a single tear, plucked and extinguished between two fingers like an ember. Among so many resentful or passionate tears, this was the only one whose pearly weight Fanny would have wished to ignore all her life long; also the only one which could make Fanny once more a new, rejuvenated, self-assured woman in the clear, breathable atmosphere of unhappiness.

Quietly she got out of bed, exercising as much skill and precaution as if she were moving in the dark. Farou sighed in his sleep and turned over, moulding the whole sheet over his body like a great fold of a wave. A score of times malicious gossip, and Farou's own carelessness, had forced Fanny to imagine that masculine body striving after pleasure and taming a soft feminine body. . . . Many a corner of her memory hid recollections of bitter little tears, sleepless nights, letters purloined from Farou and restored without his knowledge. Christian names, unknown handwriting, blurred sketches . . . Fair weather spells speedily followed, she could count of them, and awaited their coming with composure.

"I know nothing more worthy of admiration than Fanny Farou's arrogant indulgence towards her great tom-cat of a husband!" Clara Cellerier would exclaim at the top of her old woman's piercing pseudo-young voice.

'It isn't very difficult to be arrogant or even indulgent when you reign supreme over something, even if it be a betrayal. How long have I not been the only one in my house to suffer at the hands of Farou?'

With a twist of her arm she gathered up her cable of black hair, which now seemed inconvenient.

'Oh, all this hair! Three snips of the scissors . . .'

She envied Jane her short hair—silver, honey, barley—which the wind fluttered over her forehead.

'Well, Blondie must be finding the time drag up there. She weeps so easily. I must be badly in her way.'

She felt her cheeks reddening, pressed her clenched fist

72

against her teeth, and shot an angry glance at the sleeping man, whom the grey morning light, rosier every moment, did not disturb. Lying there on his back, mouth open and rounded, his whole face expressed an impressive simplicity. Fanny was seized by a contemptible fit of gaiety.

'You'd almost swear he was going to break into song!'

She scanned in detail Farou's broad nose, the flat space cleft by a vertical furrow which separated the eyebrows, the short straight lashes. The relaxed jaw was beginning to show signs of age, but the face itself, invigorated by an enigmatic happiness, the neck round as a tree trunk, the nest of tangled hair, displayed a serenity, suggestive of a faun or some mythological creature. Fanny turned away from the open mouth.

'He smells like a menagerie, before breakfast, like everyone else.'

Farou's large hand, palm uppermost, lay extended beyond an arm with veins like vine tendrils, and opened towards Fanny as though in trustful homage. In her surprise, she could almost have melted in tenderness over this nail-petalled flower.

'Ah, I must beware of everything now. I must keep myself in hand, think things over, come to a decision. . . .'

Tense with wariness, dully wrapped up in her brand new widowhood, with noiseless steps she made her way towards the bathroom.

SIX

"Come, Jean, don't lie there! Jean, get up! What's the matter? If you're not ill, I will not have you indulging in these antics another minute! Jean! You fell! . . . Did you have a fall?"

Fanny dared not shake him, but she felt indignant that the child should lie there on the bank beside the path, fully conscious, prone and pale as a stricken fawn. His long slender body straddled the top of the slope, his hair and feet dangling on either side. A strange colour made his face look almost green and served to accentuate the pallor beneath the lunular freckles on his tanned skin. Fanny could just catch sight of the moist blue gleam in his upturned eyes.

"Have a fall!" he murmured. "You may well say so, Mamie! I'll say I had a fall."

She lifted a limp hand that did not grasp her own.

"Where does it hurt you?"

"Nowhere, thanks."

He closed his eyes again and took a deep breath. As she looked him over uncertainly for traces of a fall or blood smear, Fanny could hardly help suspecting the inertia, the lifelessness, the very pallor of this secret-ridden child.

"You were a very long time in the village, Mamie. . . ."

He spoke in a monotone and did not open his eyes.

"I like that! With all the things I had to buy. . . . In any case, how do you know I've been a long time? And then, the mail wasn't sorted, so I had to wait. How was I to know that I'd find you on the roadside like a scythed flower! And then, there's exciting news. If you only knew what's in the telegram I've brought back for Farou! Ah, that's made you wake up, I see!"

Jean had just sat up without discomfort: but a sort of mauvish smudge persisted under his eyelids.

"A telegram from the Vaudeville! Now don't let on that you know about it before Farou has seen it! '*My dear master, return earliest, urgent start* Impossible Innocence . . .'"

"Lord, how I hate that title!" Jean muttered.

" '. . . *rehearsals. November first opening. Affectionate admiration. Silvestre.*'"

"It really reads 'My dear master' and 'affectionate admiration'! Oh, good God!"

"Why not? It's only proper."

"Most proper. And what about the 'option' on his next play promised by contract to Trick and Bavolet? What sort of a schemozzle has there been, I'd like to know, between them and Silvestre?"

"They're not ready."

"Not ready? As if that couple were the sort of team who wouldn't always be ready!"

He was becoming himself again, and expressed his conjectures in decisive tones.

'Everyone knows more about what's going on than I do,' thought Fanny.

"Well? Are we leaving?" little Farou asked after a pause.

"Yes, but don't let's talk of leaving. . . . Here comes Fraisier. Fraisier, carry my parcels up to the house. If the Master is not working, ask him to come down here and meet me; if he is working, don't disturb him."

"He's not working," Jean whispered behind the chauffeur's back.

75

"What are you saying?"

Fanny stared so savagely at her stepson that he lowered his eyes and sprang to his feet as though to avoid a blow. She stared him out of countenance as he stood there untidy, shamefaced, and sullied now by the knowingness he had vouchsafed.

"If he's not working, he'll come down here. I shall rest here, where the ground's level. You know he doesn't like sick people. Since you are feeling better, go and wash and make yourself tidy. I don't want him to see you in this state."

The child obeyed and climbed the hill path. He was struggling against shortness of breath after his fainting fit. Specks of humus and sand still clung to his fair hair, as to a youthful corpse risen from the dead.

Only when he had disappeared from view did Fanny feel any indulgence towards him.

'He's just a wretched young boy. At his age the change is so rapid from cad to hero to desperado . . .'

She elicited pride from having dealt with him judicially, and sat down to rest on the wooden bench beside the path. The sky, only partially cleared by the morning's rain, was about to open on the setting sun: mountains and tattered wisps of cloud shone with the same reddish violet, a special Franche Comté purple that rivals clematis and stock. Before she had turned her head round again, Farou was beside her.

"What's wrong, my Fanny? You're not ill? I wasn't working," he added. "There's so little needed now to finish it. . . . Some things must never be written down, they come of their own accord, just like that, written on the air, sung in the train, invented at the same time as a piece of stage-craft."

He was describing figures against the sky, and in his

76

yellow eyes and appeased features—as well as in the smell and sensuous warmth of the body leaning over her— Fanny recognised the complete state of well-being that permeated Farou after love-making. She steeled herself and did not burst into tears.

"All the same, you'll have to write them down in double quick time, my dear Farou. Look. . . ."

He read the telegram, gave a couple of little neighing snorts, both vindictive and satisfied, then frowned.

"I shan't have Charles Boyer, then . . . Bernstein'll never release him."

"But Bernstein is so sweet."

"That's got nothing to do with it. Sweet . . . sweet! This habit of talking about Bernstein as if he were a bullfinch or a kitten! Sweet indeed! Jane!" he called, raising his head.

"What do you want with Jane?"

"I want her because we're returning to Paris, of course. A telegram to Blanchar! A telegram to Marsan! Oh, and that infernal little Carette to play the barman. Quinson has his address."

He tore at his hair with both hands and suddenly relaxed.

"It's going to start all over again, this eternal hunt after actors. . . . Thirty names, and when it comes to the point, not a single one available! Jane! What the hell does that girl get up to as soon as she's wanted? Re-doing her hair again I suppose, or in a little pink apron making jam. The Angel of the Hearth! The Good Genius of the Vacuum Cleaner! Jane!"

He radiated ingratitude and a natural ferocity. Fanny listened to him in silence, and, for the first time, overwhelmed. The yellow eyes came to rest on her.

"Well, Fanny! You don't look as if you had the

slightest notion that our whole coming year, and perhaps future ones as well, are now at the stake, my dear! Trick and Bavolet postponed! Upon my word, there is a God! Bestir yourself, my girl! Can we catch a train tonight? Jane!"

"No matter what it is, you're surely not going to make us catch the train at three in the morning, Big Farou? It has no sleeping berths and is always crowded with Swiss! Isn't that so, Fanny?"

Jane had come racing towards them, but without exerting herself unduly.

"At a pinch, you could travel on it alone."

At this there was a minor explosion.

"Alone! Since when have I travelled alone when it wasn't necessary? And once back in Paris, with the house shut up, and the gas to be turned on, and all the other chores. . . . Oh, well, do as you please. Oh, you women! After all, I'm very longsuffering!"

He lost patience, as he did each time he gave way, and went off up towards the house with a sweeping gesture that repudiated the two women.

"Let him go," said Jane quietly. "I'll reserve seats on the day train tomorrow. We'll be home by eight tomorrow evening, and from nine till midnight he can talk with Silvestre. What would he do with the whole afternoon to himself in Paris tomorrow? Like all men, he must always have things arranged for his own good despite his protestations. At all events, there'll be no Yvonne de Bray. . . . Oh, he ought to have had Yvonne de Bray."

She laughed excitedly.

"In another moment, the way you were going, Fanny, and he would have pinned us down to leaving tonight. 'Yes, my dear . . .' Fanny, I shall want Fraisier, to take the telegrams. I'll type them out at once. All we have to do is each to pack her own trunk and Farou's. If we could get hold of Jean again, I'd send him to the station. No, I'll do it quicker than he would. The washerwoman is late with some of the laundry. Fraisier can collect it while I'm in the post office."

She calmed down, and tactfully assumed a bright girlish manner.

"Fanny, I do so want you to have a marvellous gown for the dress rehearsal! Clear the decks for action! Just see my nostrils quivering!"

Fanny, unmoved, peered down into the valley, where the first autumn crocuses had sprung into flower after the rain. A low, slanting ray of light picked out the purple heather.

"It's odd," she said at last, "I thought I hated this country. Now that I know we shan't ever come back to it, I find it endearing."

She tried to summon up energy enough to hide her feelings, but a degrading meekness was all she could achieve.

"Don't regret it, Fanny. You'll find lovelier places. Don't listen to Farou next year. Next year . . ."

As she stood shoulder to shoulder with Fanny, she lowered her voice with a resentment that did not seem feigned. Fanny detected in Jane's voice a note of complicity, of an ill-will aimed solely at Farou. She accepted the support of the arm offered her, a flexible arm, tapering at the wrist like a serpent's neck and hollowed at the crook, soft, deft, officious.

'That too serviceable arm! But if I were to hate all the women who have been intimate with Farou, I should shake hands only with men.'

Her courage returned as her scruples left her and she

satisfied her self-respect by speaking to Jane in a rather superior tone.

"Jane, would you be so kind as to find the inventory of the furniture of the Villa Déan for me? Old Déan is such a fussy character."

Jane, who was holding her elbow as they climbed the steepest slope, answered with a vague yes, yes, while keeping one eye on the door of the study, from which came sounds of a typical Farou commotion—the slamming of cupboard doors, the scraping of a table across the parquet floor, and the plaintive grumble of a servant being scolded.

The evening and half the night were spent in an uproar. At eleven o'clock Farou took it into his head to revise a scene of the fourth act and to dictate it in the hall. His voice, which reverberated from one bare wall to another, his set look of an inspired madman, the hammerstrokes of his steps pounding up and down the creaky floorboards, the docile piety of Jane who was taking it down in shorthand, all combined to drive Fanny into exile on the terrace. The stillness of the night and the rising damp held a scent of reeds hanging in the evening air, together with the sickly vanilla of buddleias.

In front of the open door giant moths whirled like a grey snow flurry, and Jean Farou struck down the largest with sweeping blows of his hat. Sometimes he jumped straight up in the air like a cat, and Fanny's attention wavered between the child's graceful dance and the difficult, impromptu work which must not be interrupted. She admonished herself to be a coward and turned her head aside whenever Farou's face, as it passed through the rectangle of light falling over the terrace, reminded her that it was her duty to suffer.

'Another Farou play. . . . Uncertain manna. . . . What

80

shall I do in Paris? Does this present affair between him and Jane spell complete ruin for me, or is it a passing sickness which will work itself out as it came, without my noticing it?'

Her hand was touched by a warm cheek. Jean Farou had just sat down on the ground at her feet, in perfect silence.

"What do you want?" she asked in a low, irritated whisper.

"Nothing," said an invisible pair of lips.

"Are you unhappy?"

"Of course I am," the shadow admitted cautiously.

"You deserve to be."

"Am I complaining?"

"You're nothing but a little wretch."

"Oh, Mamie, you've no team spirit!"

The cheek, now damp, pressed against her hand.

"No," Fanny breathed with a touch of pride.

She was beginning to discover a firm spot, a small callus of lonely strength within herself, and she took as great exception to complaints as to conspiracy.

"What's all this nonsense, then? Get along with you!"

The toss of her head shook loose her hair and she felt it slither on to her back, cool as a snake.

"How lucky you are, Mamie," the shadow sighed.

She scraped the gravel with her foot.

"It's not a question of my luck! It's no concern of mine! You'll never get me to admit that I'm concerned in it. You're sixteen and a half, you're in love, you're unhappy. It's all perfectly normal. Sort it out for yourself."

"Sort it out, indeed, sort it out for yourself! Oh, Mamie, do you really consider that sound advice?"

They were whispering vehemently but with extreme

caution, prevented from giving their anger full rein by
Farou's pacing up and down; at times he would come
right through the front door out into the night, chewing
over some such phrase as "er . . . er . . . *Pull yourself
together, my good Didier* . . . er . . . *Be once more what you
were before this vile day dawned.* . . . No, that's nonsensical.
*Be once more the decent little chap who was brave enough to say
to me yesterday* . . ."

He took no notice of Jane as he dictated, and would
come striding out towards Fanny as if he would trample
her underfoot, unseeing. She had never cared for these
sudden attacks, rare as they were, of working in public,
which she likened to a form of exhibitionism.

"*Pull yourself together, my good Didier, I implore you!
Those are not your words, they are hers, which she has put into
your mouth* . . . er . . . *I implore you* . . . Oh, that's more than
enough! Why did you let me dictate such stuff, Jane?"

"What stuff?"

"*I implore you* and *Pull yourself together*—have you ever
called anyone *My good Didier*? As a matter of fact, I
believe you're quite capable of doing so. Just say 'My
good Farou!'"

Ears cocked, Fanny and Jean caught Jane's strangled,
unhappy little laugh.

"You've no wish, then, to call me 'My good Farou'?"

"None."

"*Didier, I implore you* . . . We mustn't forget that the
Vaudeville is a sort of popular theatre. *I implore you, pull
yourself together.* . . . By eleven forty-five the whole house
will be in a state of high expectancy. The end scene follows
as you have it typed. Good night! Fanny, I'm going to
bed!" Farou shouted.

Behind him, Jane gathered up the sheets after levelling
their edges, then replaced the cover on the typewriter

ready for the journey. She looked pale and sexless as a tired employee, and Fanny could discover no signs of secret triumph about her person, or even of familiar intimacy with love-making.

'Shall I never think of anything but her?' Fanny asked herself fearfully.

At that moment Jane looked up anxiously as though to catch her eye beyond the light of the room, and Fanny rose to her feet, leaving Jean Farou a crumpled, sheepish heap.

"Are you going up, Fanny?"

"Oh well, yes . . . I've already had enough of to-morrow's journey. . . . And all those Paris characters we shall have to see again. . . . Farou has kept you working late."

"It's my job. But it's unbelievable, all the fuss about that tag-end of the scene. It's becoming childish."

She was defending him and at the same time accusing him, with bad grace. She slipped her arm through Fanny's.

"Fanny, why do you never take my arm, but always let me take yours? I'm very tired, Fanny."

"With good reason. . . . You've been hard at it from early morning."

'As hard at it,' thought Fanny as she checked back, 'as a housemaid, courier, secretary, butler, plus half an hour of love-making—I'm being generous—into the bargain. It's true! I perfectly see the disadvantages of her situation, but wherein lie the advantages?'

She felt she was being rather coarse and this cheered her considerably. But her optimism faltered when, lying not far from Farou, who slept with the soft, flute-like whistling of a kettle on the boil, she found herself faced by the bluish screen of the uncurtained window. The previous evening it had been a blank; now, patterned with gold and very dark red, at the moment when, between rebellious eyelids, the gaze focusses by degrees on fantastic fairylands, the night-darkened window was decked with a rime of rising images at which Fanny stared, motionless, lying on a haycock of black hair, lulled by an invalid's hope.

'Is it no more than that? Is it no more than that?'

SEVEN

At the moment of their departure she was the least cheerful, but they were all accustomed to Fanny's shivering clumsiness that caused her to linger at station entrances and slightly hampered her movements when getting into a motor car. When the time came to hand over the keys of the Villa Déan to the caretakers, she seemed to wake up; she tied the two ends of a scarf under one ear and crammed down her felt hat, already pushed out of shape by her large bun, to the very bridge of her nose. With hesitant steps, she wandered to and fro on the terrace and put a hand on the padlocked door.

"No, Fanny, no! You really haven't left anything behind," Jane called to her.

'I would like,' Fanny said to herself, 'I would like to start the summer all over again, fortified by the knowledge I now have. I should see the house in another light, and the landscape and the people and myself. These empty chairs already have a different look; this great gimcrack house is less hideous; the plan of the rooms and the two storeys is now clear to me, as though the front of the building had been blown in.'

She heard laughter and saw Jean Farou walking away, piled high, as a joke, with all their overcoats and looking just like a conical haystack on the move. She joined in their laughter, tripped and twisted her foot.

"It's always your butter ankles," Farou scolded.

"You'd do better to give her your hand," Jane retorted.

She brought up the rear, graceful in her girlish, pale blue silk waterproof. Farou stopped and waited for her. He slipped his hand through the tight white leather belt round Jane's waist and dragged her along.

"Gee-up! Ktt! Ktt! little blue horse!"

As always at the end of his holidays, he looked as if he were wearing borrowed clothes; his coat and waistcoat buttons undone, his hat pushed to the back of his head. A wiry tuft of hair curled above his forehead like the crest on a bull-calf. Jane took exception to his uncreased trousers and loosely knotted tie; but Farou, bright-eyed and grinning broadly, laughed and archly succeeded in scorning sartorial convention.

"Ktt! Ktt! little horse!"

'The innocence of it!' Fanny marvelled. 'And what was it she said to him just now? That he would do better to give me his hand. . . . How often in the past three years—no, four years—has she made the same kind of remark? I used to pay no attention to them. "You would do better to give her your hand!" '

The path was smothered in spider-webs; by seven-thirty the morning sun, still low and red, was not strong enough to absorb the dew. A sere and golden autumn was licking the feet of the lower hills like a flickering flame. As she passed, Fanny leaned over the kitchen-garden hedge and picked some mauve Michaelmas daisies she had scorned the day before.

In the train, Jane wanted to prepare "Fanny's corner". She unrolled the light kasha rug and slipped a paper knife between the pages of a brand new novel; but Fanny desired neither her attentions nor sleep.

"I'm quite comfortable, thank you, I'm quite comfortable," she repeated in a listless voice.

Her lovely, rather bovine eyes wandered over the

fields. A violet arabesque on the tips of her scarf and the bright lipstick on her mouth combined to make her fair-skinned brunette's complexion appear even whiter.

On the platform, Jean Farou promised to leave the wheel in the capable hands of Fraisier, promised not to drive on after nightfall, promised with speed and insincerity all that he was asked to promise.

"What newspaper would you like, Fanny?"

"None for the time being, thank you. I'm quite comfortable."

'And the best of it is that I'm not in the least uncomfortable,' she went on to herself.

The first little Franche Comté stations, their vines laden with tight bunches of black grapes, sped past the train. Farou read the papers after his fashion.

"They haven't announced it: it's not announced yet. . . ."

"What's that?" asked Fanny, startled out of her reverie.

"That it's gone into rehearsal, of course. Where are your wits?"

"You know what I'm like when you get me out of bed at five in the morning."

A curve in the track brought back to her line of vision the distant hill she was leaving, the square villa she would never see again. She leaned forward to watch one of the very few houses which, since her marriage, had sheltered her for two successive summers, slowly vanishing into the distance.

EIGHT

"Has he had his lunch? I'm sure he hasn't lunched!"
"Of course he has! He said he'd have something brought into the theatre. As if it were a habit of Farou's to let himself starve! You make me laugh!"

"All the same, he's not been in bed by four in the morning for the past three nights."

"So what? It's nothing unusual."

"Oh, what a Spartan you are! The Spartan Wife—that fits you exactly. No one would guess it to look at you. What's more, how grand, how noble! Such strength of mind, such scorn of material comforts, such . . ."

The assembled women had not quite reached the stage of begging for "a tiny corner, at the dressmakers' special rehearsal", but they put on church-going, anguished faces, intended for Farou *via* Fanny, and had already assumed that air of cynical ecstasy which hovers ostentatiously round the playwright and actors of repute. They did not mention Farou by name; they said "He", or else "The Master".

'Well, what of it?' thought Fanny. '*He* has written a play; yes, he's finished another play. If he were a cabinetmaker, or if he had invented an electric cleaner, a fly-swatter, a serum, would these women be bowed down as if before a Christmas crêche?'

She preened her rather plump chin and kept silent, hoping that these beggars for favours would go. But assiduous as they were, they showed no concern for her.

"Is it a play on much the same lines as *Atalanta* and *No Woman about the House*?"

"The opening will be delayed, will it not? Mademoiselle Aubaret was saying to me, the day before yesterday, that . . ."

"Oh, really, Jane! You were saying, the day before yesterday?"

Fanny turned on Jane her Paris smile, well made-up and full-lipped, and Jane, whose fair hair lit up a corner of the room, was instantly extinguished.

"Who knows nothing, says nothing, Fanny. The Master leaves me in total ignorance, as he does you. But Madame Cellerier has ears everywhere."

Clara Cellerier was smoking, manly as a schoolboy, and exhaling with a long drawn "ph-e-e-w". A hat of chip straw, brimless and shaped like a small coal-scuttle, provided the only jarring note in a black and grey ensemble and endowed her with a chin unfamiliar to Fanny. The aged actress dressed daringly, with a kind of provincial bravado that for thirty years had inspired the respect of the *Comédie Française* audiences. That day she brought to Fanny's house one of those young actresses skilled in ringing up a playwright early in the morning, running into him in lifts, becoming speechless under his gaze, dropping a swift, awkward kiss on his hand—and dying of shame afterwards. Eager in the shadows, Clara Cellerier's protégée ardently hoped that Farou would return home for dinner. In silence this flaming blonde confined herself to afflicting her countenance with a consternation near to sobbing, when she heard that Farou, for the past week, had hardly slept, eaten, or come home.

"You'll soon find out what it's like, child, you'll soon find out for yourself what this last minute fever of rehearsals is really like," Clara Cellerier had promised her.

"Oh, Madame! I should be so happy to know. The slightest chance of my spending my time . . ."

Fanny considered her with a graciousness at once cold and familiar.

'I know her kind. Perhaps this one will get her small part—she's so persistent.'

Jane did not get to her feet to relieve the aspirant of her empty port glass.

A few of the women were waiting until it was time to go to dine.

'They'll leave,' thought Fanny, 'when it is convenient for them to go home or join their friends at a restaurant. They'll go away and say that they had "a very pleasant time at the Farous' ". I don't like that barrister's wife, or that high-class dressmaker, or the Farou cousin, who thinks it her duty, whenever she comes here, to make up her eyes and plaster herself with rouge which she wipes off again on the Métro stairs as soon as she possibly can. What a bore my house has become! And this furniture! It wouldn't even be acceptable as a set for the second act at the Scala! I ought to . . .'

A sort of metallic-green bird-woman, exposing a pair of sinewy legs, crossed the depressing square salon. Although a music-hall comedy star, the bird-woman ached to play in straight comedy, or tragedy. Even with its make-up, her little waif's face seemed the least important accessory of her acrobat's body. She strutted like a feather-legged pigeon, so accustomed was she to pacing huge stages, dragging dappled trains and a foam of feathers behind her, and shooting out at each step a small artificially cultivated, heart-shaped muscle on her sailor's calf. She seized Fanny's hands between her green gloves, emitted a sigh and a refined moan, and her respectfully sympathetic retreat put new life and a little gaiety into the company.

"The typical tart," said Clara Cellerier. "And to think she'll probably get the lead in Farou's next play *New Skin!*"

"She's a box-office draw," said Fanny.

"The contract isn't signed," said Jane.

The young actress shifted uneasily on her chair.

"Put on your cape now, child, I'm taking you off," Clara Cellerier ordered her.

The young actress took a few steps with hanging head, as if condemned to exile, and Clara Cellerier clasped Fanny's head between her hands, like an egg, in order to imprint a kiss upon her forehead.

"My dear Fanny, what have you done with your nonchalance?"

"My nonchalance?"

"Yes, your . . . How can I put it? Your *morbidezza*— what a pretty old-fashioned word!—your utter detachment. . . . I see that you are wide awake? Naturally, these last days are a great strain upon your nerves. But what a relief it will be, after the triumphant success! Lovely eyes so full of care . . ."

Gently, under her palms, she drew down Fanny's great eyelids, which reopened after the caress.

'The sharp old creature, she misses nothing!'

Fanny studied the bold features of the old trouper, her hard, precise make-up which austerely restored the faded contours of her face, her hat of chip straw, and her youthful black dress. . . . She was about to give some random reply when Farou entered the room. The young actress shut her eyes, as though wounded, parted her lips, and her hand flew to her throat. Farou's first glance was for her. Utterly exhausted, covered with dusty patches, his forehead damp and his collar a rag, he emerged from his rehearsal as if he had been taking part in a boxing match in a basement, or had fallen down the cellar steps. But at the sight of the young actress, the weak, happy smile of a convalescent spread over his face and he grew younger in a matter of seconds, by degrees, by leaps and bounds.

"What a state he's in!" sighed Clara Cellerier.

Impatiently Farou snapped his fingers at her. He was looking at the young actress and trying to put a name to her.

"Pour him out a glass of port," Clara Cellerier breathed into Fanny's ear.

Fanny shook her head, and with a tilt of her chin drew attention to Jane, who was fiercely crushing sugar into raw egg yolks before sprinkling them with marsala.

"By Jove," whispered Clara Cellerier, "whatever she's up to over there, Mademoiselle Aubaret doesn't appear to be getting much fun out of it!"

They exchanged a little laugh, which made Fanny feel slightly humiliated, and at last Farou spoke.

"Good day to you all! I beg your pardon, Clara, but I'm dead to the world. But surely that child there is young . . . Come now, I only know that she's the young . . ."

He was holding the young actress by the tip of her little finger, and was swinging the pretty, defenceless arm up and down.

"Young Inès Irrigoyen," Clara Cellerier prompted.

"A pretty name for a blonde!" Farou said.

"But it is my name," confessed the tremulous young woman.

"All right, all right, you're forgiven. But why on earth are you all standing about like this?"

92

"We're just off, we're just off," said Clara. "At such a time . . ."

Her well-timed false exit brought the lingerers to their feet and drove them out, even the Farou cousin. In their rear, Clara kept on repeating, as she pawed the ground, "Come along, come along, let's be going. . . . At a time like this . . ."

"Did it go all right?" Fanny asked.

A vindictive memory caused Farou to knit his brows, and his yellow eyes threatened a whole horde not present in the room.

"Yes, yes. . . . Oh, the swine! All the same, they were wonderful. . . . They will be wonderful. . . . Especially——"

"Especially who?" asked Clara avidly.

He eyed her with professional mistrust.

"Nearly all of them were wonderful."

"How lucky they are!" hazarded the fair-haired disciple. "Three lines in one of your plays, Master, would be a star part."

He laughed at her point blank, maliciously, to show that he was not to be taken in. Fanny knew that somewhat negroid smile, that open-faced grimace with wrinkled nose and grinning teeth, which Farou overdid in photographs and at important business discussions.

"Three lines? Would you care for them?"

As though seized with vertigo, the young woman called Inès clung to Clara's hand and held her breath.

"Three lines, and a nought after the three? The small part of the shorthand typist? . . . Eh? Eh? What's this abomination, Jane?"

He pushed aside the glass which Jane was holding out to him.

"Your raw egg concoction again? Pass it on to a consumptive, my dear. A small port, if you please."

He drank and his manner changed.

"Mademoiselle . . . Inès, will you kindly remember that the rehearsal is at one o'clock sharp," he said coldly. "Favier has the part, he will give it to you. Mademoiselle Biset threw it up this afternoon."

"Threw it up?" Clara Cellerier repeated ostentatiously. "My dear friend, what times we live in! Threw it up! Biset threw up a part?"

"Yes. Actually, I threw her out, if you prefer it."

Clara drew herself up like a soldier.

"Yes, I certainly prefer it! For the honour of the theatrical profession, I prefer it! Will the dress rehearsal be postponed, Farou? No? You'll open on the date fixed? That's splendid! Come, child. How happy you've made her, dear Master!"

She dragged away the fair young woman, who took great pains over her exit, stumbled a little, stammered, went all childish as she reached the open door and clapped her hands.

"Not bad, not bad," adjudicated Farou as he tore off his tie and collar. "She has the artificiality required for the part."

"There's also the concierge's daughter," Jane put in from the back of the room.

Stupefied, Fanny's eyes sought her out, and saw that she was pale, with dark-rimmed shining eyes.

"As for you," Farou replied quietly, "please go and tell the maid to run me a bath and put out a clean shirt and a pair of socks. And confine your theatrical accomplishments to those tasks."

Jane disappeared without a word, but slammed the door behind her.

"How can you speak to her like that?" said Fanny, embarrassed.

"Don't worry about it, Fanny-my-Poppet!"

He lay, bare-necked, in the hollow of the divan, and closed his eyes. He was exhausted and sure of himself, victorious in his repose.

"Are you going out again?" Fanny asked in a small voice.

"Certainly I'm going out again."

"Are you having dinner?"

"No. If I had dinner, I'd be too tired and I'd be dropping with sleep. I'll have something to eat when I get there."

"Are you pleased with it?"

"Fairly."

He limited himself to that brief word and she insisted no further. What could she have tried to find out? She knew some of the scenes of the play, the surprise ending she did not care for, the end of the second act about which Farou had asked her opinion with affected indifference. She felt constrained, and more than ever a stranger to her husband's professional life.

'There you are—almost twelve years of married life, and such an awkwardness existing between us, such difficulty in finding the right words.'

"You are lovely, standing there."

She gave a start, and hurriedly smiled at the handsome golden eyes that were staring at her.

"I thought you were asleep, Farou."

"You are lovely, but you look sad. Perhaps you are sad, after all."

He lifted a hand and let it fall back limp on to the divan.

"What an odd moment to choose, Farou!"

"Fanny, my dear, what makes you think that one

chooses? I have come from a desert," he added, rising and stretching his arms. "Oh, those people over there! One of them can play his principal scene only if he shows his right profile. If I make him change sides, he acts badly. One of the women plays her scene of despair with cropped hair glued down with brilliantine. If you could only see her rolling her head about on her lover's knees! No, no! And on top of that, Silvestre! What a menagerie! You have the lovely face of a human being."

He placed his heavy hands on Fanny's shoulders and took pleasure in studying the pale face with its round prominent eyeballs, which might have graced a lady of the harem. She suffered him to look upon her with profound uneasiness, pleasurable as sensual pain. The floor creaked and warned Fanny that Jane had just come into the room.

"I am glad to note," Farou said without turning round, "that sometimes you know how to close doors quietly, Jane."

He received no answer. Leaving Fanny, he walked vindictively towards Jane.

"Eh! Kindly imp of Dundee marmalade! You've calmed down now, it would seem."

Overwhelmed by fatigue, he laughed almost drunkenly, as if to get his own back for the lengthy arguments and muffled outbursts of the Punch and Judy show that had ebbed and flowed across the footlights.

"It seemed to me that you didn't take kindly to blonde actresses. Eh, Jane!"

Fanny went over to him and pulled him back as if he had been leaning over a chasm.

"Be quiet, Farou!" she begged hastily.

She kept her eye on Jane, an exasperated Jane, strangely pale and on the offensive.

"If you think that's going to stop me!" Farou said very loudly.

And Jane gathered herself together as if, fearing a blow, she was already trying to return it, while warding it off with white forehead and immaterial hair. A strange grimace distorted the childlike bow of her mouth and her eyes were filled with misery and hate.

"Jane!" Fanny cried, holding out her arms.

Her cry and gesture loosened the tensity of the frail body, whose hostile rigidity brought to Fanny's mind a young Fanny of long ago, bullied by Farou, and so closely resembling this enemy, this gallant, sheet-white woman.

"Go away!" Fanny ordered her husband. "Yes, you heard what I said. Go away. You've work to do elsewhere. And another time you'll vent your wrath on me, if you please, not on others. Not on others, at least not in front of me. . . . You're . . . you're impossible before a new play. In three days' time you'll be . . . you'll be feeling much better."

She stuttered a little and felt her chin trembling. For a very long time she had not known what it was like to be angry, and while struggling with herself she smiled vaguely, as do certain animals when they take pleasure in their own fury. Farou misinterpreted that smile and gave in with the grace of a guilty man.

"Dreadful!" he sighed. "I feel I'm dreadful! What a brute!"

He underlined the word and repeated it in a conciliatory tone. Fanny was recovering her breath and clenched her teeth to stop her chin from quivering.

"Jane, would you mind, please . . ." he began in a gentler tone.

But Fanny interrupted him.

97

"No, not tonight! Everything will be better tomorrow. Go to your rehearsal, and sharpen your claws on Tom, Dick and Harry, on Silvestre, on the programme seller, if you like, but leave us alone!"

"There are no programme sellers at rehearsals," said Farou shocked.

"Go, Farou, go to your bath, go!"

He left the room and Fanny immediately set about gathering up the empty port glasses and continued to talk so that Jane might remain silent awhile.

"Oh, good gracious! No really—really—what a ghastly profession his is! You know, in his present state, the small amount of port he's just drunk is enough to make him lose his self-control."

Meanwhile she thought: 'I escaped by the skin of my teeth! How could Jane let herself go like that? She was going to speak, shout, say things . . . especially . . .'

Having repowdered her face and redone her hair, Jane was applying lipstick to her mouth. Automatically she bit her lips, chewing the fresh rouge, then painted them again.

"Oh, you know," she said suddenly, "I could have answered him back quite easily! He may be Big Farou, but he doesn't frighten me. I've been through a lot worse!"

She cast defiant looks at the door which Farou had closed, and the words that fell from her lips were those of a quarrelsome woman of the streets, or a disgruntled workman. The little smooth grimace once more altered the shape of her mouth, and Fanny shivered, feeling lonely and uncomfortable.

"Jane, shall we have dinner? I hate these hysterical outbursts. We are alone. Jean has gone to the meeting of his 'Active Youth League'."

Jane took her arm. Her fingers, still tense, danced on Fanny's arm and she gave her an anonymous kiss behind the ear.

'Two months ago,' thought Fanny, 'I might have sat down to table alone, or I should have given the young woman a good dressing down. But now that I know they are guilty, I feel shy. . . .'

She was faced by a stoical companion who drank, ate and talked. But at moments Jane was transparent and speechless. Then Fanny was able to diagnose the passing of pain or anger, as she might have guessed from the face of a pregnant woman the secret movements of her child.

A little later in the evening Jean Farou came home. He smelt of tobacco and of a male scent which was not his own. He was still vibrating with the shouts uttered by a hundred insolent young throats around him and the senseless and vain words he had hurled into the smoky atmosphere. Dressed in new clothes, with a badly chosen tie, a peevish puffiness under his eyes, and a new shadow over his lip, Fanny compared him to a bruised fruit. His entrance broke in on the great silence, in which the two women had taken refuge with their needlework and reading, sitting almost elbow to elbow under the family lamp.

"Are you pleased with yourself? Did you yell your head off? Did you drink a lot of muck? Did you establish certain principles and throw out others? Are you feeling sick?"

Fanny did not wait for his answers; she was interposing herself between Jean Farou and Jane; but, unerring, Jean's gaze never left Jane's face. He turned to Fanny simply to enquire with his eyes, 'What's the matter with her? What's happened? What have you done to her?'

With a shrug of the shoulders, Fanny, at the limit of

her patience, replied: 'Oh, for goodness sake, leave me alone!'

Little Farou dared not speak to Jane, whose scorn kept him at a distance and who was separated from him even further by her attitude of monogamous repulsion.

"Yes," he said finally, without being aware that no one was asking him any more questions, "it was all very brilliant. We were a credit to our fathers. They would certainly not have disowned all the stupid things we said. What a bear garden!"

He had been changing since his return from the country: he was acquiring an assurance that depreciated and somehow lessened him. At times, Fanny, in an access of maternal affection, looked at him sadly.

"Is my father at the Vaudeville?"

"Of course," said Fanny.

"Are things going well over there?"

"So he says. Hasn't he taken you there yet?"

"No more than he has you, Mamie. And you, Jane?"

"No preferential treatment for me," Jane answered, her eyes on her book. "Since rehearsals started at the Vaudeville, I've heard scraps of readings, grinding of teeth, arguments between Silvestre and the stage designers. Really, Farou hides his work on the stage, as——"

"As a cat hides its retirements in the sand," said Fanny, who wanted them to laugh a little. "And really, I wonder why?"

"Because he's shy," said Jean.

Jane raised her head at the sound of this word, only to lower it again immediately with an evil little smile.

"You're not going to make me believe, Mamie, that you've never noticed that my father is shy?"

"I confess," said Fanny, annoyed, "that this . . .

characteristic, has never . . . precisely struck me up to now."

But she spoke haltingly while she reflected.

"I believe you, Mamie, I can believe you quite easily. Jane, most likely, can't have noticed it either."

This indirect attack did not ruffle Jane. Jean's glance greedily devoured Jane's shoulders, her arms, Jane's knees, Jane's hair; but in the inflamed blue of his smoke-reddened eyes, Fanny read only a glutton's stare and hopeless resentment.

'Perhaps he's beginning to hate her,' she thought.

Little by little he was losing his stepmother's goodwill and was aware of it. Available for looking after his material welfare, she still scolded him with a Nanny's bluntness. "Have you at least cut your toenails and taken your Eno's Fruit Salts? I know you! Your motto is 'Silk socks and dubious feet'. 'Clean teeth and a coated tongue.' "

But for nothing on earth would she have sat down opposite those blue eyes, clairvoyant, technically trained and intense in colour, to ask: 'Explain to me how you know that your father is shy! Tell me exactly—you who do not live with him, who talk to him so little, who are not his ally—tell me what you claim to know, what miraculously you do know of him!'

The mysterious and unhappy young creature shifted from one leg to the other, picked up the newspapers, shook an empty cigarette box; but Jane neither stirred, nor took her eyes from her book, until she heard midnight strike on a distant clock.

"Well, what now? Are you both staying here?"

"Farou has enough to keep him busy all night. Silvestre is keeping to his dates. Friday, the matinée for the dressmakers. Friday evening, dress rehearsal——"

101

"Saturday, twenty-four thousand francs box-office takings," continued Jean.

"*Inch'allah!*"

"Who came today, Mamie?"

"Various people," said Fanny laconically. "Clara, the Farou cousin, some other people—nobody much."

Jane, struck by the names of Clara and the Farou cousin, feared that of Inès Irrigoyen and advanced a peevish, aggressive countenance, but at that moment, Fanny did not even remember the fair-haired young woman.

"And on that, children, I'm going to bed."

"Me too," said Jane.

"Remarkable how . . . Remarkable unanimity," mocked Jean.

He had not dared to say 'solidarity'.

Jane heard him and took the offensive.

"Yes, indeed! Master-Little Farou, yes indeed! It is a remarkable solidarity! Have you any objections, Master Little-Farou?"

"Me? No. . . . Not at all. . . ."

Losing all his affronted child's swagger, little Farou gazed in terror at his first enemy.

"Hush, hush! Peace! Peace!" Fanny ordered softly. 'Oh, these Farous, how tired I am of them!'

She pushed Jean Farou towards his room. "Sleep well, child."

But at the moment when Jean turned on reaching the door, she could not prevent him from seeing Jane, in an attitude of deliberate frailty and defiance, leaning against her shoulder.

NINE

THE following days brought Fanny her full share of excitement, surprise and unexpected minor incidents. Esther Mérya, the star, caught cold; Henry Marsan sprained his ankle in a trap-door; a new set, vetoed by Farou and insisted upon by Silvestre, again delayed the dress rehearsal. At each fresh incident, Fanny remarked calmly: "The same thing happened with *Atalanta*. We had the same trouble with *Stolen Grapes*."

But Farou, forgetful, touchy, sick to death of his too often repeated lines, broke out in honest indignation.

"Where have you ever seen such a mess? Where? Do they go on like that in Berlin? Do they go on like that in London? Such a muddle! Such inefficiency! Such——"

"What about your little Irrigoyen? How is she getting along in all this?" asked Fanny, out of the blue.

"Who did you say? Oh, yes. She isn't doing anything, thank God! Biset has resumed her part."

"Really!" marvelled Fanny. She ceased to marvel as she noted in Jane a renewed and growing happiness which brightened her eyes, her complexion, the tone of her voice. At Fanny's slightest request, she hastened up: "What do you want, my Fanny?" like a golden-haired pink-and-white young girl, winged and busy as a bee. A little song, barely audible, never passed beyond her closed lips. Often, when addressed, even as she answered "What is it, Fanny?" her face betrayed the candour and hope of a betrothed bride.

At the same time, as soon as he turned his back on rehearsals, on experimental lighting, and on Esther Mérya's bedside, Farou recovered his sweet temper— which sometimes soared and sometimes plunged abysmally—as well as his pacified golden glance, even the scent which emanated from him when he was voluptuously satisfied, and Fanny became moody again. Treachery had left the lower levels and was creeping up on her again. Farou's pleasure ceased to be a passing phase, a caprice born in the street—of the street—of the theatre— gratified no matter where. She reached the point of childishly working out the grades of the adulterous hierarchy.

'The young Asselins, the Vivicas, the Irrigoyens and all the small fry are Jane's concern. She can storm, weep a little in corners and—if she dares—row with Farou. But what about Jane herself, my home, my poor domain of a woman who possesses nothing of her own?'

For the first time in her life, during sleepless nights, she longed for a room where she could have slept or lain awake alone. The flat contained only one spare room, which Jane occupied. Little Farou slept in a room which, had he not been there, would have been called "Madame's boudoir". At night, Fanny and her husband slept side by side. A single frame of English woodwork, of the Bing period, enclosed their twin beds. For years their tamed bodies had floated side by side during the night. Farou, unfaithful and a creature of habit, demanded Fanny's presence, her warm stillness, the spreading sheaf of her black hair into which he could thrust both fists and tumble it by stretching out a hand in the dark. His sleep required Fanny's slumbers, her prominent eyes so closely protected by the broad lids, the foolish expression her mouth assumed in sleep, and the whole of her utterly feminine body with its undulations, as she lay on her side, her elbows close to her knees.

"Nothing is more self-contained than you, when you're asleep," he would say to her.

'He used to call me a tramp, because I curled up like a retriever. He said that I must have once wandered along the high roads and slept in ditches.'

Sad and cowardly, then wise and dissembling, she relied on her face, rounded and soft as a child's, not to betray anything but deep emotions. She alternated between irritating unhappiness and a state of dreading anything in the nature of exterior upheavals, screams, confessions, convulsed faces and bodies.

Occasional visitors, whose appearance was as seasonal as that of starling or swallow, took her mind off the subject. They passed through the house—open to all and sundry—announcing that the stormy period of rehearsals was nearing its end and that the play was at last going to see the light of day. Fanny caught a glimpse of one of Farou's colleagues who specialised in recrimination. Behind a closed door she heard loud and tearful reproaches.

"No, old man, if you make a practice of pinching the subjects I'm working on, or of systematically taking up those I've staged more or less successfully, you should say so! Your *Impossible Innocence* is my *Woman Warrior*. Come now, nothing else than my *Woman Warrior*. What's that! Doesn't love belong to everyone who writes plays? I agree, old man, but it doesn't prevent similarities being there! Flers and Croisset are already shamelessly using my *Rosine*. You must admit that disaster dogs me!"

"Your plays are nothing but a disaster," replied Farou, who promptly became 'unkind to the man', as Fanny used to say.

105

Before her eyes passed young actresses who hushed their voices in order to instil ideas of intrigue into Farou's mind; resounding duennas, a very handsome young man who departed all swollen with tears, like a rain-drenched rose.

"What's the matter with him? What have you done to him, Farou? He's crying!"

Farou roared with laughter. "I should jolly well think he is crying! It's Crescent!"

"Who?"

"Crescent?"

"Who is Crescent?"

Farou raised his arms.

"Oh, it's just like you not to know the Crescent story! I haven't time to tell you now. Ask Jane!"

Fanny never knew the Crescent story. Finally came the crack reporters and photographers for advance publicity. For both species Farou sported his faun-in-the-sun grin, as he leant over his desk, resting on his fists. There came, separately, Henry Marsan and Esther Mérya, protagonists with bitter complaints about one another. There came unknown actors with faces like beadles, who having conscientiously and modestly rehearsed for a month, declared that they would not act "under such con-ditions".

"What conditions, Farou?"

Farou made a gesture of despotic indifference.

"I don't know. 'Under such conditions'—'In such cir-cumstances'—'And this being the case'—they are compulsory and expletive formulas."

"Is it serious?"

"Not in the slightest, my Fanny. God, how simple you are! It's quite usual. They'll act, and act very well."

"Then what's the point?"

"Ah, what's the point! And what of vain imaginings, Fanny? And the need to increase their importance in my eyes and in their own?"

He changed his tone and spoke briefly.

"Fanny, you're coming the day after tomorrow to my last technical rehearsal. If you see my son, it would be kind of you to inform him that he can accompany you."

"And Jane?"

"She has been told."

'This,' thought Fanny, 'is a summons, not an invitation. Let us sort this out. Why does he adopt that tone when he decides to show me a new play? "Because he's shy," Jean Farou would say.'

"You will doubtless be pleased to note that I've toned down the safe scene. Branc-Ursine still steals the letters, but he commits the theft off-stage, in the next room."

Fanny suppressed a shriek of laughter and bit the inside of her mouth. Farou could only bring himself to talk to her about his plays by using a harsh, schoolmasterish tone.

'Because he's shy,' she thought promptly. 'That merciless child was right.'

But she began to laugh secretly. 'He commits the theft off-stage . . . that's delicious!'

"So that," Farou continued, as if he were at the blackboard, "the audience is sufficiently informed by seeing the bundle of papers in his hands, and silent action can be far more impressive than an exclamation. It's the curtain. Do you understand?" he concluded, relieved.

"Excellent, excellent!" approved Fanny. "Much better. Much less——"

"Yes, yes, I know," interrupted Farou. "Hop off to your 'final fitting', to your Fanny-fitting. Shall you be beautiful?"

She mimed an Andalusian belle, her eyes velvety under her black band of hair.

"Irresistible! Irresistible and discreet. Lace—skin under the lace—a red coral flan right in the middle of the corsage—your grandmother to the life!"

"Cheers! I'll make love to my grandmother!"

Long afterwards, she remembered how, that day, his glance had wandered, his right eyelid had twitched nervously, and how passionately he had longed for holidays, vulgarity, stupidities and celebrations—all of which could be perceived through the fog of exhaustion. He smiled at Fanny in a womanly way and lowered his voice.

"They say there's such a charming film at the *Aubert* . . ."

And she was just a little sorry for him, remembering that he was short of sleep, freedom, leisurely meals, fresh air, and that, nevertheless, he never shirked any professional responsibility or dreary task.

"You're not going *over there* this afternoon?"

"Not for my weight in gold! I'll only go there tonight. In any case, they rehearse better without me. I seem rather to put them off their stroke. Yes, I put them off their stroke," he repeated sadly. "It's strange—I can never help them right up to the end."

"Well have a rest and then dress yourself up to the nines—Jane, are you coming to my final fitting?" she called.

Jane emerged from the dining-room, her sleeves rolled up and an apron tied over her skirt, looking very pretty.

"Fanny, you're crazy! And what will the new maid do? She doesn't even know how to lay the table. You'd think that in her last job her employers never ate! And I'm also ironing my petticoats . . ."

She was waving an electric iron tethered to the end of its flex and Fanny went off alone.

She returned, tired out after playing the part of "the author's wife" in front of icy young saleswomen and lively, gushing old saleswomen crowned with red or white curls, bursting with false emotions and deadly tittle-tattle, and burning with an old-fashioned passion for the theatre, actors and smart plays. These asked a hundred questions, pausing miraculously on the verge of the most outrageous indiscretions. She liked those sly old know-alls, bristling with claws, as satanic and maternal as attendants in a special hell for the convalescent damned.

When Fanny returned home, the house smelt clean. A vinegary scent carried the news into the hall that Farou had relaxed in a bath. He was singing in the distance, going to and from his study to the once white bathroom, yellowing now and old-fashioned in its fittings.

The new maid, full of zeal for the first two days, was following the houseboy about, memorising the instructions he gave her in a low voice. With devoutly hushed footsteps, they circled the laid dining-room table as though it were a death bed. But Fanny already knew that, in the kitchen, the new servant smoked and stubbed out her cigarettes with her thimble. Never mind! This evening the house was like a home, provided with a master, adorned with a friend who was probably devoted to her and so little guilty, probably. . . . A need to be able to love in peace, to shut her eyes to things, to grow old, softened Fanny's heart.

> "*When the season of crisis is again to the fore*
> *And Rip, Pierre Wolff and all the Bourdets*
> *Are on the rocks once more,*
> *And Mirande proudly awaits his encore . . .*"

sang Farou, who was not superstitious.

109

A peal of laughter from Jane greeted his improvisation. Fanny had just put a large cardboard box on the bed before switching on the two dressing-table lamps. Against the lighted background of the bathroom she saw Farou in his shirt sleeves and Jane, protected by her maid's apron, rinsing out a shaving brush.

"What?" said Farou. "Isn't that a pretty song, then?"

"Stupid!" Jane replied in her angel voice.

"Ah! Really stupid?"

He pressed Jane against the wall, hiding her entirely with his tall thick-set body. Nothing could be seen of her but two small feet and a bare elbow resting on Farou's shoulder.

Placing his hand on her forehead, he tilted back her head and kissed her mouth in comfort, without lingering.

"And that—is also stupid?"

The young woman disguised as a servant shook herself free with an air of coquettish bravado, looked at herself in the mirror and answered in rather a husky voice: "It's worse than stupid, it's bungled."

She moved out of the clear background of the bathroom and Fanny trembled with fear. 'She'll see me—she's coming in here—she'll know that I've seen them.'

And she fled into the dining-room where, to keep herself in countenance, she was drinking a glass of water when Jane found her.

"Water before meals? Are you at last being sensible, Fanny? Have you just come back? Where is the dress?"

"I've brought it back."

"That's much safer. But don't drink so quickly! What's come over you?"

"I'm rather cold," said Fanny.

Jane took the half-filled glass from her.

"Cold? Ah, no, Fanny! Nothing so foolish, please!

No influenza before the first night! But I don't like the look of you at all, now you're back! Give me your hands!"

Fanny's hands allowed themselves to be roughly examined by two hands which retained the vinegary scent of Farou's bath; two dark grey eyes, steady and searching, looked straight into her own, seeking for signs of a possible illness. She coughed away a sob and tears rose to her eyes.

"Your throat! Of course! Aspirin, quinine, bed, hot drinks—Farou!"

"Leave him alone."

"Nonsense! Farou!"

He came, his cheeks and ears white with talcum powder and his little improvised song on his lips.

"She's ill," Jane cut him short.

"No," said Fanny struggling.

"No?" said Farou.

"She-really-is-ill!" affirmed Jane. "Big Farou, are you going *over there*? Then stop at the all-night chemist and send back by the car some English aspirin, a box of plasters and some tincture of methylene. I'll write it all down and you can give the list to Fraisier."

She left the room while Farou bent over Fanny, repeating: "Well, my Fanny? Well?"

'Ah! Well never mind—it's easier that way,' thought Fanny.

She gave Farou a slight, apologetic smile, closed her eyes and slipped full length on to the carpet.

Her sham fainting fit gave her respite and repose. Entrenched behind her closed eyelids, she listened to the sound of voices and rapid breathing. Farou picked her up bodily, clumsily, with powerful arms. She abandoned herself to those masculine arms, made to ravish and

111

wound. She knew he would knock her feet as he went through the door, but that he would hold her firmly. Always that vinegary scent of bathwater. . . .

"Here, get out of the way so that I can pass," he said to Jane.

"I'm holding the door open to prevent it closing on you. Don't shake a fainting woman about in that way! Wait till I turn down the bed! Go and tell Henriette to fill a hot-water bottle!"

"Shall I telephone Doctor Moreau?"

"If you like. At the moment he can do no more than I can. The first thing to do is to get her conscious again quickly. There's nothing wrong with her lungs, her breathing is steady."

They spoke quickly, in whispers. Fanny prolonged this moment of secret watch, of relaxation, of false pretence. She had managed to let her head fall into a position that enhanced her beauty and the bedside light shed a rosy glow on her closed eyelids. A hand slid the flabby, burning hot-water bottle under her shoeless feet.

"It's boiling," said the maid's voice. "I will take off Madame's stockings."

"Then—shall I go?" asked Farou.

"Yes, go. Don't forget the chemist!"

"What a thing to say! Shall I 'phone from the Vaude-ville?"

"If you like. Personally, I think it's only a very minor complaint."

"But she doesn't usually suffer from minor complaints," said Farou, perplexed.

"That doesn't mean that she hasn't any right to have them, does it? Go quickly!"

As Jane's hand sought for the hooks of Fanny's dress, it lightly touched her breasts and Fanny could not repress

112

the jerk of a fully conscious woman. Filled with shame, she opened her eyes.

"Ah, there you are!" said Jane. "There you are! Well, really!"

She wanted to laugh and instead burst into nervous tears. Forgetting the gesture that prostrated her, with her head rolling in Fanny's lap, her tears broadcast, Jane wept where she stood, quite simply, dabbing her eyes with her handkerchief. With one hand she made a sign.

'Wait, it will soon be over.'

She was not embarrassed by Fanny's big eyes, dark and expressionless, which were staring fixedly at her. She sat down on the bed and pushed back the band of black hair which fell across one white cheek.

"Now tell me. How did it happen?"

Fanny clenched her clasped hands and summoned all her strength in order to remain silent.

'If I speak, Jane will exclaim: "What! Because of that? Because of Farou and me? But that goes back to the dawn of time! But surely you're not making a fuss about that? But you yourself have said a score of times . . ." '

"You aren't in the family way, by any chance?"

Her words seemed so inappropriate to Fanny that she smiled.

"What was so funny in what I said? Do you think you are proof against all kinds of little Farous, boys or girls?"

"No," said Fanny, feeling extremely awkward. All that was most commonplace and sensitive in her nature considered for an instant the picture that moves all women—a child, indistinct and small. Fanny placed her hand on Jane's fair forehead and was hesitatingly imprudent. "It would . . . it wouldn't . . . Well, you wouldn't . . . mind if I gave birth to an unkind little Farou?"

113

Jane lowered her eyes. The dilated white nostrils, the quivering corners of her mouth, the chin which revealed the movements of her throat as she gulped with emotion —every feature in her face fought and triumphed.

"No," she said, opening her eyes again. "No," she repeated, refuting some claim which she was stifling. "No."

'I don't think she is lying,' Fanny decided.

She did not remove her hand which was stroking the fair hair. In this way she kept at a distance, at arm's length, a head and body which, in a muddled feeling of equality worthy of the harem, she would have taken into her arms and embraced.

A little later, she extorted the small perquisites of her position. She represented one of the two powers revered by domestic servants: sickness and wealth. She had a cup of clear soup, cold stewed apples soaked in red gravy from the joint, grapes, and magazines strewn on her bed. Jane remained in the salon so as not to tire "the invalid".

'What a fuss they're making of me,' thought Fanny.

She practised lying flat on her back, her bare arms flung out on the coverlet, seeking the cool air.

'I'm probably slightly feverish. No, the aspirin is making my head spin.'

A tide of sound, ebbing and flowing, approached and retreated, and with it rose and then receded a picture, whose significance she did not very clearly perceive at this particular time: Jane flattened against the wall, almost hidden by Farou's vast body. She fell asleep and awoke towards eleven o'clock. In a hushed voice, Jean Farou was asking Jane's permission to enter the room. Jane, on the threshold, was keeping him prudishly in his place.

"You'll tire her. This is hardly the place for a boy. Tomorrow, if she has a good night."

Rested by her short sleep, Fanny no longer enjoyed being treated as an invalid and called out:

"Yes, yes, you can come in! Sit there. There's nothing wrong with me, you know."

"Nothing?" protested Jane. "She fell like a log, look, just here where I'm standing! She had come back from her fitting, I hadn't even heard her come in and we were even thinking that she was rather late in returning."

Jean, who was already as bored as if he had been at a hospital sick bed, intelligently raised his head.

"Who do you mean by 'we'?"

"Your father and I. Your father didn't go to his rehearsal. His actresses were all with their dressmakers. He had a bath and a shave and titivated himself like a blushing bride. . . ."

But Jean was no longer listening. He had ostentatiously ceased to listen, and he remained silent when Jane left the room.

"I'm able to talk," Fanny said to him when they were alone. "What's more, I'm quite all right now. I stayed in bed because it's comfortable here and I don't want to look ugly at the dress rehearsal; people would think I'd got stage fright."

He did not answer. After a moment's silence, he stared point blank at Fanny and shot at her the words "And so?" in so pointed and bitterly searching a manner that she blushed.

"And so—what? And so—nothing!"

She tossed about in her bed and pushed up her pillow.

"And so," repeated Jean, "they were there when you came in?"

115

She did not answer, her eyes strenuously avoided the stony blue of the eyes that were tracking her down.

"And then? Then, you were . . . you fainted? How?"

His words summoned up for her the picture of the child lying on the slope of the hill, head and feet dangling limp, the fair hair spattered with grit. But now the child had become this stranger, mad with grief, selfishly drunk with the need to hurt himself more and ever more. No shadow of pity moistened the blue eyes which questioned her, heedless of her feelings, and on the innocent mouth there trembled but one shameful question—the same, ever the same.

"They were—where?" he stammered.

She could never have believed that he would come to this.

No shadow of pity. She turned her head sideways on the pillow to hide her tears.

"When you came in, were they . . .?"

Between her lashes, clotted with her tears, she could see the child whom she had looked after, in sickness and health, who had grown up at her side for more than ten years. Obsessed with his first sorrow, he lived only to nourish it.

'How cruel is a child without hope!' Fanny said to herself. And her tears, flowing more easily, hid from her the fair face and the bitter curiosity of the blue eyes.

"Were they in here?"

As she was silent, he made a movement of angry impatience in which was apparent his contempt for tears.

"If I were you, Mamie . . ."

Jean's dramatic, threatening gesture which brought him to his feet was redeemed by a child-like haughtiness.

'A child,' thought Fanny. 'A child that I brought up. He was so gentle.'

116

She exaggerated the common sentimental links of the past in order to increase her tears; but all the new, recently awakened elements in her did not tolerate this procedure for long.

'Brought up! We'll go into that later. And as for his gentleness! He hasn't a shred of pity for anything, not even at this very moment for the woman he loves.'

Contact with this ulcerated child was calming her and when she spoke her voice was steady.

"You will never be me, child. Don't think you ever will be. And let me rest now. Good night, child, good night."

But he did not go away. His glance wandered over all the surrounding objects and seemed to call for help, witnesses, allies, a universal clamour. He rose, with swift obedience, only at the sound of Jane's voice.

"This late visit has lasted very long. Isn't he tiring you, Fanny?"

"A little."

"Jean? Do you hear? Clear out at once, child."

He went out of the door, carefully avoiding contact with Jane, and Fanny, delivered from the aggressive child, from his rigid, frenzied mind, which battered itself against the very walls, was able to breathe again.

The solitude and the silence were broken only by street noises, and by the coming and going of Jane, tall and luminous, and by the hardly perceptible breath of air which carried to the bedside the rhythm of her dress and her unctuous, slave-girl movements.

A lamp in the avenue below served as a nightlight. Open and ghostly, Farou's bed also lit up the room.

In its early stages, insomnia is almost an oasis in which those who have to think or suffer darkly take refuge. For

117

the past three hours, Fanny had been longing for darkness and, precisely, for insomnia. All they gave her was the vivid picture in natural colours of a group pressed against the wall of the bathroom. She examined it in detail—the bare arm resting on the masculine shoulder, Farou's hair like a bunch of mistletoe against the wall, two corners of the apron fluttering. In short, nothing very terrible, nothing indecent, nothing sensual, which would justify the presence in Fanny's breast of those uneven heart beats, that imagined hardening of the heart, not the uneasiness and exaggerated fear that the pair had guessed her presence there.

'I must speak to Farou. To Farou, or to Jane? To Farou and Jane.'

She no longer recognised herself.

"Your'e much too simple," Farou would say. "You're a monster."

'Where was this Fanny, this monster?'

'Yes, I must speak to Farou first. No screams, no rows, just make him straightforwardly face up to the situation. . . . Come, that's impossible! We're no longer very young lovers; I shall therefore not take the line of physical jealousy which only enters into it in the very smallest degree.'

But an elaboration of that very small degree reminded her of Farou's good nourishing healthy mouth and the breath of his nostrils when he prolonged a tenacious kiss. She sat up abruptly, switched on the light and seized a mirror from the bedside table. The expression of an angry woman superimposed on a gentle face, endowed her with a double chin and a pouting lower lip, which she corrected. Except for her fine obstinate eyes, she considered that she looked ugly, but the evidence of her own violent feelings did not displease her.

'I can still lose my temper,' she thought, as she might have said during a siege, "Ah, we've still got a three months' stock of sugar!"

She smoothed her cheeks and her chin with her hand, and pushed away and settled her angry face into the background. 'In case of need, you never know.' She became quieter, with her sense of security restored through having seen and touched on her face, unchanged and ready for all emergencies, the innate savagery of the female species. A wave of loyalty brought about a truce.

'Later. In any case, after the dress rehearsal.'

So she turned out the light like a good little girl and when Farou came home, towards three o'clock in the morning, she remained motionless beneath her hair and peeped at him.

In the gloom, he wandered about aimlessly, coughing with fatigue and nervous exhaustion. Then he cast aside his garments like a defeated warrior. His broad back was bowed when he ceased to think about it and the weight of his arms dragged his shoulders forward. At the sight of this physical distress she, an inalienable ally of other days, nestling under her great curtain of black hair, nearly flew to his rescue, to offer beverages, smiles, words, all the consolations tested and found worthy during the past ten years. She controlled herself, suffered strangely, and feigned sleep.

TEN

"WILL anyone else but us be there, Farou?"

"Of course. Cellerier is coming along. I couldn't refuse her."

"Why?"

"She has a certain influence—*ex officio!*—at the *Comédie Française*! If the . . ."

"Wherever she goes she pretends she's the power behind the throne," interpolated Jane.

"—if *Stolen Grapes* goes from the *Gymnase*, where it's been stuck for three years, to the *Français*, I'd rather have Cellerier on my side."

"Oh, yes. . . . And who else?"

"Their Ladyships, the dressmakers, their Lordships, the dress-designers. The bootmaker. An American agent. A couple of fellows from the German theatres. Photographers. Silvestre is also bringing some people. And Van Dongen, because he's painting Esther Mérya's portrait."

"I see," said Fanny, annoyed. "In other words, the dressmaker's show! The whole of Paris. You should have warned me. Oh, that telephone!"

Farou looked at his wife in surprise. He had never before seen her nervous or temperamental on the occasion of a new play. The telephone had kept Jane with one elbow on the table and the receiver at her ear since morning.

"The critic of the *Echo de la Péripherie* is asking for a seat at the second performance," Jane transmitted.

Farou did not deign to reply. Egotistically and uninterruptedly idle, he had spent a painful, interminable afternoon.

"Why didn't you go *over there* today?"

His smile was forced. "Because no one needs me any longer. Jane, find out who has just rung the door-bell. Ernest is so stupid. After that, get Silvestre's office for me. What's been done about the flowers? Has anyone thought about Esther's red roses?"

"Yes," said Jane.

"And Marsan's cigars and Carette's note-case?"

"Yes," said Jane.

"Abel Hermant's seat in the dress circle? Have you seen to——?"

"Yes," said Jane, "exchanged for his favourite lower box."

"What are those papers under the crystal paperweight?"

"Requests for seats, of course."

Farou became nervously fussy. "But I haven't seen them! You must always show them to me—always! Why didn't you show them to me before?"

Jane held the papers out to him and he pushed them away. Fanny listened silently.

"Is that rain you can hear?" asked Farou suddenly.

"Yes," said Jane, "but the glass is going up."

"What's the time?" asked Fanny in the midst of a silence.

"Oh, Fanny!" said Farou through clenched teeth. "It's always too early! Esther's famous costume change in the second act will be enough to land us in for an hour's fitting, screams and hysterics this evening. . . . We're having something to eat beforehand, I suppose? If Jean doesn't get back in time, you are not to wait for him."

121

"Jean will meet us at the Vaudeville," said Fanny.

"And where is he dining?"

"With his committee."

"He's on a committee?"

"He's seventeen."

As usual, whenever Fanny showed signs of a sense of humour, Farou raised his eyebrows and was careful not to smile.

"Had I known that there were going to be so many people, I would have dressed," said Fanny. "Will Silvestre be in front?"

"Yes," replied Farou, "and also on the stage and also in his office, not to mention the flies and the prompt box."

"What does he say about the play?"

"I don't know."

"What? You don't know?"

"No. We're no longer on speaking terms."

"But you never told me! Why?"

"We're on the eve of a dress rehearsal. We've been rehearsing for forty days. He's the producer and I'm the author. There's no other reason."

He was tapping the windowpanes streaked with long tears of rain. He yawned plaintively.

"To have finished a play is not as amusing as one might think."

*   *   *

On the stage, with the curtain up, an endless argument was in progress between the stage hands and the stage manager. It had been going on for half an hour and might well go on for ever. The flute-like voice of the portly chief property man maintained a courteous tone and vocabulary. The stage manager, who looked like Barrès, took up the challenge and exhibited an invincible politeness. In a lower box, Jane and Fanny already knew by heart the details of the set for the first act, notable for its genuine antique furniture, English silver and "real" bound books, and they retreated to the back of the box, chins nestling in their fur collars, shoulders hunched, as on a station platform. Towards half-past nine, Jean Farou slipped in beside them and asked, "Hasn't it begun yet?" and received uncertain signs in reply. Interrupting his dialogue, the stage manager turned towards the auditorium and addressed the black vacuum and the vague parallel rows of seat covers.

"Is Monsieur Silvestre in the house?"

After what seemed to be a very long pause, a sentence floated down from a tenor-voiced seraph, invisible and flying at a great height.

"Not here yet!"

The rain pattered steadily on the dome of the theatre.

"What are they doing?" asked Jean.

"Waiting!" answered Jane. "Oh, there's Farou!"

The stage made him look taller. He exchanged a few words with the impassive stage manager, took the bloated and floating chief property man into a corner. The latter disappeared and returned with two skinny stage hands. Thanks to their ministrations, a blue settee flanked by a Chinese table disappeared and a ministerial desk and two chairs took their place. Then the stage manager swep back the Barrès-like lock of hair, put on his hat and left the stage. From a vast basket presented to him by the property man, Farou fished out a little Louis XIV wall clock, a Japanese vase, a desk candlestick, which appeared to be made of silver, and a morocco-bound blotting pad. He placed the ornaments here and there, ruffled up the artificial roses in a vase, then he stepped back to judge the effect, altered the position of a piece of furniture and readjusted the angle of a flower. Fanny watched this frivolous task unsympathetically, as if she had been watching Farou make women's hats, or embroider on the tambour. Jane touched her arm.

"You'll see—they'll forget to put the stick of sealing wax into the drawer."

Fanny noted that she was serious and attentive, and jealously tried to imitate her.

A white-gloved hand rose from a scrum of people clustered round the cameras in the middle of the auditorium.

"It's Cellerier, to let you know she's here," said Jane.

"Cellerier and who else?"

"People she brought with her, no doubt."

"What cheek!" said Jean.

"The first hands from the couture houses are further on, under the dress circle. Therefore Mérya is dressed and so is Dorilys. I therefore wonder what they're waiting for?"

She was biting her thumbnail. Fanny, overcome by an attack of recurrent yawns, gathered her coat about her shoulders and crossed it over her legs. Jean Farou left the box and came back with some whitish sweets, tasting of old vinegar. With little sideways dance-steps, the guests slipped between the rows of the stalls and greeted each other in low voices, as if in church.

From gaping boxes, which Fanny had believed empty, escaped sounds of a cough, a laugh, the snap of a bag closing.

On the set, between two leaves of the folding doors, a woman's head peeped out, shining with all the colours of a bouquet, and was withdrawn immediately.

"It's Mérya," said Jane in a low respectful voice.

"She's blonde now," remarked Jean.

"And a superb make-up. Did you have time to notice it?"

"Yes. Luminous. She looks ten years younger. At least, so it seemed to me."

They whispered feverishly. In the uncomfortable box, Jean leaned towards Jane, touching her with his shoulder and knee and inhaling an atmosphere saturated with her scent and her blonde warmth. He relaxed in the darkness, but stifled a little piercing laugh when his father crossed the set with a Spanish shawl over his arm.

"Ah, there's Marsan with Farou. Do you like Marsan's smoking jacket?"

"You can't like a smoking jacket. Why is he wearing one?"

"He's screamingly funny," decreed Jean from the height of his new suit.

"Fanny, do you remember your wild attack of giggles at the dress rehearsal of *Atalanta*?"

"My wild attack of giggles?"

"Yes, because of Grault's smoking jacket, his seducer's jacket of bottle-green ottoman silk, my dear! You just couldn't stop."

'My wild attack of giggles . . . I couldn't stop. Yes, I still want to laugh irrepressibly. I shall get over the state I'm in. You get over it, like an illness. I want to——'

"Mérya is making her entrance," whispered Jane. "Oh, that is a lovely dress! Just look at Mérya's dress. Fanny—eh?"

"Black is always distinguished."

"Will you go round and see Esther Mérya in her dressing-room after the first act, Mamie? Can I go with you?"

"No, no," said Fanny quickly, gathering her coat closely about her and contracting her breasts. "I shan't go. You can go with your father."

"Her real name is Mayer, isn't it, Mamie?"

"Of course."

As he bathed in the artificial light of the theatre, she saw the young boy's face glow, in spite of himself, the moment a couple of actors' faces in their traditional make-up appeared. He professed extreme coldness and distaste for Farou's profession, but in the presence of actors and actresses, grease paint, stifling boxes, the preparation and celebration of theatrical rites, he became once more a dazzled child.

"Farou is green about the gills," remarked Jane.

"In contrast," said Fanny, "Marsan has put on a sun-tan foundation. What a queer idea!"

"It gives a virile effect."

"Really?" asked Jean anxiously.

Fanny smiled as she noticed how simple he remained beneath his passion and hostility and how much import-ance he attached to Jane's slightest word. The curtain fell; a cold voice requested silence and added: "Persons not concerned with the play are asked to leave the stage."

"Who's speaking?" enquired Fanny.

"The box at the back of the theatre. The one with the yawning black cavern. It's Silvestre, who has just arrived. It's Father he means by 'persons not concerned with the play'."

The "fireman" struck twelve quick blows on the boards, then three solemn ones; a lazy little roll of dust swept along the surface of the floor under the curtain; the imposing furniture reappeared and the rehearsal began. Fanny leaned her head against the partition of the box and closed her eyes in order to listen. She opened them at a muffled exclamation from Jane.

"Oh, her scream misfired badly! What luck it's today and not tomorrow that she's muffed it! But in such an experienced actress, it's inexcusable. Farou must be simply furious! What do you think, Fanny?"

Fanny said nothing. Dumbfounded, she was emerging from a deep sleep which had appeared to be of short duration. 'Is it possible? I was asleep!' She gauged the isolating depth of her anxiety. Following suit, she repeated as the curtain fell: "It's really inexcusable!"

The auditorium was once more faintly illuminated. Palid, Jane was furiously biting her thumbnail. The door of the box opened under Clara Cellerier's gloved fist.

"Nothing serious, children!" she cried. "Only she must be careful tomorrow. An old warhorse like me knows why these things happen, these purely vocal accidents. The heat of the dressing-rooms and fatigue as well—I grant you fatigue. If Mérya had brought her voice a little more forward—d'you see? 'Hin, hin, hin,' like that!—it would never have cracked. Ouf! That's over!"

She sat down. The weak diffused light deprived her of her high colour and reduced her face down to the great shadowy holes of the eyes and the deep ravine of her mouth. For a few moments, Fanny imagined that her sleep had lasted long enough to age Clara Cellerier by twenty years.

"Let's talk about the play. By Jingo, what a masterpiece! That direct manner of entering straight into the plot, eh? Farou is a thruster! What an attack! I must confess that Marsan is first-rate. And the rogue remains a handsome devil. Between you and me, Fanny, when Mérya despairingly answers him: 'So many women have come to this office to beg you to save them, but I shall not leave it until I have ruined one or other of us,' don't you think that—gives it away a little too much?"

In the shadow, Fanny blushed; that dialogue had not disturbed her sleep. Jane forestalled her and answered

127

with some heat, "Oh, Madame, a woman like the beautiful Madame Houcquart could not express herself in any other way. She's sure enough of herself to be in a position to unmask her batteries."

"Madame Houcquart is neither an inexperienced girl nor an *ingénue*," insisted Jean. "She doesn't demean herself by trying to play canny with a fellow like Branc-Ursine! Does she, Mamie?"

"You make my head whirl, the lot of you! I shall have to see the play through at least twice. I'm not as quick-witted as you," said Fanny out of cowardice.

She was dreading Farou's arrival; he came in almost immediately. He no longer seemed irritated, or worried, or even disappointed. Perhaps he felt already that languorous distaste which, after the first performance, kept him away from theatres where his plays were running.

"How do you do, Clara? It went well, didn't it, except when Mérya's voice went—a purely material mishap!"

Clara hung on to his shoulders and gave him her accolade. "What a masterpiece! What a structure! Real Farou granite!"

Farou tried to catch Fanny's eye.

"Oh," he conceded limply, "perhaps its only conglomerate. Fanny—you like it? Or not?"

She took his hands, pressed them and tried to satisfy him by a fervent silence.

"You shall tell me later. You are my stern little judge. I'm all of a tremble."

He was joking uneasily and Fanny thought he lacked his usual arrogance. She hated anything which resembled humility in Farou and took it out on her stepson.

"Well, Jean! Aren't you saying anything to Big Farou? You were enthusiastic enough just now! I could hardly control them," she said, indicating Jean and Jane.

"Oh, bravo, Father, bravo!" Jean applauded with affectation.

"Yes?" said Farou absent-mindedly. "Let's wait for the end. You're very sweet. Whereupon, children, I return to my stoking."

"If Marsan could hear you!" spluttered Clara.

In the gloom, her joyous laugh carved out the black, cavernous grin of a skull.

In the orchestra pit the photographers erected their limp magnesium balloons and Clara yawned.

"They'll be a long time. What about going outside to smoke a cigarette and drink a grog?"

"No, no," said Fanny quickly.

She corrected herself. "Not I, at least, I'm chilly, on edge. You three go whilst I rest. Yes, I insist, go!"

Left alone, she again leant her head against the partition and waited. Her sorrow was unsatisfactory. At times she would have preferred a young girl's grief, shrill and distraught, outside all self-respect, while at others she regretted her light-heartedness of the previous year and the bitter little mystery of the absolutions she granted Farou. She could not forgive her sorrow for being bearable and for taking its place, between despair and indifference, in a spiritual region which allowed of diversions, pleasures, scruples, and compensations. She was ceaselessly surprised that treachery had not changed Farou in her eyes and that Jane herself—'Except that I cannot bear *that*, I wish her no ill. At least I don't think I bear her any ill will.'

Clara Cellerier returned before Jane.

"Were you asleep, lovely darkling! I'll leave you. No? Let me tell you the local gossip, young woman! Marsan is starting a boil and a temperature. Up aloft, Dorilys and Biset are saying—saying! they're yelling—that Choquart only gave them a job here to have both of them conveniently at his disposal. If you could have seen Farou restoring peace! He held Dorilys with one arm and Biset with the other: you can well imagine they took advantage of the situation, especially Dorilys. It was enough to make you die of laughter."

'When one has no friends,' thought Fanny, 'from whom does one seek advice? From no one. And anyway, of what value is a friend's advice? This old Clara would give me advice in accordance with tradition, her tradition, in a manner it makes me sick to think of it. She would give me Francillon's or Mimi's advice."

"It has stopped raining!" exclaimed Jane. "I knew that the glass wasn't lying! It's fine and warm."

She brought back with her fresh air with a touch of damp in it, and the sooty scent of Paris rain. Her cold hand immediately sought Fanny's.

"They're starting, Fanny. Be off, Madame Cellerier! Silvestre said he would decapitate anyone who opened a door or put down a seat after the curtain was up! The same set is used for the second and third acts, so one can hope that by two o'clock at the very latest . . . I left Jean Farou with one of the Silvestre boys, but as they are twins, I can't tell you which it was."

She bent over Fanny, peering at her under the brim of her hat.

"I don't know why, but I've got a feeling that you're not well. I'm not happy about it. I don't like leaving you alone. Take it—here's a little bunch of violets. All they lack is the scent of violets!"

Without seeing it, Fanny touched the tiny bunch, dewy with water, stiff, still alive and smelling of ditch water like a tiny animal from the hedgerows. She thanked her with a motion of the hand and a tight-lipped smile. The only human being to whom she could have spoken with a hope of being understood sat down at her side. She drew her coat more closely about her and made room for Jane.

"In the café next door, they say that it promises to be a very powerful play."

"Yes, yes—as usual!"

"As usual?"

"But of course, of course: 'A powerful piece of writing', 'a powerful third act', 'an irresistible force drives the tragic characters to their fate'. We've read enough of them, those clichés, you more than I, since you paste up the press cuttings. Farou's 'power' is Farou's flesh and blood. It's his physique, his manner. I've always thought that if Farou had been a skinny little thing with a pince-nez, we would have read something different—'acute perception', or 'many-pointed ironical shafts'. Don't you think so? Tell me!"

"What does Farou think of your point of view? Have you mentioned it to him?"

"It isn't easy to talk to Farou. Have you never noticed that?"

"I have," said Jane.

The curtain rose. On the stage, Mérya and Dorilys were attacking their big scene, the latter pitching high her colourless, nondescript, childish voice, the other using a slightly rasping, velvety contralto. The one intended to keep the lover whom she would not marry, the other fought to possess the same man. On two occasions, isolated and vigorous rounds of applause burst out here and there amongst the half-hundred spectators, like gorse pods in a fire.

"It's good, that!" whispered Jane.

The two actresses redoubled their fictitious coldness and their feigned pride: they sensed already tomorrow's success. Their acting became tinged with that excess of natural behaviour and conviction which brings the theatre down to the level of the basest enthusiasms. Fanny heard Clara Cellerier's voice call out "Bravo!" during a pause which Farou had inserted just to allow someone to shout "Bravo", and the bitter dialogue went on again. This time Fanny listened irreverently.

'Perhaps he really does believe that it would happen like that in real life. He makes me laugh!'

Sheltered from observation, without turning her head, she looked surreptitiously at Jane. Jane was biting her nail and her eyelashes fluttered.

'She is moved. Perhaps she too thinks that it would happen like that. Which day must I choose for her to learn, and I myself to learn, that it does not happen like that?'

Tragic cries assailed her ears. Mérya weakened before a Dorilys who defied her in a Joan of Arc attitude, tense and visionary.

"*You do not know—you no longer know, Madame—what a young girl is like. All the virgin strength, all the untapped innocence I bear within me, the most heinous sin I could commit, the finest deed I could perform—I hurl them all against you, I cast them into the battle for him!*"

In the depth of her soul Fanny was looking at two real, rather dreary, women, self-controlled, careful to avoid raising their voices, to escape a servant's curiosity, to save appearances.... She shivered. '*It must come soon.... It must come soon....*' A hand passed across the back of her neck and turned up her fur collar, then slipped under her arm and remained in its warm fold, as if asleep.

'Always that hand! What can I do with that hand?

And what if, some day soon, I have to cast off that hand, forcibly open the fingers which will perhaps clutch at my arm, at the material of my dress?'

She was more concerned with that hand than with the end of the act. On her side, Jane watched the coming and going of the actors with a rigid vigilance, as if she felt herself guilty of not listening properly. Jean Farou entered noiselessly and sat in the corner seat, left vacant by Jane now pressed close against Fanny, and until the end of the act he lived only for those linked arms, to curse them, to glower at Fanny, to compel her to release the refugee arm. With never a word, obstinate, Fanny fought back, and the curtain fell without her having yielded.

"Oh bravo!" cried Jane, a second late on the audience's frenzy.

The curtain was going up and down as at a first night. Mérya already displayed all the signs of an emotion which would do her credit on the morrow and, as she bowed, Dorilys became once more the eternal adolescent on which the theatrical world could count for another twenty-five years.

The third and fourth acts, linked by two tableaux, exhausted Fanny's patience and strength. They absorbed half the night. Traditional disorder, routine upheavals, classic technical accidents, delayed the time when Farou, freed at last, with the frigidity he displayed for each of his works when the moment came for him to let it fall, fully ripened, upon the public, could say: "There is nothing more for me to do here."

Fanny and her two companions joined him on the stage. Beside him an assistant stage manager was enumerating once more: "The stick of sealing wax forgotten in Act I, the pocket battery torch which failed to light in

Act II. The door-bell to ring close at hand in Act III; the coffee did not steam in the cup, also in Act III; less steel in the moonlight (that's fixed with Julien), and the type of telephone to be changed. Can you think of anything else, Monsieur Farou?"

"No, no, old man—oh, the lamp-shade in Act II, not deep enough, the bulb blinds the people in the stalls."

"Monsieur Silvestre has already noted that."

"I can't think of anything else. Good night, old man! And thanks!"

His patience was unimpaired, but his eyes wandered with expressionless activity from left to right and from right to left over the stage, which had been cleared as if by magic.

"Where are they?" Fanny was asking. "Where are they all?"

"Who?"

"Well, Mérya, Chocquart, Dorilys, Marsan?"

"Gone."

"But why? It isn't possible, the curtain is only just down. I would have liked to . . ."

Farou shrugged his shoulders, strangling himself with a woollen scarf. "Gone, I tell you. Ouf! They're perfect, but I can't bear the sight of them—until tomorrow. Neither can they bear the sight of me. We're sick of each other, you can understand . . ."

He slipped his arms under the elbows of the two women and dragged them away.

"It's a great success," said Fanny pensively.

She wished to judge dispassionately and to be just to Farou for having, as usual, worked alone and loyally. Since she lacked enthusiasm, she tended to evaluate the work according to the fruits it bore.

134

"Yes, it's a great success," she repeated. "I'm certain of it."

They separated to go down a narrow staircase. Farou went ahead, swinging his arms. He cleared the last three steps at a bound and stretched his arms until they cracked. 'What a pity!' sighed Fanny to herself.

She sighed with a confused regret, as she did each time she saw the man who wields the axe, drives a machine, holds the reins and the oars, a close-kept prisoner in Farou's nature. Jean Farou followed the group and cast a shadow with bowed head on the wall.

Once outside, Farou sniffed the rainy air. "Oh, to walk home!" But he flung himself violently into the back of his car, curled himself into a ball and never stirred.

He kept Fanny on his right and Jane on his left. His indifferent hands, for lack of space, lay one on each feminine shoulder. On a tip-up seat, Jean Farou gazed fixedly out on the streets, empty at two o'clock in the morning. At each street lamp, Farou's hand, dangling over Jane's shoulder, appeared out of the shadow, and Fanny could not help watching for this abandoned hand and Jean's obstinate profile each time the light flashed by.

"Half-past two," announced Farou. "Tomorrow . . . a foul day!"

"Oh," protested Jane, "success is certain."

"Doesn't prevent one dying of sleep. Eh, Jean?"

"I'm dying," acquiesced a feeble echo.

The journey seemed long to Fanny and suffering assailed her once more. She feared that the intermingling of her own tension, Jane's agony and Jean's irreconcilable silence would explode into a kind of premature catastrophe before shelter and closed doors had been reached. Farou yawned and stretched out his long legs, let fall two or three trivial remarks and congratulated himself on seeing a veiled moon running between the clouds, heralding fine weather. Untouched by subtler weather signs, he, nevertheless, conjured up by some human reverberation everything which could, there and then, threaten his serene and patriarcal immorality.

ELEVEN

"IT's funny that they can never type the figures opposite the printed names under 'Authors'. Look, Fanny. Because the typed column is out of alignment, it reads as if we had taken 2,440 francs the night before last, and the Mathurins 22,000."

Jane held out the sheet of box-office returns to Fanny.

"Have you the first week's returns, Jane? Give them to me. Twenty . . . sixteen, seventeen thousand four hundred; eighteen thousand four hundred; twenty thousand three hundred and twenty," Fanny read in a low voice. "That's good, isn't it?"

Jane tossed her head.

"Good? I should say so! It's a fortune, Fanny! And the holidays will soon be here."

"Holidays?"

"Christmas, of course. Three matinées, two midnight performances—and the revival of *No Home* at the Antoine —and the *Grapes* touring in the suburbs! Oh, that Farou! Already he's made it impossible to speak to him," said Jane rather sourly.

"So it's . . . it's really a success?" persisted Fanny. "They're sure now?"

"What a question to ask! Why are you so eager to . . .?"

She noticed that Fanny, whose head was bent over the returns, was no longer reading. She also noticed that she was wearing a new blue frock which slimmed her and made her look as if she were paying a discreet call or going away, and that the sheets of paper were trembling in her hands.

"Well," sighed Fanny, "well, let's get on with it."

She raised a troubled and almost suppliant glance to Jane. The lipstick round her mouth had left exposed a little margin of lip which was a strange mauvish white, and the low December sun darting through the trees in the Champ-de-Mars made her blink.

The same sun bleached Jane's head of young-maize-coloured hair to the palest green, and with a quick movement she slipped out of its rays.

"Let's get on with it," repeated Fanny in dejected tones. "You see . . . My poor Jane . . ."

The beating of her heart and the blood drumming in her ears upset her plan of action.

'What have I said? "My poor Jane"—that was not the thing to say!'

But she was dealing with a rival who would never consent to be over-ridden and who allowed her to utter only a few more words.

"You see, Jane . . . I've found out that you . . . that Farou . . ."

"Wait!" Jane interrupted her. "Wait! Just a moment!"

Sternly, she summoned up her strength. A suspicion of very pale pink rouge, usually invisible, showed on her cheeks, defining their elongated oval shape.

"What are we going to do?" she asked.

Because of the "we", Fanny blushed.

"How do you mean—what are we going to do?"

"Well . . . Is Farou to decide the matter or are we? If you don't mind, I'm going to sit down. I don't feel very certain on my feet."

Once seated, Jane was obliged to raise to Fanny a face

138

which at first appeared calm enough, being simply devoid of its usual candour. In order to fight more freely, she seemed to be keeping nothing but the essentials in her features, on which could be noted the approach of the thirties, the changing shape of the mouth under her rather long nose and the very fine eyes of a jealous woman.

"Have you spoken to Farou about it?" she continued.

"No, you would have known."

"Not necessarily. I am grateful to you for taking the initiative."

"The initiative? Were you going to speak to me about it?"

Jane's hand sweepingly dismissed the suggestion of such a step.

"No—oh, good heavens, no! I meant, for speaking to me about it first. So . . . what do we decide?"

Even if assumed, such assurance caught Fanny off her guard. She knew herself capable of improvising, but only when moved by anger. For want of anything better, she smiled.

"It seems to me that what we shall decide is obvious," she said.

"Good, I understand. But then, it is *your* decision, Fanny, and your decision only."

Her imploring grey eyes warned Fanny that she must not take into account the arrogance of the words, but sense their underlying motive. Nevertheless, Fanny's white nostrils dilated and her whole countenance was lit up by the onset of anger.

"Don't lose your temper, Fanny! Goodness, how careful we must be about what we say! Are you going to leave Farou out of our—our discussion? Will he remain in ignorance of today's conversation?"

"Come now, what an idea! That's impossible!"

"Have you thought about it, Fanny?"

"Very carefully."

She was lying. She had merely thought that after she had exclaimed in some fashion or other "I know everything", matters would either be settled or would be fatally disrupted. But all she saw before her was a reasonable young woman, certainly upset, but already arguing, and doubtless preparing to make use of her practical experience and cunning submissiveness.

'She—she's experienced,' thought Fanny. 'She's fought more than one woman over more than one man.'

"I fear," said Jane, shaking her head, "that you've thought less about it than I have."

"Not for as long as you have, probably."

"If you put it that way!"

But Fanny liked neither her pliancy nor her ease of manner. She lowered her head like a horse about to be blinkered and doubled up her chin.

"What is he going to do?" asked Jane in even quieter tones, as if speaking to herself.

Fanny smiled, showing the pale outline of her scarlet lips.

"Are you afraid?"

"Afraid? No! . . . Perhaps I am, after all."

"Afraid of what?"

Sadly, Jane looked into Fanny's eyes.

"But of everything the future may hold, Fanny, of everything which may happen to change our life."

"You can always see him outside," said Fanny in a nasty voice.

"See who? Oh, Farou—I wasn't thinking of Farou."

"That's very ungrateful," said the same voice.

"I owe Farou no gratitude," retorted Jane, raising her eyebrows.

"It's fortunate that you have not claimed him for your own in my presence."

A convulsive cough cut short her breath. Jane made a discouraged gesture, put her elbows on the table and rested her head on her hand. The December sun had already gone from the room and the translucent, aquamarine colour of twilight gave Jane's extraordinary hair a tint of green, revealing a flat, over-broad interval of cheek between nose and tiny ear. A tear streaked the flat cheek and reached the corner of her mouth which absorbed it heedlessly.

"Three and a half years, four—nearly four years," Jane counted to herself.

Aided by a spasm of anger, Fanny threw off her rigid pose.

"I do not require detailed statistics, you know," she shouted.

The tear-stained countenance turned round sharply and Jane surveyed her friend.

"What do you believe, Fanny? Do you really believe that for four years I've been . . .? That Farou is . . ."

"Don't mince your words! And as for the length of time—we know that has nothing to do with the matter, don't we?"

"Oh, but it has, my dear, where Farou is concerned!"

She raised her shoulders as if she were laughing.

"Fanny, you see before you one of Farou's very ordinary caprices . . . nothing could be more ordinary."

Jane's humility and the bitter distortion of her features revolted Fanny as if they had been low comedy antics.

"That's untrue! Have the decency not to lie! Am I threatening you? Am I complaining? Let us at least finish what we have begun decently—suitably. Yes, suitably."

141

She was growing hoarse from shouting and, with a wild pleasure, relied on her anger to carry her further. But at the same time, she repeated the word "suitably", attaching to it a moderating virtue. She was met with the shock of seeing Jane, now on her feet, advancing a bold face towards hers.

"What? How do you mean, it's untrue? Then what on earth am I supposed to be? The woman Farou loves, perhaps? You think that I am humbling myself to melt your heart? My poor Fanny! You excused me from giving you statistics, otherwise I'd not have concealed from you the number of weeks which have gone by without Farou condescending to treat me other than as——"

The violent slamming of a door in the flat interrupted her. The pair of them, their hands on their hips, in a pose of acrimonious argument, listened to it.

"It's not him," Jane said at last. "If it were he, we'd have heard the outer door first."

"It makes very little noise since the new draught-excluders were fixed," said Fanny. "In any case, he never comes in here before dinner."

With the sudden cooling off of their anger, they moved away from each other, as if they had tacitly discarded any plan of battle. Fanny went to draw the double curtains across the two windows and light the lamps on both the tables. She sat down, poked the embers and loaded the andirons with logs. She felt the cold of early evening, crystalline and wind-whipped, and shivered despite the central heating and the wood fire.

Now that her spasm of anger had passed, she was less inclined to confront, even "suitably", Jane and the truth, or Jane and untruths. Wisely, and lacking in will-power, she was already saying to herself:

'We were better as we were *before*. Neither of us will reap profit or happiness from what is to come. It would be better if Jane were to remain silent.'

But Jane spoke once more.

"Ah, Fanny, if I could make you understand me. You don't know. You don't know!"

Fanny raised her white forehead with its touching lock of black hair.

"But I'm going to know," she said in dull tones. "I don't see how I can stop you from telling me, now. I beg of you, don't let us be drawn into exchanging the kind of thing—the things which women insist on telling one another about their lovers, their monthly periods and their illnesses—revolting things."

She swallowed her saliva with repugnance. And in contradiction, she added all in one breath:

"Besides, I know enough. And anyway I saw you one day in the bathroom, while he was kissing you, the day you wore an apron and were doing your ironing. . . ."

Shame forbade her to go on. But Jane paid little heed to shame or silence. She pounced upon that memory with a glutton's eagerness for confession and resentment.

"In the bathroom? The day I was doing my ironing? Oh, of course! Ah, that's something we can talk about! Ah, you've certainly hit on a good instance there!"

She began to walk up and down, slapping a flexible paper knife against her palm.

"Yes, yes! Oh, of course—that day! He kissed me as he would have kissed the housemaid, d'you hear what I say? And when I say a housemaid, I'm less than a servant in his eyes, less than all the Asselins and the Irrigoyens in the world! And yet you know what Farou's infatuations are like, come now, Fanny! You've talked to me about them enough, you've demonstrated to me often enough

your superior wisdom, your indulgence—your con-
donation."

Jane stopped for a moment, shook back her hair and
sniffed up tears of irritation. Two meagre little tears
shone at the corners of her eyes and she continued to
make a smacking sound with the paper knife. The closer
Jane came to losing control, the more Fanny returned to
an inopportune state of calm resolve, in which she
decided that violent emotions did not suit Jane.

'She is made for moderate emotions, ash-blonde
sorrow.'

"Really, to hear you, Fanny, one might think you
didn't know what Farou was like!"

"He is my husband," Fanny replied.

She had introduced a note of rather pompous simplicity
into her retort and this did not please her. It did not
produce the reaction on which she had counted, either,
for Jane exclaimed:

"Thank God, Fanny!"

"I didn't imagine I should have to thank anyone for
that," said Fanny. "Not even you."

For the first time, Jane seemed to be frightened and
looked about her distractedly.

"I meant, thank God you were there too, there with
him. You feel so terribly lonely with Farou," she concluded uncertainly.

She added in the same hasty and hesitating manner:

"Of course, you feel lonely with other men as well.
But much more so with Farou. It is perfectly true that I
owe Farou no gratitude. But I do owe gratitude to someone——"

"Charming way of showing it to me!" Fanny burst out.

At that exclamation, Jane subsided, as if it were her
turn to be calm and collected.

144

"I showed it to you, Fanny, as best I could. It was not easy. For the past four years, I've thought so much more about you than about Farou."

Fanny rose, stiff as a poker.

"No," she said. "Not that. Up to now, nothing monstrous has arisen between us; everything, indeed, is extremely commonplace. But I will not stand the sentimental touch. Oh, Jane!"

She hid her face in her hands, and promptly uncovered it so that Jane should not think she was crying.

"It's not a sentimental touch!" protested Jane. "Why should I have thought so much about Farou?"

She beheld on Fanny's features the astonishment which Farou called "the gaping of a pretty fish", and continued impatiently:

"Of course it's not. You assume that anything you don't immediately understand must be a lie. You're so inexperienced, Fanny."

She became milder and stretched a cupped hand towards Fanny's hot face, as though to embrace the smooth, heavy contour of the cheek with her palm.

"So inexperienced . . . so untouched. How very different from me!"

"Yes, yes," interrupted Fanny with an irrelevant thoughtfulness, for childishly she feared the intrusion into the conversation of Quéméré, Meyrowicz and Davidson, and . . .

"You say 'yes, yes', but how can you understand in your present state! Oh, yes, this state of inexperience, this virginal state in which you pass your life. For you, there's Farou, and again Farou, and only Farou, and no other man but Farou. That's all very fine—and then again, I'm not sure that it is very fine—but where I'm concerned, I do not see, I have never at any time seen Farou through your eyes, let us even say with the same feelings as you. It didn't take me very long to distinguish between the two of you, Fanny, and from the moment I did, then . . . Oh, then . . ."

She was growing heated and changing the tone of her voice, as if she had finally reached and almost surmounted the most painful part of their discussion. With her hand she pushed aside, then recouped, all that she wished to express. Sincerity came and went about her like a temptation.

"So, you see, it didn't take long! It didn't take long!"

"But what didn't, after all that?" asked Fanny.

Jane's shoulders twisted under her frock with an affected and provincial awkwardness which Fanny noticed for the first time.

"I find it difficult to say, Fanny. I don't find it difficult to talk to you about Farou. Farou—Farou is a man, an attractive man, a well-known man, who is very gifted. In short, Fanny, I confess that it takes less than that to seduce a girl like me, who has no reason to live by strict standards, to remain chaste and lonely. There is nothing surprising in my having so easily fallen in love, become jealous, unhappy, in fact all that you saw in me. But on the whole, apart from the fact that Farou is Farou, there's nothing particularly remarkable about him as a man. Whereas you, Fanny, you . . ."

She sat down, took her handkerchief and began to weep copiously, easily and discreetly, in a way which seemed to be new and agreeable to her.

She blew her nose and continued quietly:

"You, Fanny, are a much finer person as a woman, than Farou is as a man. Much, much finer."

"Oh," said Fanny with superb haughtiness, "how little you know him!"

146

Jane turned on her a sharp feminine glance.

"And by the same token," she said, half smiling, "you nearly made me believe that he was incomparable."

"That's it," said Fanny, shaking her head. "It's all my fault now!"

"Yes and no. In a certain way."

No doubt she wished to explain, to expound to Fanny the state of a new and elegant race of serfs, unattached and wandering like winged seeds in the air, with all their adaptability, their anonymous attractiveness, but she gave up in the face of the dark-haired, obstinate female, rooted to her seat, who based her claim on a more ancient code.

"I'm talking about the early days, of course. After that——"

"After that, you became my friend," Fanny answered with a sweetness that boded ill.

"No," retorted Jane definitely. "I was that before. I could not stop being that."

"For so slight a cause?" suggested Fanny.

"Indeed," continued Jane, "there is nothing about me of the siren. Neither am I a mercenary slut, nor an ambitious woman. You can grant me that much. What risk do you run with me? Not much."

"Yes—you would have liked to be the only one to betray me."

Fanny made her point with the same sweetness of tone.

"But your indulgence towards Farou, your damned indulgence, your so-called understanding of Farou, was against me, against us! Your mania for showering him with praise, and curses which were even a hundred times more flattering. Your 'superiority' which consisted in putting Farou at the disposal of all women—did you think that was honourable? I didn't. Ah, no! I didn't! It is a trait which disfigured you, which lowered the opinion I had of you. You," she said as she looked at Fanny with demanding admiration, "you were a finer version of myself."

She moved away, raised the window curtain for an instant and promptly let it fall back, as if to hide what she had seen in the grey night. She returned to place her hand on Fanny's shoulder and shook it slightly.

"And just now you asked me if I were afraid? But I'm shaking, I'm ice cold with fear, Fanny! You, you're just thinking of getting rid of me, you think that petty physical matters of love are crimes if I'm mixed up in them, you think you're going to tear Farou away from me—as if he hadn't attended to that himself long, long ago! You think you're going to cleanse your house and perhaps fumigate my room. It's unbelievable that anyone should make such a fuss about love! A man isn't so important: he isn't eternal! A man is . . . a man is only a man! Do you really believe that you meet a man, on his own, just like that, alone, free, quite ready to devote his life to you. A man is never alone, Fanny—and indeed it's rather horrible that he should always have a woman, another mistress, a mother, a maid, a secretary, a relation, a female of some sort. If you only knew the various types of women I've found round a lover! It's horrible—the word is not too strong!"

She clutched her forearms so tightly with both hands that her finger-tips turned white. Abruptly she poured herself out a glass of water which she raised to her lips first, then on second thoughts she held out the glass to Fanny.

"I beg your pardon. I'm dying of thirst."

"Me too," said Fanny.

They drank in silence, as courteous to each other as wild animals keeping truce beside a stream. Emotion had

148

affected each in a different way: Jane had red patches upon her cheek-bones and Fanny was pale, with smutty circles under her eyes, and her mouth, devoid of lipstick, was a negroid mauve. After she had drunk, Fanny emitted a lengthy sigh of fatigue and Jane again made as if to cup the curved cheek in her hand, without touching it.

"Poor Fanny, what a lot of trouble I give you! Would you like to . . . ?"

She dared go no further.

Fanny said shortly, "No thanks," and concentrated on trying to recall the exact words of a scolding Jane had given Farou long ago.

'She said to him, "You'd much better give her your hand" or "hold her hand", I can't remember exactly. She also said to him that day they thought I had fainted, "Don't knock her feet against the door", or something like that, and "Is that the way to carry a woman?" '

"You taught me the desire to serve," said Jane softly.

Fanny could not control her agitation, rose to her feet and began to walk round in small circles, as she did when she was merry, with the supple and agile movements of a plump creature.

"No," she said. "No, I can't stand it! Since everything is spoilt, you must change your way of speaking, you must stop appealing to our emotions and exploiting that bond, that past, that——"

A door opened behind her.

"A-a-a-ah!" yawned a great joyous voice. "All these women! All these women! What a lot of women I've got in my house!"

He had returned dishevelled and pleased with himself. His handsome golden eyes, languishing and inscrutable, announced that he had just come from a brief bout of pleasure or from a long spell of work. Easy money for a few months and renewed success adorned him with a youthful air, in no sense unseasonable but foreign to his nature, and he wore it like a spotted bow tie.

"I've just met Pierre Wolff," he exclaimed. "I must be looking remarkably fit, because he threatened me with arterio-sclerosis, the shaking palsy, and——"

He became aware that neither Fanny nor Jane had stirred when he entered the room. He examined the two faces, saw that they had both changed completely from what they had been that morning, and asked in masterful tones:

"What's the matter?"

"Farou . . ." Fanny began.

"Fanny, I assure you!" begged Jane.

"What's the matter?" Farou repeated intolerantly in louder tones. "Women's quarrels? Rows with the servants?"

Fanny looked at Jane and gave a little laugh. The whole of Jane's body gave fleeting signs of a kind of mimed politeness, as if to tell her, 'I'm leaving you free to speak'. To which Fanny replied with a nod, 'I'll take charge of everything.'

"Farou," Fanny continued, "Jane and I have just had a serious talk. You see that we are quite calm. We intend to remain so."

She spoke with lips over which the mauve pallor had entirely encroached, and pronounced her words with care. Farou just had time to notice the pallor of his wife's mouth, and the pervasive glaze over her too big, too beautiful eyes which no longer expressed anything. He must have thought that she was going to faint, for he put out an arm towards her, but she made her meaning clear.

"Jane is your mistress. I am your wife. We cannot decide anything completely without you."

Farou, who had sat down, rose slowly to his feet. His

150

brows were knit majestically and, for a moment, the two women were afraid only because they thought him handsome. Both waited for they knew not what thunderbolt to fall.

"Which of you brought it up?" said Farou at last.

"I, of course," declared Fanny, offended.

His glance rested upon her without anger, but with already calculated mistrust.

"Had you known it long?"

She lied from a kind of bravado.

"Oh, a very long time."

"And you hid it so well? Congratulations!"

She considered this a vulgar counter-offensive and shrugged her shoulders.

"But," Farou continued, "if you really have been hiding it so long, what astonishes me—yes, what astonishes me is—why didn't you continue to do so?"

Thrown off her balance for a moment, she recovered herself and cried:

"Do you think one can keep a thing like that to oneself —that one can be silent for ever?"

"I'm certain of it," said Farou.

She made a gesture of appeal to Jane as she stammered, "Well, that's the limit—that's the limit——"

"You especially," added Farou.

"Accustomed to it, no doubt?"

Until then Farou had watched Fanny's trembling hand, but he now saw that her eyes were filled with tears, and gained confidence.

"Accustomed to it—if you like to put it that way. Whatever I may have done, have I ever abated one iota of my affection for you during the past twelve years?"

At these words, Jane stepped smoothly and softly forward into the light, and Farou started.

151

"I am well aware, Jane, how particularly painful this scene must be for you. But I beg you to remember that every word you utter will make it more painful still."

"But I did not wish to speak," said Jane.

"What's more," Farou continued, "I am ready to assume the entire responsibility."

He was interrupted by a sharp exclamation from Fanny.

"What do you mean? Responsibility? What responsibility? Who asks you to be responsible? That's not the point, Farou! Say what you want, do something, pay some attention to us, but not in that way! Quick, Farou, quick!"

She was horror-struck that at such a time he should have been able to control himself, and was already accusing him of respecting the age-old convention of a man caught between two women. How was it that Farou had not yet stormed, dispatched human justice and delicacy to the devil, as well as any feelings Jane and she might have, and carried off in his arms the object, if only temporary, of his burning choice. 'How slow he is! God, how slow he is! Violence—but a passionate violence for one of us, never mind which! Despair—but a passionate despair! Are we all so old that he should remain so calm, that he hasn't even sworn at us?'

"We are not lunatics," said Farou. "I am only a man, but a man who has decided to preserve a sense of proportion in a situation in which so many men and women lose theirs. If, in regard to Jane, I have been——"

"I don't enter into the argument," Jane intervened. "I'm not aware that I've made any claims? I only enter into the argument if Fanny wishes me to go away, which is quite natural."

He acquiesced with a grave nod. Behind his male

152

strength, bold outline, beneath his mane of hair, Fanny sought for a manly decision, a trace of the emotion which Jane's words had roused within herself.

"Fanny knows perfectly well," said Farou.

He corrected himself and addressed his wife.

"You know very well, Fanny, that you are my dear Fanny. And for my part, I have always been fortunate in your affection for me, whatever our ups and downs, for more than ten years. Those same ten years should be an assurance to me that you will be able to spare the woman who deserves to be spared. I thank you in anticipation."

"The woman who deserves to be spared" received the end of the speech and Fanny's stupor without so much as a flicker of the eyelids. She even pursed her lips and indicated a whistle of ironic admiration. Since Farou's entrance, she seemed to have lost the power of feeling deeply or of being astonished, and her eyes narrowed as she watched Fanny and Farou's movements.

"What does that mean? Farou, what does that mean?" murmured Fanny in consternation.

She turned again to Farou just in time to see him stifle a yawn of nervous exhaustion.

'The longing to be far away from here is oozing out of his very pores!' thought Fanny, white with fury. 'He's going away! He's going to find an excuse for going away. Is that all he's got to say? Is that the way to finish, or begin, a new chapter in one's life?'

"Farou!" she called in sorrowful anger.

"Why, yes, my Fanny, I'm here. I'm listening to you. Would you like us to have a talk alone?"

"Farou!"

She rejected the gentleness, the thoughtfulness with which he treated her like a delirious invalid. She would willingly have dug a knife into Farou so as to see

153

something spontaneous, irrepressible, gush out of him, blood, curses, suffering.

Farou took the risk of putting a hand on her head, and bent over her as he tilted back her forehead. In the depth of the large yellow eyes, Fanny saw the desire to convince her by sensual means, but beyond that again, it seemed to her there lay a spirit of precaution, hidden, wary, and rather cowardly. Her madness retreated to the depths of her soul and, bending her neck, she caused the heavy hand to glide over her hair.

"Listen, Farou! I'm in no state to talk to you. You came in too soon, do you understand? That's it! You came in too soon."

"All the better," said Farou with great dignity. "My place is here. Let's get all this settled."

Fanny looked thoughtfully at him, her courage fled. In her turn, she wanted to speak to him in tones of deplorable kindliness.

"No, Farou, let it go. All Jane and I have to do is to finish our conversation and come to some practical arrangement tonight, without fail. Nothing shall pass between Jane and myself to make us raise our voices— isn't that so, Jane?"

"Of course," said Jane. She was still standing in the same place, slightly behind Fanny, her eyes watchful.

"Good," acquiesced Farou. "Good. I see nothing against it. I hope that you have no objection to my staying next door, in the study? I can be sure that nothing which concerns the three of us will give rise to public scandal? Not even to servants' gossip? Can I be absolutely certain?"

He took advantage of his unfinished question to make slowly towards the door, walking backwards, impressing each woman in turn with his dominating yellow glance.

"Yes, yes, yes," Fanny repeated each time. She nodded impatient assent and, in the end, the black cable of her hair uncoiled itself. She hastily gathered it together with both hands.

Farou's attention never wavered from the two unhappy faces and from the thick flowing hair which was being twisted by white arms. Through his eyes passed an offer of peace, unseen by Fanny, but such that Jane advanced aggressively towards Farou.

"Yes, you can be certain. But let us talk to each other alone."

Farou obeyed with a strained little smile. Jane followed him to the door, shut it and came back to Fanny who had just finished putting up her hair again.

"And that's that," said Jane, drily.

"Yes," sighed Fanny, completely overcome. "That's that!" She let her arms fall to her side.

"Have a rest, Fanny. There's no hurry."

Fanny went back to her armchair beside the hearth and huddled over the fire. The entrance of the maid, passing through the room, obliged Jane to sit down and run through Farou's mail and the documents of the Authors' Society, which she pretended to sort out. The maid came back through the drawing-room again, carrying Farou's dinner jacket and shirt.

"He's going out," said Fanny in a low voice.

"Yes," said Jane, "it's the performance for the dressmakers at the Gymnase. Are you going to it?"

Fanny did not reply. Hunched up in her chair, her breasts against her knees, she stared at the fire. Jane, barely leaning against the back of her chair, appeared to be waiting for her relief from sentry duty. She made some entries in a notebook, seemed to be making mental calculations, and looked at her wrist-watch.

155

At about seven o'clock Jean Farou came in. Fanny answered his "Good evening, Mamie," automatically and did not move. But such an outrageous and tell-tale scent emanated from Jean Farou that both women raised their heads simultaneously.

"Is it you who are smelling like that?" asked Fanny.

"Like what, Mamie?"

It was to Jane that the boy dedicated his dark-circled lids, his shining, feverish, swollen mouth and his youth darkened by its fall, directing them to her like a mulish insult. His laugh was harsh and he brought the vulgar scent, the scent of another woman which at long last announced his deliverance, for Jane to inhale.

"Go and change," Fanny ordered him. "You make us sick."

He went out, proud of being understood and blamed.

"Would you believe it?" said Fanny. "How nasty a little boy growing into a man can be! For two pins he'd bring her here. So proud to have a mistress all for himself!"

"For himself and against me," said Jane.

"That's true."

They felt themselves strictly alone and spoke without restraint.

"He does his best. He does himself an injury so as not to love you any more."

"Oh, love me! Perhaps enough to wish to injure me. Perhaps he has already done so. I'm not asking you any questions, Fanny," Jane added quickly. "If you are willing, while we are undisturbed, let us speak briefly and to the point. Let's say that I leave tomorrow——"

"No, no," Fanny interrupted her, "later, after dinner. Can't you hear that they're already laying the table."

Jane gave her friend a long look.

156

"You wish me to dine here?"

"But of course. Come now!" said Fanny at the end of her tether. "Don't let's complicate matters."

"Very well. You're right. I'm going to put some things away in my room. If you need me . . ."

When she returned she found Fanny in the same place beside the dying fire. She whispered to her: "Fanny, dinner!" And Fanny, after a summary toilet, made her way to the dining-room, in which lingered, although less strong, the scent Jean Farou had brought back with him. With exceptional courtesy, Farou stood waiting for his wife to be seated.

Fanny noticed that he had shaved closely, had combed his hair and discreetly dusted his face with ochre powder. His dinner-jacket fitted tightly over the hips and his head was held high above well controlled shoulders. 'Who the devil is he after tonight?' she asked herself. 'Perhaps it's me?'

Once seated at the table, she felt completely exhausted, cowardly and ravenous. She ate a large meal, to the surprise of Farou, who watched her as he talked to his son. Jane also talked to Jean, who, not without impertinence, paused with marked surprise before replying. As Farou ceremoniously tilted the bottle of champagne towards his wife, she laughed at him.

"I don't know why, but tonight you look like a young tragic actor playing a comedy part!"

And she began to laugh easily as do the convalescent or the very weary. She was thinking: 'And my sorrow—what becomes of my sorrow in all this? When shall I have time to nurse it? Today there has been a place for reason, anger, for everything except that. They'll finish by taking it away from me.'

Farou's departure from the house was subtly contrived,

157

and carried out with agility while talking, lighting a cigarette and putting on an overcoat. Fanny thought he was
in the hall and Jane thought he was in the bathroom when
he was already crossing the street. Facing Jane alone again
and slightly tipsy with the dry wine, Fanny shook her
head.

"That's what I call, by way of an exit, the charwoman
style."

"What?" asked Jane, taken aback.

"Haven't you ever noticed that one never knows the
exact moment of a charwoman's departure? She vanishes
like a sylph. It's because she always takes away with her
a small memento, a slice of veal for her husband, what's
left of the coffee in a bottle, the scrapings from the sugar-
bowl."

She laughed again. But in the salon in which she took
refuge, someone had already revived the fire and spread
over the arm of a favourite armchair the big vicuna wrap,
and sorrow in its most selfish form sent a lump to Fanny's
throat. The idea of being left alone, the threat of being
alone so soon, dispersed the transient warmth which she
owed to her copious meal. 'One is so lonely with Farou.'
She sat down, placed the wrap round her legs and closed
her eyelids over two tears.

"Am I in your way?" asked Jane in a low voice.

"No, no," said Fanny without opening her eyes.

"Would you rather we had our talk now? Yes? I can
get Delvaille by 'phone tomorrow morning early. She'll
really be delighted to get her job back."

"Who is Delvaille? What job?"

Fanny was taking the comb and pins from her hair and
laid her head back on its streamers of black damp seaweed.

"Why, Farou's former secretary, don't you remember
her?"

"Not Delvaille, Jane! No, no, not Delvaille!"

"What has she done to you?"

Beneath her unbound hair and her oriental pallor, Fanny opened eyes that were as moist, wild and gentle as those of a drowned woman. She gathered herself together with difficulty to drive away the image of a former Delvaille, short, plump, active and pregnant. Delvaille at work. And Jane? And Jane? Jane not there, Jane vanished.

"Nothing," she confessed. "But there are really more urgent matters than sending for Delvaille. Can't Farou's scribbles wait? Farou's scribbles can go to the devil!"

"I don't mind them going to the devil, but not if they land on you! Think it over."

"Exactly. I'll take time to think it over."

She fell back on her pillow of hair. When Jean Farou, dressed to go out, came in suddenly, she moaned.

"Are you still ill, Mamie? You're ill much too often. Why not see a doctor? I only came to say good night to you."

He kissed her finger-tips and she noticed that he had changed the way of doing his hair. On his wrist he wore a thin gold chain and in his shirt a jewelled stud, which she had not seen before. The two women read, as if writ large, these hall-marks stamped on him by a woman.

"Luckily I leave you in good hands. Good night, Jane."

He went out with a light-hearted, cruel expression.

"Now he's pleased," said Jane. "He's made his exit, if I mistake me not, with a 'poisoned shaft'."

"Poor kid!" said Fanny absent-mindedly.

"Oh, really!" Jane took her up. "You've better things to do than to pity *them*."

Her use of the plural made Fanny thoughtful. The

159

crackling of the fire and the regular pecking of a needle made her drowsy.

"What are you sewing?" she asked, suddenly waking up.

"I'm restitching my thick gloves," said Jane. "This leather is so tough, you can't wear them out and they're very useful for travelling."

"Ah, yes."

Fanny shuddered at the word "travelling". She visualised the cold, the whistling wind, arid white platforms, and saw the hotel bedroom with its naked bulb hanging from the ceiling. She was not the kind of woman to exile herself voluntarily; she could imagine no other form of loneliness but to be ignored, nor any other form of decision but to wait.

The houseboy came through the room bearing mineral water, oranges and two glasses for the bedside tables.

'Oranges and two glasses?' Fanny said to herself. 'It's true, Farou will be coming home.'

She was apprehensive of the night hours, of the beds and the twin bodies, of Farou, and perhaps of his amorous strategy which was not without its dangers.

'I know him,' thought Fanny humbly. 'He'll be more brilliant than he was this afternoon. Oh, this afternoon...'

"Jane," she exclaimed, "couldn't you tell me . . .?"

The seamstress waited, needle in the air. She had not concealed her real face behind the mask of a young-girl-on-the-verge-of-thirty, and she smiled with heavy sad hollows in her cheeks.

"I can't see what there can be I couldn't tell you now, Fanny."

"Then tell me if you don't agree with me that, today, Farou showed himself to be incredibly . . . That he was . . ."

160

She could bear it no longer, rose, and allowed herself the relief of exclaiming: "I thought that he was beneath contempt, but also beyond contempt! Why was he beyond contempt?"

"And how then would you have liked him to be?" retorted Jane pointblank. "Did you expect him to be witty? Or that he would beat you? Or throw me out of the window? A man in such circumstances! But not one man in a hundred ever gets away with it to his advantage, if not to his credit!" She shook her head.

"It's much too difficult for them," she concluded without further comment and as if keeping the most illuminating part of her experience to herself.

"Why?" asked Fanny feebly.

Jane bit off her thread.

"Because . . . it's like that. They're shy, you know," she said, still using the same unflattering plural. "And besides, they're so made that when involved in what we call a row, or an argument, they always see at once the chance of getting rid of us for ever."

Fanny did not reply. She was harking back to long past, passionate days, when she wept and screamed with jealousy before a silent, detached Farou, who had retired to one of the mountain fastnesses from which the male antagonist watches his dearest possession, his superfluous encumbrance, whirling and falling through space. She walked from one window to the other to ease the stiffness which numbed the whole of her body. She stopped in front of Jane and looked at her searchingly.

"Have you a definite purpose in speaking ill of Farou to me in this way?"

"A purpose? No."

"Or at least a motive? A plan? An intention, an idea? Come now!"

161

Her hands moulded her loose, deep-rose gown over her hips and she shook a smoky cloud of hair over Jane.

"Do you mistrust me?" asked Jane, her lips quivering.

"No, I don't mistrust you yet! But why do you speak ill of Farou?"

Jane narrowed her eyes, focussed on the study door, but she clung to an original grievance, as if it would have taken longer to explain the man than to accuse him.

"It's out of resentment," she affirmed, meeting Fanny's glance steadily.

'Out of resentment,' Fanny repeated to herself, 'just as in the case of Quéméré, of Davidson—and so?'

She could not understand that Jane could treat Big Farou like a mere Meyrowicz, or that Jane could use only the word "resentment" to describe the ingratitude, the sardonic harshness, with which the female of every race repays the male from whom she has escaped, though not unscathed.

"Out of resentment," Jane insisted, "out of resentment. It is so. You don't even understand, do you? It's because you are Fanny. You're much too clean-minded for all that sort of thing, dear . . . dear Fanny."

She had at last dared to capture the hanging hand and was pressing it against her cheek. The hand protested agonisedly, slithered and grew limp so as to escape, and Jane took up her needle again.

'It is here,' thought Fanny in front of the black window pane. 'Now the hour has come when I must decide if I shall force open that hand I was expecting. That hand closed over my wrist, resting in the hollow of my own, cupped under my elbow, that hand on my arm, that hand clasping my own during our walks in holiday time. I was certain I would have to deal with that hand which brings me the vicuna wrap, pulls up the collar of my coat, tends my hair, the hand that met my own under the damp sheets during little Farou's illness. It is the same hand, dyed with duplicating ink, which stained Farou's fingers purple and denounced him to me.'

"It's freezingly cold between the two windows, Fanny."

'But,' Fanny continued as she returned obediently to the fireplace, 'where shall I find the scales, and if I did, what right have I to weigh what I owe to that hand against what it has taken from me?'

She fell into a long reverie which at times was close to slumber. Whenever she opened her eyes again or turned them away from the fire, her glance wandered round the room, strewn with tall lampstands and large shades.

On one of the tables, Jane placed documents and files. "Farou's scribblings."

"Is everything there important?" asked Fanny.

The round head of hair, shining with clear gold and silver, and the young, tired face turned quickly towards her.

"Not in the slightest. But he insists on everything being kept. It's a mania. That's his look out. You may be sure that I'm leaving everything in apple-pie order."

The warm silence closed in again, attacked by unobtrusive noises from outside and protected by the low, even chatter of the fire. Towards eleven o'clock Jane rose, taking the documents and files into the study.

'Tomorrow,' mused Fanny, 'tomorrow, if she goes away, I shall be like this, alone beside the fire, like a woman who has come to the end of the greater part of love. Perhaps Farou will take it into his head to keep me company—that would be the worst of all. For he would batter the walls from the window to the fireplace, break down the panels, or fall asleep with his head on his shoulder in that armchair. Or else he would work next door, seeking Jane at every moment and cursing the pair of us. At the end of the week, he would have replaced her. But I, I shall not so easily replace her. As for him, he is bound to find another of the kind he prefers, a passing favourite. He will once again recover his innocence, his loneliness and his profession. But what about me? Where am I to find someone once again to keep me company? Two of us are not too many to be alone with Farou—to stand up to Farou.'

She raised herself from her armchair and looked for a book or a pastime; the green table was folded and no longer awaited the litter of cards.

'Before the days of Jane, there was at my side a fair-haired little boy, very sweet, who played cards with me. For a long time he was twelve years old. I've lost that little boy. He was charming and the sound of his voice, his shyness, his frail health, used to bring something feminine into our home, where henceforth there will be only Farou. I am no longer young enough, or rich enough, or brave enough to remain alone with Farou—nor far from Farou.'

She tried to form a clear picture of Farou, stripped of its conjugal glamour. But the effort wearied her as if she had been straining upward to follow the flight of one of those silent birds which fly in great circles round a nest on which they never alight. She considered a few stead-fast couples and tried to assess how large a share of a man women can get for themselves.

'Pooh! The only certain thing they possess is to be able to talk about their man, complain about him, boast about him and wait for him. But everything they flaunt could just as well be done without the presence and existence of a man!'

She was aware that she was denying the remains of a

pure religion, whose faithful lived solely by waiting for their god and by the childish ritual of their cult, and she turned again to the help which could spring only from an alliance, even if it were uncertain and slightly disloyal, from a feminine alliance, constantly broken by the man and constantly re-established at the man's expense. . . . 'Where is Jane?'

"Jane!"

Jane came at once. Although her face was grey with fatigue, she was ready to sit up all night, to answer each call, to work with scrupulous care.

"Jane, don't you want to go to bed?"

"Not before you do."

"Are you waiting for Farou?"

"Not without you."

She sat down on the other side of the hearth, facing Fanny, and thoughtfully poked the fire. She was listening attentively to the after-midnight sounds, and suddenly kept still because a car slowed down as it passed along the street.

'When I flay Jane, I find Farou again in the first drop of blood,' thought Fanny. 'Tomorrow, the day after to-morrow, later on, the same will happen to me if she happens to strike me.'

The heavy front door was heard to close downstairs, then the gate of the lift on the landing. Jane's eyes questioned Fanny nervously and she rose.

"Where are you going? It's only Farou come home," said Fanny with exaggerated calm.

But Jane, her face sheet-white, confessed her fear by stammering.

"A scene . . . So painful . . ."

"A scene? With Farou? My dear," said Fanny, who was resuming the advantage of her seniority, "it's out of the question. Why have a scene with Farou? We have mixed up Farou far too much in everything that concerns us. It's my fault," she added with a slight effort.

They listened to the slow fumbling of a key. Footsteps in the hall made towards the study, stopped, and returned thoughtfully towards the salon. Then their sound changed, they became light, and faded away.

"He's going away," Fanny said very softly.

"He saw the light under the door. Perhaps you ought to go to him?" Jane suggested.

Fanny shrugged her shoulders. With the fingers of both hands she lifted the weight of her hair from her neck to cool it, put her feet closer to the fire, and peeled an orange.

"There's no hurry," she said at last. "We've plenty of time. Is it very late?"

"No, no—barely half-past twelve," Jane assured her. "It's so cosy here," she said with secret anguish. "To-morrow, I'll——"

"Hush, Jane! Who's asking you to think of tomorrow? Tomorrow is a day like any other. It is cosy here. . . ."

After that, they exchanged only a few desultory, commonplace words. As one pretended to read and the other to sew, their sole desire was to refrain from speech, and allow those inner reserves, which the man had not dared to affront, to subside and sink to rest, relying on silence to foster their frail, new-born security.

THE BLUE LANTERN

1

WE should not be unreasonably perturbed when our
precious senses become dulled with age. I say " we ",
but I am the text of my own sermon. My chief concern is
lest I should mistake the true nature of a condition which
has come upon me gradually. It can be given a name: it
keeps me in a state of vigilance, of uncertainty, ready to
accept whatever may fall to my lot. The prospect gives
rise to little that is reassuring, but I have no choice.

More than once of late, turning my eyes from my book
or my blue-tinted writing paper towards the superb
quadrangle that I am privileged to view from my window, I have thought ' The children in the Garden are not
nearly so noisy this year,' and a moment later found
myself finding fault with the door bell, the telephone, and
the whole orchestral gamut of the radio for becoming
progressively fainter. As for the china lamp—not the blue
lantern that burns by day and night, of course, but the
pretty one with flowers and arabesques painted on it—I
was for ever scolding it unjustly: ' What can this wretched
thing have been eating to make it so heavy?' Discoveries, ever more discoveries! Things always explain
themselves in the long run. Instead, then, of landing on
new islands of discovery, is my course set for the open
sea where there is no sound other than that of the lonely

heart-beat comparable to the pounding of the surf? Rest assured, nothing is decaying, it is I who am drifting. . . . The open sea, but not the wilderness. The discovery that there is no wilderness! That in itself is enough to sustain me in triumphing over my afflictions.

Four years have gone by since *L'Etoile Vesper* was published; years that sped speedily enough as they must when the mornings are all alike and the evenings are spent in a kind of glass retort, with some unpredictable little incident at the centre, like a kernel. I was honest when I called *L'Etoile Vesper* my last book. I have come to see that it is as difficult to stop writing as it is uncomfortable to go on. Beneath my blue lantern, my life-line grows ever shorter and shorter, my physical torment ever more persistent. Yet how many changes of scene—other than on foot—are still permitted me! Uriage in '46, Geneva and the Beaujolais in '47, Provence, albeit against doctor's orders, in '48. From my seat in a car or a wheel-chair, I proudly compiled a census of the landscapes, streams and shores I have rediscovered. 'After all, I can still visit these.' Visit! Yes, in a manner of speaking and, above all, of experience. During the final infirmity of her life, Anna de Noailles saw more cities, hills and oceans than I, against the backcloth of her perpetually lowered blinds.

I wanted this book to be a journal; but I do not possess the knack of writing a proper journal, that is to say of stringing together, bead by bead, day after day, a rosary whose value and intrinsic lustre are relative to the writer's powers of exact observation, of assessing his own importance and that of his time. The art of selection, of noting

170

things of mark, retaining the unusual while discarding the commonplace, has never been mine, since most of the time I am stimulated and quickened by the ordinary. There I was, vowing never to write anything again after *L'Etoile Vesper*, and now I have covered two hundred pages which are neither memoirs nor journal. Let my reader resign himself to it: this lantern of mine, burning blue day and night between the pair of red curtains, pressed close to the window like one of the butterflies that fall asleep there on a summer morning, throws no light on events significant enough to astonish him.

It is twenty years, or a little more, since Princesse Edmond de Polignac, staunch friend of music and musicians, passed sentence with a glance and a single word on the little four-legged table-desk that used to follow me from Paris to Saint-Tropez and back, taking up its position on the bed at my night's lodging. I set great store by this piece of furniture, originally contrived for me by Luc-Albert Moreau—painter, engraver, and master carpenter —so that I could write other than in a sitting posture, my feet dangling, which has always had an adverse effect on my comfort and my work.

"I have," Princesse de Polignac said to me, "a little English piece which, if enlarged, would be just right for you."

She was not mistaken. Widened, made higher, reinforced, and stripped of most of its English eighteenth-century elegance, it bestrides my divan-bed and indeed, for a quarter of a century, has gladdened both my leisure and my working hours. An adjustable desk has been let

171

into the solid mahogany table and takes the weight of the things I turn to for relaxation from my own writing: telephone, fruit, portable radio, and bulky illustrated volumes. This contraption glides easily from the head of the bed to my feet. Including the all-purpose knife with its scorpion handle, the bunch of fountain-pens and various knick-knacks of no particular use, I have assembled on its back a fair number of good and willing servants.

All round me a litter of papers; but a litter belied by its appearance, with more often than not, to add to the confusion, a boiled chestnut, a half-eaten apple, and for the last month a seed-pod—from some exotic plant, no doubt —the capsules of which retain for a while and then expel, almost with violence, a delicate silvery follicle weighted with a tiny seed and lighter even than thistledown. One by one these feathery tufts break loose, drift up to the warm air beneath my ceiling, float there for some time before descending, and should one of them happen to be caught by the draught from the fire it yields at once, a consenting victim, and flings itself deliberately into the flames, there to perish of its own volition. I do not know the name of the plant which scatters its winged spirits abroad in this fashion, but it has no need of a label to take its place in my dunce's museum.

What has become of those whom I wanted to last for ever, firmly attached to their own lives and mine? How could I ever have conceived that Marguerite Moreno would abandon me? She was kindly treated even by fatigue, and she would laugh me to scorn in my praise

172

of idleness and the forty winks of a siesta. . . . But Marguerite goes and catches cold, and succumbs within a week. But Luc-Albert Moreau, happening to meet a friend, exclaims cheerfully "Hullo, old chap, how pleased I am to see you!" and dies on the spot from heart failure. And before them Léon-Paul Fargue who, on his death bed, grumbled about the blue of his sheets which he had had dyed: "Far too blue . . . won't do at all." And others there are too whom I must give up trying to name, or even count. In my heart of hearts I blame them for dying, calling them careless, imprudent. How could they deprive me of their company, and so abruptly, how could they think of doing such a thing to me! So I have banished from sight and mind the vision of them lying prone and lifeless for ever. Fargue turned suddenly to stone? I'll have none of it. My Fargue is still wearing his dusty walking-shoes, still talking, scratching the head of his black cat, is still ringing me up, still tramping from Lipp to Ménilmontant, and berating his bed for its too maritime blue. . . . Marguerite Moreno's feet still shod with static gold? Certainly not! They live in my memory as they were, wayward, restless, vulnerable and never tired.

My juniors in the prime of life sometimes look sternly at me; they feel anxious. They gather the recalcitrant fold of a shawl across my shoulder with a "You're not feeling a draught?". No, I am not feeling chilly, I am not feeling *that particular* draught you have in mind. My thoughts are too out of joint for me to feel it. I have so many reasons for avoiding what you tactfully call "the dangerous draught". Chief among them is pain, pain ever young and active, instigator of astonishment, of anger, imposing its rhythm on me, provoking me to defy it; the pain that enjoys an occasional respite but does not want my life to end: happily I have pain. Oh, I know perfectly well that by using the adverb "happily" I sound affected, like someone putting on the brave smile of an invalid! Very few invalids do remain entirely natural, but I would not like it thought that I am making my infirmity an occasion for sinful pride, that I require respect and special consideration, or that it fosters an inferiority complex, that root cause of acerbity. I am not referring to those who pretend to be sufferers, who are of no interest and are in any case a small minority, nor am I alluding to a category of sufferers who are far from reluctant when surprised or discovered in the very act of suffering. My doctor-brother summed up in a few words the pleasure enjoyed by such as these. "It is," he said, "a kind of ecstasy. It's akin to scratching the hollow of your ear with a match-stalk. Aphrodisiacal, almost."

A prominent politician, who was lame, once confided something to me which I had no difficulty in understanding, though at the time I was myself in excellent health. This man of politics liked to elevate my mind to the realm of general ideas, at least he made a good try. I struggled to follow his line of thought, but not for very long. I believe he would have found me mediocre all in all had he not so enjoyed one of my books, *Break of Day*, and had he not wished to expand (I would have said 'restrict') the scope of my life by the help of some great idea that should serve me as, in a sense, religion, high purpose (his phrase), inspiration. Out of malice and to get my own back, I asked him one day whether he could

174

conceive of what a life laid waste by a single idea would be like, and I was astonished by his unhesitating reply: "Perfectly well, since all my life long, every day and almost at every hour, I have remembered that I was lame."

Up to the time of his untimely death he endured with great fortitude one accident and operation after another, and his legacy to us was a considerable corpus of learned works entirely devoted, as had been his life, to political matters—all, that is, save one, a story of some length, in its way a masterpiece, a single story whose hero was a cripple.

So, as luck will have it, I am fated to suffer pain, which I reconcile with a gambler's spirit, my ultra-feminine gambler's spirit, my instinct for the game of life, if you prefer it; the Last Cat, towards the end of her life, gave every indication by the movement of a paw, by the smile on her face, that a trailing piece of string was still for her a plaything, food for feline thought and illusion. Those who surround me will never let me want for pieces of string.

II

GENEVA 1946

I AM just back from Geneva, where life is brisk and not too noisy. To start with I found little resemblance between the peculiar existence of an invalid-under-treatment in the heart of a foreign town and my customary way of life, adapted over the years and so ungrudgingly to the dictates of a disease with its contrasting ups and downs, and to a beloved city where I hardly had need of pain to equip me for an imitation of the thebaic life in Egypt, with its discretionary solitude and chance sociability.

Confined to my downstairs quarters, I neither heard nor was affected by the teeming life of the Swiss capital. True enough, its roadways are well laid and its traffic largely consists of noiseless vehicles. Early in the morning a hand-cart collects the leaves and twigs from the little square. And the waste paper? Certainly not! In Geneva no litter is left lying about. The little hand-cart rolls along on two large pneumatic tyres. My window looked out on a length of embankment, a street corner, and all I could see from it were sleek automobiles gleaming like brand new pianos.

The first weeks of a prolonged treatment brought me both renewed pain and respite from it, if prostration can be regarded as a lull. I only had to recall my brief periodic visits to Geneva thirty years earlier, in a family pension where theatrical and music-hall artistes, whose purses were as modestly lined as my own, frequented a table d'hôte. A Geneva under pouring rain. My pockets were stuffed with cigarettes for the needs of others (I don't smoke), and tiny gun-metal or nickel watches costing ten francs apiece, in the days when the Swiss franc and the French were equivalent.

Back in Geneva in 1946, while timid April reluctantly approached, I looked forward to the return of some of my strength, or rather of some of my optimism—the two are really one and the same—if not the decisive killing of my pain; and also to the time when an almost exclusively physical dread would so far yield as to grant me a keener perception of the town and its inmates. Had I, then, been reduced to such straits that, to start with, the mountain of solid silver on the far side of Lac Léman appeared to me as no different from its picture postcard replicas? Believe this I must, for I regarded the towering plume of water which, spurting from the lake, remains erect and brandished aloft before constantly returning to it, as little more than a glorified toy, a blade of corn, or seed-corn at the mercy of the wind yet ever resistant. Believe it I must, for at first I could not bring myself to curb a sense of dependence and humility in front of the therapeutist who had undertaken to act in my defence.

In the first place I learnt how a patient should behave under treatment: for this my doctor friends had not prepared me. I learnt how to accustom myself to punctuality and the daily round, to the hours of visitation from an all-powerful, well-intentioned, inexorable stranger. . . . The hour of fearing a certain man, a man unknown, although he was answering my summons. It happened to be the hour that was highly charged with a persistent coquetry, that called for a rose-pink petticoat, a new ribbon in the night-dress, a freshly ironed dressing-gown. The moment that precedes the entry of such a man with healing powers quickens the pulse more than his maltreatment of the limbs—injections, massage, pommellings, vicarious deep-ray therapy, to which his visible presence acts as alleviation. After the cry of agony wrung from me or the muttered oath, I indulged in a wry laugh seemlier than a sob, a hearty swear-word, or an indecent joke for which the doctor made allowance. After that I would enjoy a most agreeable conversation for a minute or so, friendly, light-hearted, when I forgot all about myself, and . . . " Good-bye till tomorrow, my dear doctor ".

I had indeed forgotten my Geneva of other days, since on my first carriage outings as the April dusk was falling, I was utterly astonished to find that the town had unleashed a rush of pedestrians, cyclists, and noiseless American cars: surprised at the concourse without hubbub, activity without collision, haste without confusion. And—greatest surprise of all to me after six years of confinement in the blue of a Paris cellar, with the black-out of war and the red glow of a shaded torch—the bright carnival of electricity! Bathed in a wealth of rosy light, the small dwellings were transformed into a quivering, teeming thoroughfare, brimming over but well ordered, where the shop windows displayed a congeries of goods—lace, footwear, scents and food. I never ceased to register surprise. What! Chocolate for the asking, and gâteaux, in pâtisseries still abundantly overflowing when all had eaten their fill! Also, for the asking, to quench my lips that are parched for it, can that be milk, MILK, pure and held in reverence, sold at every door! Milk that in Paris, following the war restrictions even for the old, is bluish and rationed drop by drop. Is it really true that all and sundry, myself included, can sit down here in a garden-restaurant or ice-cream parlour, and ask for a cup, nay, two and three cups of milk and be supplied! Permissible for anyone to drink it out of a red cup blobbed with white, or one blue as a periwinkle! Drink it, invisible yet palatable, from a large galactite goblet as milk-white as itself! Or ask for it at any hour in my hotel room, either iced and tasteless or warm and evocative of glossy udders, stain it with coffee, lace it, foaming and heated, with vanilla, with sugar and rum! It will be some time before I tire of seeing milk in shining canisters being carried by children all over the town, of surveying it as so many landmarks on my wheeled outings, left unprotected at the half-open wicket of a chalet, or balanced among the unripe cherries on the lower branch of a tree, or sitting in state on the little boundary wall under the watchful eye of a cat!

For anyone not able to dawdle along a pavement and indulge the fortuitous whims and luck of the stroller, there remain only superficial sights, cities that dwindle from view, buildings enhanced by alluring optical illusions. Not only am I determined, from now and henceforward to remain satisfied with this state of affairs, but I am stimulated by the prospect. What have I to lose? Nothing now. The very contrary. Illusions crowd thick upon me. What I take to be a hedging implement, can it really be the latest invention for making coffee! And surely that pretty object so elegantly curved that it looks the ideal prop for a climbing polygonum cannot possibly turn into a trouser-press! In this country a practical invention works wonders. For how long, I wonder, will certain shops, that modestly style themselves 'ironmongers', be inaccessible to me? I would dearly love at least to press my nose against their windows, become intoxicated with varnished woodwork, red beechwood, enamelled iron and aluminium, so effectively does Swiss ingenuity, at the mere sight of it, stir and quicken the idea of art and harmony. On the other hand, the less said about the arty shops full of assorted trinkets the better. . . .

But no one has suggested that I turn art critic, and enumerate landscapes, pink-fleshed nudes, still lifes; and goodness knows what use I could have for an embossed leather writing-pad or a slab of ornamental crystal! Let us give art a miss; I get as much from passing slowly in my chair in front of shops where everything on display has a new-laid look. Art, in this country means a state of innocence, the jealous care for reputation, the honest saleswoman; art and display here take the form of paper—crinkled, serrated, pleated, gilded—paper in abundance, white as snow, blue as a glacier. Compared with it and its healthy profusion, the linen of our poor France in her time of penury, eked out to the extent of using one corner of a towel after another, will be found slightly abhorrent.

Bananas, late-season but still juicy apples, early strawberries, oranges, eggs, cream whipped or plain! Against that, no cheese—other than by the gramme—no rice, no butter, except by trickery or arrangement. "What, no gruyère in Switzerland? You can't mean it!" We simply burst out laughing. We took it for a joke at our expense as newcomers, until the staid solemnity of the local inhabitants changed the look on our faces: "No, we have none for the moment," said the charming young lady, a native of Geneva. She wore well cut clothes and jewellery; but she could not procure either butter or cheese. Brought up to respect restrictions, it never entered her head to get round them. Perhaps the devil does not exist in Switzerland!

And gorged with other good things we would console ourselves with bread alone, *pain-gâteau, pain-brioche, pain-gourmandise*. So good was it that we feared giving full rein to our appetite and dared not, at table, ask for a second helping more than twice.

I have advanced only by small relays, if I dare so to express myself, in getting to know what amenities Geneva has to offer. Spring was hesitant, and from a bed of suffering one does not take any but a restricted view of the lives of the hale and hearty. My strength was at a low ebb by eight in the evening, when the tray would arrive set with raw salads, grilled meat, green vegetables and fruit —don't we all know by heart the list of a prescribed menu!—and after that came my illuminated entertainment. Through the open window, framing a blue that subtly deepens with the shades of night, I can see a stretch of the lake which reflects a bridge and quaysides, and till past midnight its confines are delineated by multi-coloured electric lamps, street lamps, and strings of fairy lights. Tomorrow the early morning haze will restore to my view the iridescent cathedral, seeming almost to quiver as it is hoisted above the rooftops with its strange glazed domes that brood over its inner sanctuaries. Tomorrow I shall have the peace of a misty sunrise and the curvetting swallows. In the evening, the banners of multicoloured light dip in the lake and ripple over the surface. One particular "advertisement blue" glorifies the national clock-and-watch trade and where this azure strikes across an absinthe-green its colour is enhanced, while a deep crimson spreads out as far as the prow-like breasts of three swans poised above their own reflection.

Certainly it is a pleasure to lie facing a spectacle of lights and shades without so much as having to raise oneself on an elbow, without craning one's neck or sitting up in bed, and never to take one's eyes off it till the curtain of their lids is lowered. Whatever is easily come by is always a pleasure, even when distilled by a drop of bitterness: if I did not suffer—here and here, and again here—this . . . well, this agony, I should never have thought of positioning my bed, calculated to a nicety, in the corner where its occupant is afforded an untrammelled view of three horizons. Those who are fit and agile have no need of such convenience.

"I shall go off by myself on a shopping expedition," said a woman friend who was staying a few days in Geneva, "to buy you whatever you think might tempt you here. Let me have a list."

No sooner said than done. For a long time I had wanted

a pepper-mill, properly made, a mill, as they say in my
quarter of Paris, "that grinds", and not one of those
tuppeny-ha'penny little tooth-wheel objects that wear out
in next to no time and can be found in any of our multiple
stores at home. I also wanted a braid of thread and a braid
of silk made up in the old-fashioned way in needlefuls of
equal length and various colours, tied tight at either end
like saveloys. I now possess them. A little too skimpy,
but a pretty piece of hand-plaiting, of real *passementerie*.
I wanted, too, some four-holed mother-of-pearl buttons for
my underclothes. Mother-of-pearl, and I refused to go back
on my word. Yes, mother-of-pearl, and may the walls
come tumbling down about me! And needles, into the
bargain, some "English" needles (when I was a child
their glazed envelopes were already printed in German),
needles which we, the mistress-craftswomen in hand-
sewing, called "taper-eyed". And some darning wool,
wound on cards. And elastic, to run up the waistbands
for stockinette knickers. And some old-fashioned reels of
cotton, waxed, for stitching leather. Have I ever stitched,
do I stitch, shall I stitch leather? That's beside the point.
And a twist of real silk for repairing the frayed button-
holes on men's clothes. . . . Is there, then, some strange
happiness to be derived from the sight and touch of
certain "requisites" which have never been drastically
changed or modified by any aesthetic concern or shift of
fashion? There is. But since I am still fairly well-off, I
do not put them to their proper use. Entranced by the
magic of contemplative evocation, I deck myself out in
the fine feathers of haberdashery. All the same you would
never have imagined that this right hand of mine, now
rather bunched up from the habit of writing, was once

endowed with the cunning to beget that show-piece of symmetry, sober relievo, solidity: the buttonhole on a male garment! I mean, of course, the buttonhole-stitched buttonhole. There is no poetry in the other, the so-called piped buttonhole.

Hunting for needles for crewel-work is labour in vain. France is a void, Switzerland a barren desert. For ages past the answer given me in the big shops all over France has been: "We don't stock such things. Of course, I'm not saying that in the past . . ." with the head on one side, you know, rather like a dog when offered an empty bowl, and as a consolation prize I am offered darning-needles! I plan, when my dearest friend takes to driving me out again and has recovered his patience, to stop at all the little village haberdashers, the proper kind, with a glass panelled door and tinkling bell, where buttons are to be found in the wool basket, wool in the boot-lace drawer, bootlaces in the zip-fastener container, where a strong smell of pickled herring is all pervasive, and where, finally, a small girl turns toward the murky back of the shop with a plaintive "Mum, I can't find anywhere the sort of needles the lady is asking for!"

Six weeks. Ought I to exclaim "Already!" or "Only six!"? The days pass, all alike, intent on running their course, each scarred at the beginning, middle, and end by physical pain, that sharp recall to life. Dear-Doctor-till-tomorrow still has his gentle voice and his big heart that takes up too much room in his big breast and makes him wheezy. The weather is fine—no, it's going to be fine. Covered by cloud, a white sun is melting the snows on

184

the flanks of the Jura. The return of winter, which has so disheartened Paris, is welcomed by Geneva with opulent serenity. In this hotel the boilers have been rekindled and, in addition to the central heating, parabolical radiators have been installed in every corner, in much the same way that amateur gardeners can't see a gap in their rockery without popping in a fern frond or saxifrage.

Yet no feigned apostasy on the part of hoary winter can outwit or discourage the Judas trees, the double cherries, the lilacs of every hue, by this time obstinately set on their forward course. The start once made, they will sleep out of doors and bloom. Another denial of winter rises at dusk, from the peacefully dormant and rarely sluiced mud at the bottom of the lake. Throughout my wheel-chair perambulations I have to hold my nose against its floating sickly-sweet fragrances. Not enough salt in it. Your true-born Genevan, on the other hand, will sigh in ecstasy "Oh, that smell from the lake! It brings tears to my eyes, each time it comes back to me after I've been away." The green vein of the Rhône, flowing in at great depth, refuses to mingle with the common eddies, and cleaves its forceful path through the waters of Lac Léman, to escape, stabbed by the golden darts of the sun at its zenith.

The sparrow, that perky pedestrian! I had not intended to speak of it. I wished simply to give it food, and leave things at that. But in Geneva the town sparrow takes the initiative and can teach me a thing or two, whether I like it or not. Generations of worthy citizens have gone to the making of generations of trustful birds.

The French bookseller, only three steps away—five or six turns of the wheel to my mode of approach—has been quick to pick up the customs of the country. "When winter comes, we divide the birds between us," he told me, "not for the purpose of eating them, but to look after them. On a night of sudden sharp frost a few winters ago, I had to get out of bed to go and free a gull which had its legs trapped by the ice at the edge of the lake, right in front of my door, the poor thing!" I too am in his debt, for he brings my fare of second-hand books out on to the pavement when I am unable to put foot to the ground, and in a stage whisper promises me "a Peter Cheyney" for the following week. He knows that for all the long days of spring the nights are not so short as the sparrows make out.

I can put up with their chirping as well here as in the Palais-Royal, for its modulation is so limited that it does not always break into my dearly acquired morning sleep. But I did not foresee that at the hour when the immaculate waiter brings in my tray and pulls aside the curtains drawn across my open window, no, I had not foreseen that at that hour my eyes would light upon not the *entry* of the sparrows into my room, but their exit. Seven of them, the colour of mice, came out from under my bed and went to rejoin their cheeping friends on the little balcony.

From that day on, I had difficulty in following the course of their familiarity, their demands upon me, I should rather say. Their appetite is unrelenting rather than insatiable. Three female birds started a nursery on my balcony for their young who had already sprouted feathers but still gave a pretty good imitation of the shrill insistence and shiverings of famished fledglings.

Jeanne Loewer brought me, from the Chaux-de-Fonds, a large round loaf of stale bread for the early morning regimental breakfast. The minute spindle-shaped females held their own against the round-breasted and better feathered cocks, their cheeks and wing plumage coquettishly marked. From watching them I have come to learn a little about that stranger, the bird, telling myself that, given four legs, it would look far more arresting than it does with its two wings crossed over its back, like Napoleon.

The mock-mahogany moulding at the foot of my bed later served as a perch for these lickspittle beggars who outstared me, bombarded me with their sharp, impatient calls and caught bread-crumbs thrown to them as would a French bull-dog. No sooner had I shut myself in the bathroom than they protested in increasing numbers that I should open the door again. The culmination came during siesta-time one warm and fleecy afternoon, when I became aware of some unusual movement close beside me, yet one that touched my heart. I found a pair of them, one close against the other, in a fold of the bed-spread. In an access of bliss, my effort to lean over them must have made too sudden a stir, for away they flew. This gave me fair warning that the time was not far off when I should discover one individual among their small, indefinite band, the particular one, the one who preferred me and was mine by preference. With the animal world, we are subject to the same perils every time. To choose, to be chosen, to love: the very next moment we are beset by anxiety, the danger of loss, and the fear of spreading regret. What an array of big words when the subject

187

is but a sparrow! Yes, a sparrow. In love, there is never a question of smallness.

In the closing days of April, prior to the cold snap, "the darling buds of May" and the kerria were setting an example in their whites and yellows to the roses of summer, and the first gentians, down from their mountain fastnesses to the florists, were refreshing themselves in my tooth-glass, their stalks on a pad of damp moss, which helps the flowers to drink. Their sole beauty lies in their uncompromising azure blue; there must be some reason why we find ourselves so sensibly affected by blue! Age-old evocations of the firmament, a moist mirage in desert eyes, all that we hold to be eternal, is readily blue. The corolla of a gentian is tight-stretched on umbrella-ribs, the cordate cyclamen leaf is lined with mauve india-rubber: the edelweiss is pure cotton-wool. None of the three thereby loses its seductive charms and emblematic character of innocence. I am not forgetting that ubiquitous intruder, the narcissus! It is everywhere. Year after year it draws its devotees to Les Avants, where celebrations are held in its honour. And how do they honour the narcissus? By killing it. It is sacrificed by the million. Let us shed no tears, that's all it is good for. Once picked it is tied up in bunches that quickly wilt unless plunged into water. Its journey down from Les Avants by car, van or cycle, has steeped the road in unchecked, horizontally spreading scent, in the toils of which we first exclaimed "How divine!" then later "How nauseating!" Surely there can be few who are put off the lilac by its sovereign if funerary scent, the lilac

188

in any of its varieties, blue, purple or mauve, or the sparse and delicate thyrsus of the Rouen lilac! My mother "Sido" used to say of this *varin* variety "I can never make up my mind whether its scent is rather nice or perfectly horrid!"

In many a plot the cherry trees here have overtopped the walls or spread beyond the party hedges. Green yesterday, the fruit is ruddy today, and tomorrow will be ruddier, rounder, heavier still. It acquires an even coating of red, almost glazed, and then it is tempting to eye, mouth and hand. Stretch out an arm, and it is mine, yours, ours for the picking. I pass the trees every day, and I notice that never a cherry is missing. In my part of France, a good shaking was just as likely to drop an urchin hidden in the branches as a good shower of cherries. "You cannot tempt the Devil," the pilferer might plead in self defence, cherries in his mouth and cherries in his pockets. In Switzerland, as I have told you, they have no devil.

I HAVE received a love letter: "*Madame Colette, I adore you! I am a very handsome fellow. If you will not say me nay, I shall pay you a call and give you a kiss on the nose.*" It was signed "Béni". I did not care to throw away my last chance of having an affectionate interview with a Prince-at-the-very-least-oriental.

He came, attended by a female slave who called herself his mistress. He evinced no disdain when treading the worn carpet of my hotel bedroom, and to start with my dearest friend and I did not know what to say to him; but he was not put out by our lack of words, nor did this deprive him of his princely expression of friendliness.

He was rose-pink—as indeed those Persians known as "Cream" should be when without blemish and, as was this gentleman, loaded with honours, medals and First Prizes. He was almost copper pink, his front paws not a far remove from the good earth, but rising in tone towards the tail. Clad like a fairy, he seemed miraculously at ease in the midst of a cloud of fur that beat against his sides at every step, and provided him at the back with breeches of insubstantial fluff. His coat was a profusion of clustered curls on chest and belly, and escaped from either ear in feathery tufts.

I hesitate to speak of his eyes, not knowing how to

capture their exact shape, the wide gleam in them of liquid gold and amber, the calm confidence with which they returned our gaze, and their latent smile, the outcome of a petted childhood. Round his nostrils too was the bloom of the same rare shade of copper pink.

To increase our speechless adoration, he spoke. The voice of the Angora is ordinarily soft and low, without prejudicing their amative periods when they are changed into howling demons. He jumped on to my quaking knees and, since he had promised it, gave me a kiss on the nose. He was pleased to display symptoms of curiosity about my bathroom and over the cheeky sparrows on the balcony, to whom he delivered a pithy address in the tremulous tones that inform the feathered race of the exact sentiments of a cat towards them. Wanting for nothing, he was without covetous desires, and when we saw him turn away from the birds to go in chase of a ball of crumpled paper, we uttered cries of delighted affection.

I held him for a moment in a tight embrace, tufted and sweet-smelling as a bunch of flowers. He gave me another kiss or two, on the tip of my nose and under my ear, and all the while his slave was expatiating on his noble lineage and the fruits of victory he brought back from every competition. She added a few relevant details: " He is unmatched for cleanliness; he not only puts up with but actually insists on his daily toilet with brush and comb; if at times it is his pleasure to show signs of abject submission, the slightest reprimand will cut him to the quick and may even ruin his appetite." I took solemn note of these " light touches " that added authenticity to his portrait; I transcribe them here in a suitably genteel tone.

Anything to do with cats, in my thoughts or in my writing, must never be treated with banter.

The musical ear of a cat clearly differentiates between familiarity and affection. It was not merely from her delight in playful fantasy that the Last Cat enjoyed my " Cat, come here at once! Cat, go to bed! " that formed part of the evening ritual. Gaily she scampered away, racing to her basket, and giving a passable imitation of a dog obeying orders. But it is true that the cat prefers the intonations of the human voice which come nearest to singing. In my few remarks to " Béni ", I observed the essential protocol. All the more since, to his other perfections, was added that childlike air of majesty which Angoras are slow to discard. Far removed from his character were the depth and intensity of the Last Cat, with her too ready aptitude to feel and express grief. For instance the year when, rather against her better nature and following a brief encounter with the shoeblack on the corner, the black and white bistro cat, and the grocer's small ginger, she produced a fine bastard daughter, striped, smiling, and half-witted, that we called Jantille. At once the Cat drove her from sight and affection out of pure jealousy, so much so that the very name of Jantille on the lips of either one of us would evoke from her a feeble little anguished cry. So we gave Jantille away as a present to the Curé of Mesnuls, and the Cat's aggrieved heart found peace.

It is to " Béni " that I owe this retrospective daydream. His resplendent presence, memories of the Last Cat, whatever acts as a touchstone to renew or remind me of cat personalities or cat characters, at once takes me back to a past climate that used to be both poignant and essential, but has since been renounced by me, prudently and with detachment.

Béni, for his part, seemed desirous of going to sleep on my knees, over which was draped my soft vicuna rug. He had already settled down to a rippling purr when his mood changed and, starting to mew in a minor key, he led his slave towards the door. The princely visit was ending with the end of his patience, the short-lived, brittle patience of the feline species that suddenly snaps and makes as putty in a man's hands the trained lion, the broken-spirited tiger in its cage, and the puma sulking in tears!

Amiable still, though distant, Béni made short shrift of farewell courtesies. He even rebuffed me with his soft cat's paw, conditioned by custom to gentleness yet ready to remind me that, dormant in their sheath—indubitably pink—it held sharp-pointed claws.

On my outings I drive along at the leisurely pace of a lady of the Second Empire. A pony-chaise could overtake me. There is always so much to look at when one travels slowly. Contrasting beauties effaced by speed fall into their proper perspective. My years and infirmities have surely earned me the right to go slow, to stop at whim beside a narcissus, a purple orchis, or a wild strawberry! No need now for my dearest friend, while at the wheel, his chin jutting out like a radiator cap, to interfere with his " No, no! No wild lavender, no honeysuckle, no cytisus! No time for a snack before Saulieu! You'll make havoc of all my timetables! " Nowadays it is he who picks my wild hyacinths for me. In the

long run there is something to be said for having
arthritis.

Thus my stoppings and startings become voyages of
discovery; I go from garden-restaurant to riverside
garden, I take stock of bowers and arbours and rose
gardens. Here the municipal gardeners are busy planting
out the roses they have kept hidden off-stage by the
thousand. Roses assume a military elegance when paraded
in serried ranks. As we pass them by, certain precocious
battalions salute us with the special scent of their species,
the unmistakable breath of " tea " and " tea hybrids ".
How quickly they go—how quickly am I going! Yet an
aged body like mine clings fast to the winter of its dis-
content and its attendant ills, wraps itself up in shawls
and rugs, derives a secret satisfaction from the chilly aftermath of the doctor's visit, profits from the anticipated loss
of strength to withdraw into itself, and forget the spring.
It is not possible to deny the spring. On a clear day the
lake, though niggardly with indigo, might well be the
Mediterranean. Children spangle the town with their
little check dresses; grown-up girls go about bare-legged.
Luxury is manifest in the spotless garment, the constant
laundering, the fluffy jumpers that are the envy of Paris.
And what a fine display of heads of hair, with never any
need for the horrible " hair-pad "! Resplendent but not
too feminine angels boldly fend their way through the
peak-hour crowds, their hair a torch, their bare knees like
glazed, crackling fruit skins.

I admire, I rejoice, I get about, I come into contact with
all these long-legged Atalantas whose praises I sing—
oh no, a thousand times no, don't run away with the idea
that I am jealous, or sad! Do me the honour of believing

that I do know how to make the most of what is left me of my part, do know how to bear lightly what would have seemed heavy in days gone by, and derive from the flaw by which metaphorically I am ploughed and furrowed a certain . . . yes, I shall say it . . . a certain nobleness of spirit. I hesitate before putting down such an expression, sounding it out, taking its measure: what if it be too grand for me! Believe, at any rate, that I have no need for all the consideration I receive, that I laugh inwardly when the kind-hearted, on my behalf, go as far as to use the word "asceticism", as though it were a fitting rank or title. Does anyone suppose that it would be easy to escape the clutches of asceticism!

Will the various remedies which the Good-bye-till-tomorrow-Doctor inflicts on me one day become a source of amusement? One of them is greasy and glacial. Another is more penetrating, has more quills than a sea-urchin. There is yet another, which the body, stunned at receiving so many steel-pointed light rays, cannot help but question.

Here I am, with two months all but gone, longing to drink a toast to what the future holds in store for me of the unpromised and unknown. Dear-Doctor-till-tomorrow, I suffer from hope, and from modesty, and I ask you as few questions as I can. After the time of roses in their ordered ranks comes, I know, the symmetrical blaze of geraniums, of scarlet salvias, and then will come the dahlias, and later the chrysanthemums. Let us look no further. While resting on shores made to bloom under civic control, I have entered again into close friendship with all the wild flowers of the Swiss meadows, which are brought in to the proprietress of this hotel swathed in a tangle of nondescript greenery. They come into my room only after they have been sorted out, picked over and tastefully arranged by her own hands. Here the funny little face of some labiate nibbles at the wing of a bee-orchis—the fringed carmine beards of the ragged-robin emerge from a blue foundation of self-heal—the golden buttons of ranunculus from meadow and stream are wreathed in the insubstantial mist of their umbels—the three "Pasque flowers", mauve, violet and white, form the gauzy edging of a large, shallow bowl filled with lilies of the valley, the last of the season—already, a suspicion of baldness silvers the crimson clover. The crimson clover already! Have I then sacrificed, aided and abetted by my dearest friend, almost the quarter of one year to ministrations of which I cannot yet compute the range or the rewards, let alone alleviation? Not a soul has mentioned a possible cure to me, yet a constant appeal is made to my moral resources. Splendid! Least said soonest mended! In any case, there are so many methods of cure —perhaps I may invent one myself. To a dash of daring add a moderate dose of arbitrariness, a liberal dose of astonishment, much after the fashion of that ingenious child who stretched a piece of stuff over two rods set crosswise at the end of a stick and shouted "Maman, do look, I've just invented the umbrella!"

IV

PARIS

THIS year, next year, some time, never! When shall
we acquire what we most want, some of us poor folk
who are almost at the end of our tether, pent within the
four walls of a room, wedged between desk and book-
case, assailed by the footfall on the floor above and the
clatter of wooden soles on the staircase without? Not
tomorrow, not this year, will Paris provide us with one
or two "Gardens for Adults". That the most pressing
need takes precedence, that first there must be "Gardens
for Children", I do not dispute. And where can a large
enough site be found? I am not to be taken in by small
talk of that nature: when Paris requires a vacant site, she
finds one. Not without first looking for it, I agree. After
which they might very well endow a site for V.I.P.s. The
garden of the Palais-Royal is the very thing for such persons. It holds few attractions for children, who have done
it infinite hurt by their presence and their games. Sand
and gravel are non-existant, the earth has been stamped
into insensibility, and it is forbidden to water the soil—
the lawns and flowerbeds alone are entitled to have their
thirst quenched, and the gardener tends these lovingly—
what we call our "Court" has to rest content solely with
the slow and time-honoured impregnations from showers

of rain, urine of dogs, and human excrement—let me put "children's droppings", to make it sound better.

Here all is an open stage, where the principal players are the children. Many are charming, most are gifted with remarkable agility. The thin-bodied outstrip the more robust. Their skill in throwing and catching a ball holds my attention as keenly as a sporting event. At my window yesterday, a Sunday, I was fascinated by a baby girl of four or so, squat for her age, who was disporting herself in the sabbatical silence with two male members of her family, her father and uncle no doubt. This child so intent on her outdoor sport repaid all the attention I bestowed on her, so deft was she at stopping the ball with her foot, at throwing it back straight—and with either hand—so adept at falling bare-legged and bare-armed on the hard ground without a word of complaint. But, as I could well see, she was an exception, as are child prodigies on the stage or in the circus, so much so that when told to do so she sat down in the wind and the sun and stayed still like an athlete. And like an athlete she had put on flesh: her face was a good colour, but far from improved by two strands of plaited hair scragged back over each ear and tied with a tag of ribbon. An exception, but a welcome exception, formed by discipline and self-confidence. It would have been beyond the comprehension, and envy, of most of our Palais-Royal children, that a small girl of four, from some sense of quasi-professional pride, could be capable of behaving with such zest and restraint.

Not all the scenes beneath my window are as pleasant to watch as that. Into my magnificent quadrangle seethe a hotch-potch of young people all full of beans who, since

198

Penny Carey

the war, intolerable and intolerant, have cast off the shackles of restraint and guidance. Quick on their feet but not fleet-footed, for their steps are conditioned by the imperfections of shoes no longer made to fit, they hop-and-go-one as sylphs might hobble if shod. Smitten from early youth with a passion for every sort of competitive game, like born neuropaths they follow their bent with uninhibited disregard for convention : they are true children of Paris.

In our royal enclosure we have never enjoyed any greater hygienic comfort and convenience than Versailles could boast under Le Grand Roi. Apart from the plush and luxury of the Restaurant Véfour and the amenities of the neighbouring theatre, there is not a single *buen-retiro* in sight. La Civette, to the greater glory of My Lady Nicotine, has pulled down its time-honoured mahogany stalls, which venerable dames used to tend with such care. Of what matter is that to the Garden's imperious guests, the children? When the need comes upon them, down slip the little shorts and up go the little skirts and . . . There are even simpler methods still. The infant in arms will pipe up from its pram with a cry of alarm; without rising from her wrought-iron chair, that indestructible relic of past ages, the mother or watcher will snatch it up and hold it at arms' length, as though it were a strainer of liquids and solids! Yesterday, immediately below my window, nine little puddle-stains all along the stone flags testified to the fact that among the chairs that afternoon nine children had slept, taken food, and . . . evacuated Oh, what malodorous incense rises in the evening air!

The war and its aftermath conditioned our children to jungle practices. A few days ago I saw two bigger boys

of about twelve coming my way. They stopped at the
first tree on the Valois side of the pleached alley. I thought
to myself ' They're going to micturate in unison '—we're
quite accustomed to that—' against one of those old decaying trees that never quite die.' Not at all. Lowering their
already man's-size trousers, they jointly deposited the
copious insignia of their brief visit. Throughout the operation they chatted amicably, without bravado and without
shame. Shame and shamelessness mean nothing to them.
But since it was broad daylight the passers-by, for their
part, did look the other way.

With a child, making a nuisance of itself is instinctive
and terrifyingly ingenious. The appetite for destruction—
in other words, invention—has to be satisfied when and
where it can. The return of spring sees the pink chestnut
candelabra cut to shreds by the stone-throwers, and brings
back the stalkers-on-the-slates so skilled in dislodging at
one fell blow the nests full of young birds from under
the ceilings of the arcade.

A generation of disheartened parents confront the
children of today. It would be easy for me to fill these
pages with shameful tales of child hucksters, schoolboy
gangsters, striplings who act as stooges for big-time
criminals: in short, of children who have never known
the joys of childhood. Will they, perhaps—in the words
of Labiche—come to know childhood in old age?

But I haven't the heart to curse them, my lively sparrows intoxicated by their own chirrupings, my whistling
little cobras, my embryo artillerymen, corn-crake-voiced
chatterboxes and maniac trumpeters, all the more because
I have never lost either the memory or the benefits of a
parental upbringing which instructed me in silence before

200

all else. I cannot spend my time abusing them, because I observe them and by observation make them my own. I do not lay claim to them in the name of a pseudo-maternity which has never come easily to me, but from my window above I recognise in them my own blood, my own race, my own past, my own faults, whether re-claimed by time or aggravated by age. Ideal greed that feeds on fancy! This naughty child secretly belongs to me, as the animal with whom I exchange some sign of recognition is mine, as one of the plants in the flower-bed is mine since I am perhaps the only one to know its name: *penstemon*. When I passed on this name to another citizeness of the Palais-Royal I received in ex-change a brief shrug and for answer " Don't make me laugh! How can I believe a name like that! " I was in half a mind to take her up: " You don't want it? Then give it me back. I shall share it only with M. Henri, the gardener, who loves his flower-beds." And having classi-fied it among the objects of my ideal possessions, along with my fillies, my newly hatched chicks, all the marvel-lous offspring of my own modest phantasmagoria, I shall put the *penstemon* to much the same use as did Théophile Gautier the flower of his imagination, the *angsoka*.

V

BEAUJOLAIS 1947

WHAT a fierce, unparalleled, interminable summer this has been, rising again and again from its ashes, converting Normandy into a parched Ardèche, Burgundy into a waste of esparto-grass, laying bare and dry the beds of all the mountain torrents, as well as the bottom mud of ponds where frogs expired and fish lay gasping! Only now, when the time has come round for the nights to turn cold, can a good word be put in for the fearful summer, responsible as it was for so many of our food shortages. In no sense to restore it to grace and favour, for it is past redemption. Its savagery began at dawn, with the animals athirst and all the herbivores deprived of sustenance. You might see a man using only one small watering-can to sprinkle a cabbage field, one of those huge fields that in good years do honour to the outskirts of a town, a single man among ten thousand yellowing cabbages. You might see a cow that, while pulling up the stubble blade by blade, had swallowed ten kilos of earth and died of it. You might see . . .

No, I shall never be able to link together a series of agreeable memories with the aid of such pictures. They blacken and reduce to cinders my favourite pastime of day-dreaming for pleasure. Forty-one degrees centigrade in Rue de Beaujolais at noon, and thirty-seven at two o'clock in the morning: how far away it all seems now when, through my high half-open windows, the December air forces a vertical passage, whitened by fine frozen snow which, for a brief moment, wreathes with a halo my blue lantern that burns by night and by day. A few seconds are sufficient for the cold to take possession of my room. Quick! Now's the moment—without making a physical movement of any kind—to plunge back into whatever of the summer's bounty was least harsh and dehydrated, there to discover something to make the mouth water, to bring colour to hand and dress, something pertaining to freshets and dew: let us return to the brief recompense, all the more real in that it was unsolicited, granted me at the fiercest moment of the ferocious summer: vintage time on the slopes of Brouilly.

Most certainly, for an arthritic like myself, the worst is not the getting about from place to place, always provided that the journey is made by car. The worst is taking ten steps across the room, walking five yards along the garden, having my night's rest broken by sudden, sharp jabbing thrusts of pain, reaching out with the quick, impulsive gesture of youth in an attempt to pick up my stick or lift down a book—oh, how inveterate is youth, its agility now purely of the mind, and chastised the moment it strains at the leash! As for the stairs, their descent is now a matter of humiliation and guile: for when a stranger passes, do I not stop and, standing still, pretend to be putting on a glove or fumbling in my bag! Once the stranger is safely out of the way, I laugh at myself and my old woman's wiles.

But put me into a car, with a cushion here and a cushion there, and away we go! You won't hear another word from me for a prolonged stretch of miles. In bygone days it was the Cat who decided, by a yawn of hunger or some discomfort of the bladder, the spot where our Ark should come to rest. She ate little on a journey, and feared travel sickness. A nip at Saulieu, a lap at Vienne, with a refresher of grass between times. My requirements are on a less modest scale than hers. When she was of the company, we hardly had time to finish our woodland picnic before she demanded to be back in "her" car to smooth every hair of her coat, blue as a storm cloud coming up from the west.

As I was saying—saying to myself, rather, though I was committing it to paper—it was a masterful decision on the part of my dearest friend that got me away, as he alone knew how, at crack of dawn on a morning that reeked of heatwave, melting asphalt and dried-up river beds, set on a course for the slopes that border the Rhône. There the small tight-bunched grapes are less decorative than the opulent Provençal muscat, that trails its six-pound allurements under the vine-stock and offers its fresh-skinned belly to the lizard.

What benefits could I hope to reap from the Beaujolais vintage? The never varying torrid heat, my very helplessness, everything seemed fated to keep me apart from such a rough and rustic festival. I would have been content to listen to the sounds with which it covered the hills, the wains creaking along the rough tracks beside which I took my morning nap. Voices hazy with early morning fatigue arose from the heights of a neighbouring vineyard and then declined, descending ever lower as the sun rose higher. I could picture the slow work of picking, the baskets filled, the increasingly parched throats of any who thought to slake their thirst by biting into a bunch. I kept the persistent summer at bay on the far side of closed Venetian blinds, on the side of the flaming ball of fire, the flies, the demented wasps, and the dusty mint plants, the side on which could be viewed a glint of a dazzling fragment of the Saône as it sparkled in the valley, far away. I exercised a modicum of patience. I listened to the red-tailed wall-creepers rustling the ivy above the fountain and cutting the thread of its jet.

But better things were in store for me. Friendship can achieve much. A chain of linked arms settled me in the car one day, and in the recesses of one of his private chambers, I bearded My Lord Wine, whose threshold I had thought never to pass.

He received me in the cool bosom of a hill without my having to put foot to the ground. It was I, seated in my chariot, who had the air of a conqueror. With its great door thrown back, his Palace had the appearance of a sequestered grotto, and from its spacious ceiling he enveloped me at one and the same time in an icy cope of motionless air, the divine and mushy odour of crushed grapes, and the droning hum of their fermentation. Lamps shone like twinkling stars along vaults a hundred metres in length; vats spumed long thinning festoons of rosy froth over their sides; a team of dappled horses, blue-tinted in the half-light, were nonchalantly munching grapes that had tumbled to the floor; emanations from the new wine, heavy, impure and but newly born, blended with the steam rising from the sodden horses.

A sparkle of ruby red flickered over the chased ribs and bosses of a silver cup which, at the end of an unseen arm, a man's hand flourished in front of me: " A forty-four in its prime, Madame. But come back and taste the forty-seven when the time comes round! It will be more than the equal of this."

Come back! How probable, how easy this sounded as I held the cold rim of the brimming cup between my lips, under the arching grotto that barred ingress to the heat outside!

As those about me were of the opinion that the *grand vin*, the starry cavern, and the shade of the hillside tunnel could perhaps be considered as antidotes, we made another trip, this time by night, taking another route to climb another slope. This time the shade was provided by a wistaria that clung to all four sides of a courtyard; issuing from a single trunk, like a huge writhing python, it rose hugely to heights where it became lost in its own foliage. The covered-in courtyard, lit by arc-lamps, rang with the clangor of voices, wheels and heavily shod feet, for the forty or so vintagers of the estate were on their way down to their repast, bringing in with them their aroma of male vigour and the juices of the vine. How dearly I should have loved to follow them down! Our cold collation on the ground floor was a feast of ham liberally padded with fat, sausages that had a whiff of new harness, and a special cheese, called "strong", that provokes an unquenchable thirst.

All honour to labour where honour is due: below stairs, the forty vintagers were to sit down to the better table, consisting of omelettes, pork, veal and poultry, washed down with a wine which, like the finest rubies when held to the light, keeps the clear brilliance of its generous, full-blooded colour.

The fatigue that follows a faultless meal, served with

a young vintage wine on a summer night with no dewfall, can be agreeable enough, provided it is not forced or pro- longed. In the court-yard at the time of our departure, under the swinging arc-lamps, the huge wistaria coiled its living spirals. But, since we were the first to leave, I could not appreciate any but the sharpest sounds emerging from the great silence that little by little was settling over the hillface: flights of brittle-winged elytrons jarring against the standard lamps at the entrance; the hoof-beats of an unharnessed horse clattering along a cross-road and, above all, soft music on the ear, invisible and held in reverence by all, the never failing babble of the freshet, the last, this fevered year, where gasping hill and parched dale could slake their thirst.

VI

FARGUE and I, confined to our respective beds, used to talk on the telephone. Not very often, but at considerable length. I dearly loved, and shall always love, his fat, rich, infinitely elastic voice, with a shade of suffocation over it caused by chronic bronchitis. My memory bears me out that our verbal exchanges were never anything but affectionate, frivolous, riddled with news of our work or of our leisure, and of course with every kind of reminiscence.

I was always curious to learn from him the manner of his suffering and the nature of his physical pain. "Today it's hammers, yesterday I was in the grip of a vice, a sort of continual grinding," he would say, and then go on to question me about my periods of sleep and sleeplessness, but I knew full well that he was reproaching me for my failure to sound romantic: whereas in his mouth an ostentatious choice of words would throw a glamour over his very disease. . . . I shall make time and space to talk further of him, as he used to be.

When he allowed me into his house to see his "Family Portraits all hung on the line," I had good reason to show my delight and gratitude. Thereafter I wanted to see more and more of him. I wanted Fargue both in the flesh and in the mind's eye, Fargue traipsing across Lipp,

Fargue strolling down the street with his soft, untiring tread, and above all I wanted to see Fargue. Arrangements were made for my transference one day last summer, I being the lesser sufferer of the two. The first stage by car, through the streets at dusk on a fine evening—the streets of Paris, Fargue's undisputed kingdom, glittering with gold-dust, rich with his insults and charm of manner—a journey at whose end I knew him to be waiting for me.

At the Rue du Montparnesse end they bundled me into the luggage-lift sprinkled with coal. The ascent brought me to Fargue. Some whim or other prompted him to be found seated at table, so that I might think him capable of rising at any given moment, I can only suppose, to offer me his arm and bring me to rest at his table.

Six guests all told; but as how many should I reckon Léon-Paul Fargue, presiding like a Buddha, with all his eloquence and gaiety? He was at his best that evening, to the extent of giving reassurance to Goudeket and myself. I won't swear that he deceived our friends Doctor Martha Lamy and Professor Paulette Gauthier-Villars and even Chériane herself. But he made a good meal, scolded and laughed as scornfully as an intolerant prince. He complained of the too blue blueness of his sheets, and depicted for us what he alone could see. He talked to the cat, affectionately, for the cat was as glossy, as dark and beautiful as Chériane. Facing me was a portrait of her, large and striking, prominent and lifelike as a guest at table. To my right the ledge of the open window cut off the trunks of the plane trees; the lover of the streets had his lodgings among the branches.

I can find nothing to say about this last evening that is either more, or less, deserving of report, of regret, or of being affectionately preserved in the memory of his friends. No single one of us, not even Fargue himself, rose to the occasion. None of us felt either the need or desire to applaud, to make an occasion of it, or to register exceptional surprise. But I know that the six guests have not forgotten a single moment of it, that in the bitter certainty of there being no next time, we, his faithful and unfortunate friends, all feel ourselves to be the poorer.

I have not been to the theatre since I went to see *La Folle de Chaillot*. Not that I have not wanted to go; but, as Pauline says, "it creates too much of a song and dance" to get me comfortably installed in a theatre or cinema. Helplessness breeds timidity. I do not mean to say that it leads one to self-indulgence. Abstinence surely does not ruin the stomach for every kind of relish! In consideration of the length of time that one or two of my senses had been deprived of gratification, I should have expected the more readily available appeal to the ear and the delights and surprises offered to the eye to have given me a rejuvenated enthusiasm. And yet there I sat as wary as when I was a dramatic critic. I had hoped to be more agreeably surprised.

On the first encounter the shock was agreeable enough: the auditorium of the Athénée, encrusted with glittering gilt. Meretricious but magnificent! What a wealth of golden fruit and swags, with as many breasts as apples, as many pears as garlands and thighs! An auditorium for a real theatre, a real auditorium for a theatre, where Bérard's rollicking blues and reds were set off by a long lustreless black figure, the figure of Jouvet standing out against the set, Jouvet with jet sewn into his black tights, a long black exclamation mark!

Last night I committed the downright folly of re-reading *Le Festin de Pierre,* the cause of my considerable embarrassment in listening to the piece. It was like listening to a musical composition with the score open on my knees. All the same I was able to enjoy unreservedly my right to give no opinion. If I were forced to form a judgment on Don Juan as played by an actor who " walks off with ", after a line or two and a couple of capers, a pair of country wenches, I should find it hard to scrap my own conception of Don Juan as sombre, self-willed—I was about to write " abstemious "—endowed with that deep-rooted misogyny which women find so attractive.

This was by no means the first time I had been tempted by Don Juan. I had dealings with him in *Le pur et l'impur,* but not at any great length and only perfunctorily. I had forgotten about Molière and how little he knew about the subject, even less than myself, since it was not enough for him that his hero should have sinned against love. The reason was that treason to love was still beyond the philosophy of his day.

The play moves along, now slap-dash, now strait-laced, dealing harshly with the heretic and driving the seducer to insult religion no less than paternal authority : I should say that we help it on its way by our strained attention— I pride myself on being one of the best audiences I know —embellished as it is with too ingenious dramatic refinements. But how good it was in those surroundings! How they foster unreality! Balconies, mouldings, ceilings, a riot of reds and gold. I had only to lean forward in my stage box to touch the strutting actors with my hand; not

211

one of them was perfect, not one could act badly if he tried. Two or three of them gave me a furtive greeting, a glance of recognition that took them momentarily out of their pretended character.

Outside the Paris rain teemed down in buckets and through it I had to pass to regain my refuge from wind and rain. A strong arm was at hand to give its unfailing support. In the thick of the crowd I knew I should again succumb to the timidity that afflicts cripples, for it is real and obliging pity that they most fear. In the time it took to cross the pavement and enter the car, I should be soaked like all the others, overjoyed like everyone else at having been to the theatre for a Sunday matinée, richer by my store of living images, and busy for the rest of the day with what was not my business but my concern, namely, the art and effort of others, and dearer still—for mistakes are more intelligible than success—the intelligent mistakes of others.

They invaded my room, each an exceptional personality, all three of them so vigorously present and alive, taking up so much space yet never encumbering a room little more than exiguous, the one sitting himself down on the prow of my raft and the other two where best they could.

They came in with their strongly defined characteristics written all over them. Yvonne de Bray, and her warm, well-bred cordiality; Jean Marais, nicknamed Jeannot, with his crest of hair and his irreproachably irregular features; and the young woman who, as recompense for having her face laid bare from ear to tip of nose, from chin to forehead, every line removed from her cheeks and thus rendered glossy as a wet-glazed jar, had suddenly become beautiful enough to play Beauty herself. Heavens! I was forgetting the dog, the dog Moulouk, who owed allegiance to one person only, to Jean Marais. Yet all the time we were together I hardly had cause to remember him; he faded into Jean's shadow, became part of Jean, took the form now of an armchair-leg, now of a small Persian rug, and up to the moment of their departure called no attention to himself, except when earlier in the proceedings he paid a visit to my bathroom on his own initiative.

"What are you looking for?" Jean asked him in an aside.

"A bidet, to drink from," answered the dog.

"To the left," I told him, "behind the bath. The tap's running, and there's always enough water in the pan for you to have a drink."

"Good," said Moulouk, "I'll find it all right, I'm neither deaf nor blind. Plock, plock, plock, plock . . . There's the proof."

Once more he parted the curtains with his wet muzzle and lay down again like a sack of nuts, emitting a sigh, for he could tell from the pitch of our voices that the visit was by no means over and that no one was going to utter the prophetic word. Indeed, our conversation was bright and far-ranging as we touched on this and that; we even rehearsed—at least they did—some scenes from *Chéri*, for a radio programme. For myself, I was perfectly content to watch them, while listening to their voices was an unearned increment. Of the three, Yvonne de Bray's affected me the most nearly. From time to time, when she was made to feel hurt, it would grate on a more enforced

213

register with the insistence of an engraver intent on his block. The actress seemed impelled by some sort of modesty to carry simplicity to excess; she introduced the tone of a family conversation to one particular scene, and broke into a sob as into a gale of laughter. Unexpected inflexions I had not indicated in the text would bring home her words to an unseeing audience. An actress so pre-eminently endowed—and one so totally disinterested —should have it in her to play all rôles.

Turning my attention away from Yvonne, I followed " Jeannot ", who diminished his huge bulk, his strong arms, and his strong legs trained to grip the flanks of film mustangs, to the dimensions required for Chéri.

Jean Marais play Chéri! And why not? In his author's conception of him, Chéri never had any traits in common with Musset's wan Lorenzaccio. And for a born actor what a challenge it is, and a rewarding one at that, to discover the means so to expand and contract his physique that a puny man can turn himself into a lusty athlete and a strapping fellow get inside the shell of a shrimp! The hardest thing of all for Jean Marais, if he is to play Chéri, will be to make temporary surrender of his natural inno-cence. He can at need make himself ugly, as in the part of the " Beast " (though in that film the grandeur of despair was hardly ugliness), but where will he go to for cunning, for soft-spoken insolence and a talent for false-hood, for the barefaced pleasure of failing, and of recover-ing only to fail again? For the moment I dreamt, as I listened to him, of seeing him on the stage. I could well imagine that it was his innocence, like a nugget of gold, that choked his big, fierce voice. Time will show. There is no hurry. For the present my three interpreters, who were close beside me where I lay in bed, were not playing what I had written, but playing with it. They were gay with the gaiety of beings whose life has one end, one vision, one light, and reckons on a succession of incarnations. They possessed talent enough to throw off time and again the watch on themselves which impedes the inferior artist. "*Nounoune chérie! Nounoune chérie!*", faltered Jean Marais. Nobody had asked of him a stage performance for the radio, yet he collapsed into the arms of Yvonne de Bray, who all at once found strength enough to support and cradle the weight of an athlete. "*Mon méchant—Ma beauté—Te voilà——*". Jeannot made himself hoarse with sobbing, as required; the dazzling blue eyes of Yvonne de Bray, as they gazed at him, were moist with tears. Was all that for me, the solitary spectator? I was under no illusion; it was all for themselves, and, in their own despite, for honour's sake.

Of course I have one, like you, like the rest of the world; but if I never let on, nobody would ever know about it, so discreet am I in my use of it. At this moment it is softly murmuring to me one of Violetta's great arias, the heroine of *La Traviata*.

That full credit may go to the soprano, the accompaniment is a mere poum, poum, poum—poum, poum, poum, in three-time. The *diva* takes advantage of this to do full justice to her soprano voice, but she is not too much for me; for I have moderated the tone, and the sound of my tiny American machine, of an apparent capacity of about a cubic decimetre, does not penetrate beyond the closed door of my room.

215

What must be must be. After going all through my cupboard of gramophone records, and finding it full to overflowing, I gave them away, and kept only " The Cat's Aria ", an American number which really did make my unforgettable Cat smile. Later on, when a bad illness took the Cat from me, I smashed the record, preferring silence, preferring above all the talent of those compassionately rich and generous people who would sit down at our ".cottage " piano: Poulenc, with " Jean Hou-Hou " and *Les Animaux modèles*, Jean-Michel Damase, with his flexible voice, in our *Rouge-gorge* and our *Perle égarée*.

After that we sold the piano to buy a book-case! One memorable day my dearest friend brought home the smallest—but is there not always a smaller than the smallest?—American radio set (no aerial required), which sang all the way up my staircase. We deposited it on my divan-bad, where it started to give a spirited rendering of *L'Enfant et les Sortilèges*: " All you have left me is a single golden hair, like a moonbeam on my shoulder ". Ever since then, it and I have been boon companions. I tone down the great voice inside the body of a dwarf, I employ its ventriloquial gifts as much on Trénet as on Beethoven, and I do not overlook its great virtues on account of its small failings.

I am too antediluvian ever to lose entirely my earliest memory and sense of the miraculous when in the presence of a radio set. How splendid that children the world over can be on terms of intimacy with this polyphonic prodigy! In whatever outdated year was it that I visited, at the invitation of General Ferrier, a hall dominated from floor to ceiling by a vast frame—hexagonal, as far as I can

216

remember—seemingly held together by strands of green silk? If I am not mistaken, the contraption swerved round vertically on one of its sides, giving out a confusion of sounds; these were explained by General Ferrier as coming from various points of origin, for he was a great expert in this rapidly evolving invention which was already one of the world's new wonders.

From within the six sides of this harp and from behind the long strands of green silk, there suddenly came to us the song, far away and limpid, for which one bird alone could be responsible. But someone said "That's Constantinople". Not a soul dared show surprise at this intelligence, for such was the immediacy of our new emotion that a nightingale heard in Paris could not but be oriental, by the same token that a flying carpet is oriental, that the moon is crescent as it rides on high above the silvery Bosphorous.

"*THIS village where we live, set about with woods and a dark fir plantation, is where I teach the village children of twelve and thirteen, telling them of your mother, Madame, and how she would taste before dawn the forbidden fruits of her household chores.* I teach them to know, which is to say to love. If ever, in the course of your existence, no bonds of vassalage have bound you to any overlord . . ."

There I stop, before I quote the whole letter, and because it concerns only myself, the writer and his office to the young. Surely this one passage is sufficient to give more than an inkling that its author is adept at turning a phrase! How delightfully we obscure denizens of the French countryside can express ourselves when we have a mind to it! I say "we" by reason of the pride I feel in belonging, as regards both native land and love of style in writing, to the same race as my unknown correspondent. He, as he tells us, is a village schoolmaster. Lucky village! Above all, lucky children, who can with confidence entrust themselves to such a guide! I hesitate to write "lucky teacher", unless he is enabled to rise above the rigours of his profession by some especial saintliness that exalts his loneliness and pride. This man has written to me in his native tongue whose crystal purity

* See *My Mother's House*, pp. 129-30. English ed. Secker & Warburg.

218

he exemplifies, being himself passionately devoted to reading, and a contemplatist; he has written to me and shows surprise that I have sent him an answer. The children in his school have also written to me. Using coloured pencils, one has drawn a flower, another a house, and a third, having also drawn a dwelling, tells me " what cannot be seen " on the other side of it. But I have no difficulty in realising what he himself sees there—the garden, two fir trees, and a lawn. When one is twelve, it is easy to see through walls.

The worthy schoolmaster is not my only correspondent. I also receive letters from schoolmistresses, some of whom love to write for the sake of writing, others with a genius for inventing games and other ingenious ploys, who are clever in winning from an unresponsive child the word or smile indicative of so many pledges, so many conquests. Then, in the hour of their success, to whom are they going to relate it? To me. You can well believe, for one day at least, I am filled with pride.

Madame Wattine has sent me a parcel of cornel berries. The good old French name for them is *macres*, or water-caltrops. But cornel sounds more horny, and has the tang of her rural Poix. Water caltrops are so little known, so unappreciated, and last so short a time, being considered a delicacy only in districts where there are ponds, that I should like to say something about them. My appetite for them is as strong as ever. To prise them open I had to make use of one of the stone stairs in the house where I was born. For this strange water fruit, of ooze and autumn bred, forms with its four protective horns when fully ripe a shell of very hard texture, definitely "Chinese" in shape according to Fix-Masseau, and the method prescribed, first to avoid cutting oneself and second to lose nothing of its mealy kernel, is one scoop with a practised hand, a good stout knife, and the step of a stone staircase. In return for which you will acquire blue-black stains, a couple of damaged fingers, and an attack of marsh fever into the bargain if, as I used to do and am still capable of doing, you eat some four hundred caltrops straight off the reel.

"And . . . are they really good?" I am asked by friends deep-dyed with incredulity and circumspection.

I thereupon assume a dreamy, sentimental, and slightly stupid look, in fact become very like the little girl I used to be, and answer "I don't rightly know, but I happen to love them."

Indeed, I know nothing to compare with the taste of these water chestnuts,

> *Prickly, tickling chestnuts,*
> *Which tickle the thighs,*
> *And prick in the pocket,*

as the solitary caltrop-vendor, sack slung over shoulder, used to cry up and down the streets of Saint-Sauveur. At four sous a hundred, and he gave good measure!

The caltrop, or water chestnut, has a bluish white flesh the consistency of a wax candle and a kernel which, like its husk, is neither almond-shaped nor spherical; moreover it neither looks like a chestnut nor does it taste like one. Even when cooked it still calls to mind the pond where it was born and the mud that nurtured it. Its long tubular stalks—the root-stock vegetates in the slime—

crisscross the bottom mud before rising to the surface, there to disseminate their delightful white flowers, flat leaves, and later the drab green fruit so quick to sprout horns. If not gathered in the nick of time, the fruit will detach itself from the tubular stalk and sink back to the murky depths, to settle down beside the small tench of which, to my way of thinking, it bears a distinct flavour. The following year it will be its turn to sprout and direct the gradual ascent of sleek leaves and white flowers at the end of a pliant tube.

On my ponds an old punt puts out here and there to gather the water caltrops during September-October. Or else a man, nearly always an old man, clad in the remnants of a tattered pair of breeches, will kick off his sabots on the bank before wading breast-high into water that has ever a treacherous appearance, inasmuch as it rises from latent springs in rippling wavelets of alternating warm and cold currents, and is the habitat of little else than stout undulating water weeds that elude one's grasp.

The fragrance of riverside reeds, of spearmint, of eddying, disturbed water mingled with the parlous and pervasive savour of caltrops, these delights are not yet destined to escape, not for this year at any rate, one who has the wits to keep them safe in her Paris room—by denomination a writer increasingly under the dominance of her malady, but each day afforded relief by the faithful memory of her brain and of her subtle senses that in old age have lost none of their cunning.

In anticipation of the time when I shall no longer be able to move, I make no effort to move.

I ride at anchor beneath the blue lantern, which is quite simply a powerful commercial lamp at the end of a lengthy extensible arm, fitted with a blue bulb and a blue paper shade. Though a permanent fixture, it has none the less suggested to my neighbours the name they have chosen to baptise it with—*fanal*—the light that rakes the seas. "Madame Colette, you can't imagine how pretty your lantern looked yesterday, shining through the fog. . . . Oh, but you can't tell me that you make sparing use of your blue lantern! It's on at all hours, in the early morning, at eight, sometimes at seven-thirty even! " There is nothing I can hide from them, not even the moment—at cock-crow, perhaps—when the beam from my lantern casts a blueness over the brown coffee-pot and the white milk-jug. I tend to make less and less distinction between the hours of night and the hours of day, the hour for reading, for writing, for looking about me, all are equally good. The hour for conjecture, for testing my memory! Before long I shall be confusing the hour for work with the hour for conjecture; wondering what Gide can be up to—my enticing Gide, whom I can never see enough or read enough—and fussing over some crazy scheme of mine, will become one and the same concern. One good example of a crazy scheme was my longing to copy the lovely rug which Jean Cocteau had bought for his house in the country. All of a sudden I felt I must have it! But the rug was at Milly! I must have it, I have to have it at once, so I summon it by telephone. I am answered by a chorus of voices: my neighbours in Rue Montpensier become alarmed; Jean Cocteau has been called abroad, Jean Marais is on some film location or other! What matter! Paul-of-the-bookshop (easier to pro-

222

nounce than Paul Morihien) shall be dispatched to Milly, they'll charter an aeroplane, they'll send the Emperor of the Indies!

At that point I begged that nobody be put to any trouble, insisted that there was no real urgency. Too late: the wheels had been set in motion on my behalf from Beaujolais to Montpensier. Then out of the blue Jean Marais sprang to life before my very eyes, tall enough to brush the ceiling with his orange—no, moonlight blue—no, auburn mop of hair! And what in the world was he trailing along behind him, slung from his shoulder? It looked like some long drag-net.

"Have you come straight in here from a fishing expedition, Jeannot? Sardines, is it, you have there? Or good fresh herring?

"Nothing of the sort, it's *the* rug. Nobody could find the time to go to Milly, Jean's somewhere up in the air between Paris and New York, Paul-of-the-bookshop is busy arranging some book exhibition, so off I hopped there."

A hop of one hundred and twenty kilometres, there and back. He certainly had lost no time, with his seven-league boots. In everything about him there was an air of breath-taking efficiency in carrying out an indisputably urgent commission, in his white rain-coat, his turquoise blue cashmere scarf, his hair rising straight off his head, and the panting mask of his dog Moulouk. How was it possible to confess to Jean Marais that it would not have mattered in the least if nobody had gone to Milly! What reverberated throughout my little room to the exclusion of all else was this haste of his, and in my imagination the sound of the full-tilt gallop along the road, the kidnapping of the rug, my staircase scaled as readily as the stairs of a convent thrown open to the Musketeers! Jean Marais, Jean Marais, hero of countless films and plays, how admirably your legend fits you, and how splendidly you live up to it! I told myself that day that I had seen you playing the lead in *The House of the Fisherman*, and that in your wake trailed the drag-net, bringing in with it the smell of seaweed and the glitter of a myriad opalescent fish scales!

From time to time I have to take stock of what has been going on in the world of the cinema, so I do go to one film a year, or two. It is not sufficient. But it is enough for me, once I have settled down again to the rhythm, to the black and white of the screen, to find myself astounded at how much there remains of crude ostentation and simple incongruity in the realm of cinematic invention and representation. After an enforced absence over lengthy periods, I ache to say to the screen "Don't tell me that you are still where you were! What have you been doing whilst I've been away?" And then I allow myself to fall under its spell once again. It is so hard to withhold one's admiration. I forget that we have every right to demand colour and "audience participation", and in the end I am content to go away with what I have retained of my journey to the other side of the world, of the human conflict, and of my own insatiable curiosity. Happy come, happy go, like the roan mare in the story books.

They (the Radiodiffusion people) one day asked Jean Cocteau and myself to record a short conversation in which " we could say what we liked ", and " promptly " the radio van arrived outside, and " promptly " Jean was here beside me, perched on the poop of my workaday raft, with the rays of my blue lantern turning his face green.

This culmination of happy coincidences did not prevent Jean and myself from exchanging a glance or two. I was quick to catch the look of apprehension in his deep-set eyes that he must have been aware of in my own. We had to improvise, and I am no good at improvisation. And I feel far from at home with that bell-shaped flower, the campanula—pear, cucumber, or whatever name it goes by —which an insidious hand was already holding out to-ward us. Too late in life I came into contact with the microphone, with all its paraphernalia that climbs in through the windows, sprawls across the kitchen floor, strangles a small table in its progress down the passage, and coils up close beside me as I lie in bed.

" And how do you feel about it, Jean? "

" Me! I have an unholy horror of the contraption. And at the present moment I'm asleep on my feet. Ever since noon yesterday I've been hard at work, right on through till one o'clock today. What's more, I've had no proper lunch. I'd far rather speak to a thousand faces and a thousand pairs of ears than into this . . . this pumpkin! At last—is all set now? "

" All's ready."

" Then you'd better begin. What are we going to talk about? "

225

"Anything you like," proposed the young man in charge of the coils.

"But I don't like. So you begin. Suppose we pretend to be taking a stroll in the Garden?"

"On my crippled legs! You make me laugh."

But I was not laughing. Neither was Jean Cocteau. He closed his eyes, hid his face behind his long elegant fingers, and courageously launched forth. I was full of admiration for his diction, his well-timed periods, the variety in tone of this musician-orator. I responded as best I could, but my best was not very good. However, the young man with the campanula was pleased to give us a " perfect! " before he rolled up his coils, detached himself from his calix, and made off, while I pulled back my bench-table close beside me with the crook of my harpoon-stick. Under the stress of emotion Jean's face had gone black and blue under the eyes, and I quickly withdrew my still icy hand from his. We lost no time in concealing our attack of radio fright. I believe mine must have been the worse, since it forecast a whole host of other pitfalls. It gave me advance warning of the voice sticking in the throat, the speck of dust in the tonsils, the unexpected spoonerism. In vain it inveighed against the major betrayal: for it is all very well, but I have never in my life spoken in such a deep cavernous voice like the one I heard, I have never arrrticulated in such an ultrrra-Burrr-gundian manner! People assure me that I am mistaken, that my voice comes over on the radio just as it sounds in "real life". I shall not dispute the point.

Jean Cocteau comes into my room, and I look at the

time by my cardiac watch, and am amazed: eleven-thirty in the morning! Had it been at night I should have had no cause for surprise. Before I can ask any questions he supplies the answer.

"Yes . . . Can you believe it, but my electricians, camera-men, and carpenters in the studio have just told me they're on strike!"

He contrives to squeeze his long body on to the poop of my raft, folds his arms and legs, and coils up his body so as to expose as much as possible of it to my sun-ray, which will shortly be coming up to noon.

"So what?"

"So nothing. I walked out of the studio."

"A holiday! Calm yourself. It's always like that."

His nose looks at me sideways, in some perplexity.

"To be strictly accurate, it's no longer like that. I've worked like a mad thing for a number of years now. Night, and day, and Sundays. On a tray, on a restaurant table, on the grass in the country, on paper. In the past it was the pressure of work that half-murdered me. Today, I no longer know how to knock off work unless a break has been arranged for me well in advance. Once again I'm being deprived of my poison, and I'm aching in every joint. It's a quarter to twelve. I'm not hungry. I never feel hungry. What is there to do at a quarter to twelve, when one's not working. I've forgotten."

"Stay here with me."

"That I can't do. Stay here with you at a quarter to twelve! It's simply not done."

"Where will you go, then?"

"To be honest, I don't know. I'm going to try to go home."

227

From the tone in which he says this, he might be embarking on some great adventure.

As the wind was coming from the right quarter, I could hear the bells for the midnight mass; then, a little later, I listened on the radio to the mass by J. S. Bach. Pauline had elected to go to Saint-Eustache, whence she returned disappointed. "The crowd was far too great and it was perishing cold. And it wasn't a proper Market crowd. For me, midnight mass must be made up of Market people." On this sibylline utterance she left the room, to see the New Year in off Auvergne cheese and a pint of champagne. I could not have chosen better myself, had I felt the least bit hungry. But I simply had no appetite for such a repast, no more than I used to have, it must be added, for my old pre-war New Year's Eve revels. How many were the *Réveillons* in the good old days that found us grouped together in some famous restaurant—the men in white ties, the women in low evening dresses—along with great editors-in-chief and big industrialists, even with deputies and ministers who considered themselves great!

We also used to see the New Year in at Madame Hessèle's among the notable artists of the day: Vuillard, Dunoyer de Segonzac, Luc-Albert Moreau and others. This was already an improvement, despite the early stages being a little too formal under the military discipline of our hostess, white-haired and dressed in white. She would have reminded us of Madame Aubernon, had that good lady not been so far removed from us. But what a lot of good painters there were to give full rein to their high spirits!

Elsewhere, in other studios, I remember how the furniture used to be moved out of and brought into the room to allow for table space for the oysters, the turkey, and the foie gras. The first wave of champagne was rough and far too cold, the second already too warm. The *consommé en tasses* was too clear, the caviar too black.

In every restaurant little multicoloured cotton balls, guarantees of reckless gaiety, began to rain down as soon as the soup came in, and into the soup, as often as not! Oh, I have a store of memories of even more enjoyable réveillons! But tonight they are dormant, and I am lying down.

A tour of my quarter, by car. Apart from the butchers' shops, apart from the silver paper and the apples, I search in vain for the quondam opulence of the *premier arondissement*. Once again I find, and can still appreciate, the stylishness with which—fine artists that they are—the gentlemen of the butchers' shops dress their meat. As he chops, cuts, slices, trims, shapes, or threads through the string, a butcher is as good a sight to watch as a dancer or mime. A Parisian butcher, that goes without saying. With his golden bang of hair atop his forehead, his cheek ruddy as the dawn and his ear pink as a rose, with his apron strings tied in the approved style and spotted here and there with just the proper amount of blood-stains; I can tell you, Madame, that a Parisian butcher is well worth your passing glance; worth more, perhaps, than that.

My promenade, were I to allow myself to make one, would turn into a melancholy pilgrimage. In Rue de

Valois, under a lovely balcony, that famous restaurant of old—*Au Bœuf à la Mode*—used to hold sway. Today the balcony is still there. The succulent beef, the excellent way of making sauces, of cooking carrots, bacon, and calves' foot, are no more.

> *Irai-je voir le bœuf gras?*
> *Irai-je voir ma maîtresse?*
> *D'un côté l'amour me presse.*
> *Mais le bœuf a tant d'appas!*

Did Gavarni himself compose that quatrain? It appears as the caption to one of his enchanting drawings, in which he has grouped a posse of "Lions", excessively tight-waisted, and ladies of the town, with sloping shoulders like Rhenish wine bottles and dark Andalusian eyes.

Next door to the *Bœuf*, let a tear be shed for the *Pâtisserie Flammang*, famed for its éclairs and Neapolitan ices, and for the departed glories of its glass panelling of the Restoration period, painted with garlands. The Flammangs were reduced to penury by selling their delicate cream-tarts and puff-pastries which simply ran away with the best butter.

I mourn the loss of the good proprietors themselves as much as that of their good confectionery. All among the flowered panels, as pleasing to the eye as those of the Grand Véfour, lived a family of ladies in black, the eldest of whom had her place at the desk. A younger sister supervised the faultless service of the waitresses, while a second generation, represented by a young woman of unobtrusive colouring, enquired after the health of the customers as she wrapped up a tartlet, a *saint-honoré*, or a *savarin*—" Deliciously moist, is it not, Madame? "—in its conical tent of tissue-paper. A little girl who never opened her mouth made out fair copies of the bills close beside the cash desk. Flammang's is now a co-op painted in bright green. The ravishing glass panels have found their way to the Carnavalet Museum. A fat lot of good that will do us—and them!

All of which is none too cheerful. If I failed to stand up for myself, I should become as grumpy as any old dotard. But I do stand up for myself, I do myself well on the black market. I go gadding off to a shop in my wheel-chair, a place known only to myself and a few others and presided over by a dazzling young lady. For nowadays you will no longer find " black " establishments run by tight-lipped shrews or gruff, sardonic young persons. Cordiality is now the order of the day. As to its where-abouts, you had far better make enquiries from Simone Berrian, or Cécile Sorel, but do not expect me to reveal to you the spot where I was once lost in admiration of the pair of them, each as agile as the other, perched like a couple of wagtails atop precipitous chests, plunging their hands into dingy drawers as though they were bran-pies, from which with shrieks of triumph they fished out a varied booty of mealy camemberts, a small bag of rancid nuts, a pair of espadrilles, a powdery cake of Marseilles soap, as well as other treasure-trove which they seemed to value far in excess of its true worth and utility. To such a pitch, that at one moment, like birds gorged on a surfeit of black currants, they neglected to notice, from their perch on high, what a fine display of their pretty legs they were exhibiting. None of this was lost on a young man, the apparent owner of the store, whose looks

231

betrayed his feelings, the entire stock of his sentiments. But for him I should never have realised how disinterested the running of a black market business can become, as much under the influence of passion as of nameless reverie!

But here I am speaking of times past and gone: all the actors on that particular stage must long since have returned to the paths of legitimate trading—all, that is, save myself.

VIII

Iɴ the room which no device could ever sufficiently heat I was born laboriously on January the 28th, 1873, and I caused my mother much pain in her travail. For close on forty-eight hours she struggled as only women in the pangs of childbirth know how to fight. The women about her lost their heads and forgot to feed the fire in the grate. By dint of her cries and anguish my mother drove me from her womb, but since I had entered the world blue and silent, nobody thought it worth while to bother about me.

There was very little of charm or comfort about that room. Curtains of flowered print, mounted on an old-fashioned triangular frame, were draped over the widely separated beds of my parents. A curious little squat boot-cupboard stood in the embrasure of the window opening on the street and could be used as a seat. The glass-fronted wardrobe of three unequal sections was made of Brazilian rosewood, lined with polished thuya, and always struck me as over-decorative and out of place.

The twenty-eighth of January came and went fifteen times without witnessing any change in the room where I was born half-choked, but showing a determined will to live and even to live long, for I have just reached my seventy-fifth birthday—an anniversary the friends around

233

me persist in calling " a great day ". It is they, let me say, who have made it so. They have given me so many things.

They have given me flowers, fruits and sweets, and offered their congratulations on my seventy-five years from morn till eve. They have eulogised me in the papers, to an extent that has led me to think that I have nothing but friends in the world. They have sent me letters and telegrams and photographs: "You can see how pretty our little girl is at three months! We have called her Françoise." And a sheaf of picture-postcards! "Madame, this is simply a little Swiss cat wishing you a happy birthday; she is seven months old and quite white." To which, kitten or pretty poppet, the palm?

They have sent me the first violet of the year: " Jacqueline had the idea of going to see whether there was not one in flower under the sheltered briar, and such enough there was one! "

Anacreon (Richard) has written to me: " Since there are not seventy-five candles in our house, nor in the whole Rue de Seine, I am sending you seventy-five carnations, one for each year."

A bottle from Bordeaux has travelled all the way here in safety, bearing on its little paunch its vintage year—1873, the year of my birth—and its cobweb of precious dust. Like me, it was kept on its back till dinner-time on the twenty-eighth of January; again like me, bless me if it hadn't retained something of its fire and colour, together with a pleasant suspicion of violets, and the Mouton wine which it brought me was sleeping peacefully on its bed of lees, from which we awakened it with care and gratitude! And my dearest friend put a circlet of gold round my wrist—my favourite metal whether it comes in the shape of a bracelet, a medal, or the links of a chain. There were many other presents too, fit between them all to choke me with emotion; there was the blue-black hyacinth embroidered on a gilt-edged card, and the pink hyacinth from Rosa, and the snowdrops from two little working-girls, who did not leave their names and made off at once; a splendid array of fruit from Pauline: " I could not have borne to let anyone else give Madame finer fruit, today of all days! " There was the spray of orchids from my daughter.

" I bet it must have cost you your shirt to buy me this spray! "

" Oh, no Maman, don't you worry. You know perfectly well I never wear a shirt."

And from my neighbours there were flowers without end for my small vases, as well as a painting of a rose by Redouté, and a wonderful sausage of purest pork for cooking.

And two American ladies have put in my hands two of those American parcels, one from the East and one from the West, which gladden the eyes no less than the palate; for the silver paper, glazed cartons, flowered wrappings, and glossy containers double the attraction of the plums, gâteaux, pure wheaten flour, Malaga grapes and the transparent sweetmeats they contain.

" I'll swap my share of powdered milk for your empty box," was the offer made to his sister by a little boy paying me a neighbourly visit.

"Don't be silly! I'm not such a fool," answered his sister. " Not even if you throw in your mint chocolates as well! "

And then the full jereboam of champagne that I had!

And the zariba of red azaleas raised all round me by my fellow members of the Académie Goncourt! And the newspapers splashed with affectionately possessive references to "Our Colette"! How I enjoy being a joint estate! Marguerite Moreno's warm voice spoke to me on the radio, borne over the air on its incomparable rhythm, rich in a great variety of overtones, with every now and then an accent of affection and tenderness—at the very moment when I was not listening. Marguerite did her best to console me for not having heard her: "It makes no difference, ma Colette. We'll have a repeat performance, you and I, in seventy-five years' time." Oh, Marguerite, I would like it well enough at this moment, now, when I know what it would be like, when to my divan-raft, loaded down with presents and lit by a blue lantern, I have welcomed a disorderly array, such warmth. and affection, and a wealth of smiles and tears not unworthy of youth itself.

Only a very small remnant of the younger generation of my sex can nowadays be numbered among my intimates. I should have more, if I let them come. But I dread them. It is in the course of nature for declining strength to be scared of up-and-coming new forces. Severity in passing judgment on the latter is not the former's lot, even supposing we possessed it.

The cocksure approach employed by the very young to hurt our feelings will always be quicker off the mark than our judicial utterances whenever we attempt, unsuccessfully, to temper enthusiasm by a little fairness.

I have never suffered from lack of curiosity. Why

236

should I go to the lengths, then, in face of the young of either sex, of denying the attraction that other forms of first appearances hold for me?

Curiosity is seldom a root cause of ill will, yet how is one to make best use of it once the days of temperamental effrontery are behind one? I have no fear of my women friends; but I fear a friend's daughter, even more so the daughter of a friend's daughter. The children who do not come to see me but who write me letters lay claim to great timidity. If they mean timidity about literary matters, which may lead them to seek advice and tips, I can well believe them. But as to timidity of other kinds, it is for me and those of my age to feel it, almost to the point of painful intensity.

I do not go out of my way to offer encouragement to my youthful friends. I do not go so far as to drive them away. They must find me lacking in conversation, since the truth is that for them I have very little to give, and I am left with nothing but a consuming itch to ask questions when I take a hand in the most exhausting of all pleasures. When I am alone with those already settled in a profession, I never end without winning from them what I best like, something of the romance of their profession. I like it the more for the fact that they do not seem to realise how moving they are when giving expression to their hopes and fears. Their pathos emerges, wrapped up as it is in the most commonplace expressions our language contains, in expletives, in hideously accurate computations voiced without a trace of emotion. Yet between them and me stretches an ever widening and worsening gulf, unbridgeable by friendly familiarity and still less by expressions of good will, in which they have but little belief. Curiosity—which in their self-infatuation they consider fair enough—serves my turn better, as does that mischievous gift for reading the heart, inherited from Sido, to which I have playful recourse. I make only playful use of it, never in the spirit of triumph. Let me stress that for all my advanced years some of my amusements are perfectly innocent.

My youthful girl friends and I find it easier to cope with topics uninvolved with intimacy, such as the theatre and its concern with dramatic art, the cinema as a means of getting on in the world, bibliophily considered as a business opening. In these fields of human activity, they beat me hands down. Young people of both sexes know all there is to know about these everyday outlets. The pleasure I derive from being astonished fills them with pride and makes them talkative; what is more, both sexes turn out to be on common ground in their pursuit of special editions, autographs and dedications, in their passion for "Grangerising" or extra-illustrating "original issues", to the neglect of fine old albums bound with a clasp-lock, and other "Golden Treasuries". Crazes of this sort are curiously interrelated with a strong family feeling, long thought to be a thing of the past; not long ago I signed a copy of *Le pur et l'impur* presented to me by a bibliophile aged five-and-a-half, whose farsighted mother had brought him along for the purpose.

In so far as I can make contact with such remote creatures, I find our young French girls to be lively and ambitious, but troubled in mind. Their self-confidence is merely a façade. They are mettlesome but quickly discouraged, like draught-horses that are not properly fed. They bear the traces of an inner conflict that has barely

238

troubled their conscience, as it were a painless wound. Among my acquaintances are three sisters and a female cousin. One of them has devoted herself to music, in spite of all and in her own despite, and nothing will induce her to give it up. When music decides . . . Another paints, but before another year is out will not, I believe, still be painting. The third is a dancer, and every day grows thinner. A question of good beefsteak, this!

The female cousin has snatched at a small opening on the stage, and is shortly to make her début in a piece in which all the characters are eighteen-year-olds; meanwhile she is doing, as the saying goes, "a spot of filming". She does not say "a spot", however, but "a sport", being still child enough to enjoy the language of mystery.

Her name is Catherine. Were she not called Catherine, her name would be Chantal, or Dominique. Her parents are lacking in originality, foresight, and historical sense. She comes to see me because her mother, who is only twenty years younger than myself, says to her at intervals: "Go and pay a call on Madame Colette, be very polite to her and do not tire her out."

"Can I ask her to put in a good word for me with Jean Cocteau?" asks Catherine insidiously.

"Yes, but make it sound as if it came quite naturally into the course of the conversation."

That only goes to show that Catherine has been well brought up. She comes into my room and, before untying under her chin the scarf which makes a hat unnecessary and keeps a permanent wave unruffled, she will say "Madame Colette, would you be so kind as to say a word for me to Jean Cocteau?"

"Yes, if you will tell me about the dress you are to wear in the first act of your forthcoming play."

"The dresses for it are excellent, as is always the case," she obliges with a specious air of condescension. "If I get nothing worse than a 'sport of bad news' in the papers from Jean-Jacques Gautier, I'll be able to live that down. Especially as my dress in the first act is in a ribbed aquamarine ottoman silk. A small bunch of mauve auriculas at the waist and a great white forehead."

"A great white what?"

"White forehead."

"Where on earth . . ."

"Why, on the forehead."

"You've not got a vast forehead, thank the Lord."

"Oh, I'll enlarge it with an electric razor!"

"How horrible!"

"It's indispensable. It's the hallmark of purity, especially in the case of a *jeune fille*. Besides everyone— every woman, that is—has a great white forehead."

"I am only too well aware of it. And 'on the day' you will also, I suppose, display in all their nakedness the little bare bumps behind your ears?"

"Why, of course!"

"Indecency can go no further. Have you never looked in a glass to see the back of your ears? In which case don't you know that even in the prettiest woman, or the prettiest child, they are a plague spot? That ever since little girls have had their hair screwed up into two tight-plaited pigtails, like lobsters' tails, they have looked hideous in back view? That behind the ears, napes, and children's skinny necks, are places in the process of formation that should be kept hidden by a providential

240

growth of vegetation, light, golden or brown? That ever since women took to sporting what Marguerite Moreno calls 'the vast encyclopedic forehead of a waiter' compatability has ceased to be possible between your face and the hazardous frivolity of your hats, between the desert of forehead and the neat wavy garland that sweeps back off it, between the barren earth and the bird perched above it, between the blasted heath and the arch features of a girl of eighteen like you?"

"There is nothing arch about me," Catherine interrupted stiffly. "And it was Jouvet himself who once told me that my future lay in wronged women."

"Jouvet and his wronged women! That may be . . ."

"Oh!" Catherine began, blushing with expectancy.

But with a gesture I cut short her budding and evident hopes. "That is not a promise, Catherine. Go on!"

"But so far I've told you nothing."

So irreproachable a repartee, so just a criticism of my flow of words, laid me flat. A very palpable hit!

"There is still some Swiss chocolate left in that box, so do help yourself. What's new in town?"

"That the fringe is coming back into favour. Very soon we shall all be looking like Lautrecs. You'll like that, Madame Colette!"

I turned on her the glowering eye of an old warrior and deluged her with a shower of truisms dear to my heart, touching on the comparison of a head of hair to foliage, and the female face to fruit; I even went so far, to put Catherine on her mettle, as to bring to her notice the superb, curl-bedecked, young foreheads of Martine Rouchard and Dominique Blanchar. A moment later I

241

was in full cry as I recalled the raven kiss-curls that so enhanced the wan and cat-like face of Rachilde. And I had good reason, for Catherine was looking at the time by my cardiac watch. Her sole reaction was to banish from her face every hair that had strayed from her ash-blonde tresses with a thoroughness which might have been taken for an impertinence, to excuse herself on the grounds of " her " rehearsal, and make an effective exit, after an " au revoir " very prettily mimed and spoken, the *sine qua non* of good manners, as they are called. As if good manners turned on a gesture and an intonation ! This fair-haired, sharp-angled Catherine intimidates me, but I make an impression on her.

She did not take her leave before offering to help me : " The rug? Your cushions? Are the sticks within your reach? " A fresh-cheeked girl, sophisticated, hard as nails, courageous, wrapped up in herself, and perhaps, in her heart of hearts, a romantic. I like the element of contradiction in her, her pleasantly acid personality, the rebellious spirit in so young a bud. It seemed to me that once man—the hand, the mouth, the body of a man—had touched her, the world around her would be aware of it . . . myself the first, naturally. Was I like that, I wonder, at her age! My memory is not clear, but I vividly recall my shudder of repugnance when I was very young—does Catherine feel the same with me?—at the touch of old people, and the wild delight with which at the end of the visit I made good my escape from Mme de Cadalvène or Mme Bourgneuf, old ladies of over eighty, whom age and infirmity kept glued to the window panes on the well-worn rim of their constricted nests. I avoided the clutches of the small paralysed hand, crumpled as a claw,

my Carey.

that offered me a stick of Vichy barley-sugar. It needed every ounce of Sido's authority to force me to pick up a detested silk scarf from beside a pair of lifeless feet shod in felt slippers. Equally detestable to me was a certain china cup, and also a certain cushion of black woven horsehair. . . . It was I, therefore, and not Catherine, who heard a quiet voice saying " You must be very kind to Mme Bourgneuf." But in those days I had eyes for details only, the very things that are now, inescapable as doom, gathering on every side of me, to wit the pair of crutches, the vicuna shawl, and my spectacles.

Oh . . . Pauline, fetch me quick my blue dressing-gown, yes, yes, the new one, and the rose-pink foulard, and the scent-spray, and the bowl of cyclamen from my table—my powder-box as well. I ought to have been given all that, goodness knows, just before my young visitor arrived. I look a perfect fright.

Rare are the days on which I receive no presents. Let us understand each other; I mean, almost exclusively, presents from those who know me well, and know how to cater for what I call my insatiable appetite. Today I have received the first chestnuts, small, hard, and dark brown, finished off with a broad, light birth-mark and three stiff little hairs at the tip, showing that they have only just reached maturity. They come from a wood quite close-to Paris, some seven or eight kilometres away, which I can see from here: a steep, wooded slope, sparsely planted with ill-tended oak and fir and chestnut. A mere slit in the road beckons the passer-by, uninvitingly, to come upon a wooden chalet, set on brick-work that is

243

losing all its mortar. What can this *dacha* be doing there? Hush! We must respect the cerebral repose of two over-worked doctors—" my doctors " I call them—who cut themselves off from the world on Sundays. On one occasion I was able to follow them into their retreat, where they gave proof of a blissful resemblance to all children who ever hid in a wood, lit a camp fire, ate off a paper plate, drank from the same bottle, and they listened to the silence perforated only by the whistle of a train and the twitter of a tomtit. Having tracked them to their lair but once, I know that squirrels frolic high above them and that one blazing hot day they covered the escape of a large grass snake. Their view consists of unpeopled tracts of the Ile-de-France and the surrounding countryside, both scoured by railway lines, both speckled with small villas, but serene and all the more expansive for the sky above them.

It is but seldom that I can accompany these two am-bitious women, who dream of putting behind them con-sulting room and laboratory for a few hours. Their several skills long since outdistanced what the untutored mind can grasp, yet they gaze in wonder at the mimetic spider simulating a pink pearl among the pink heather flowers, at the rotund puff-ball, that unspotted egg laid when the nights are freshening. They know what it is I long to see and bring it back to me: a hatful of ripening chestnuts and edible mushrooms, to appease my greed, and for my pleasure a variety of wild flowers, the matted head of the rose-gall, together with three unripe chestnuts, tight-packed in a single husk. The husk is beginning to split and through the cleavage can be seen the gleam of the three light mahogany fruits. By a trick of my peculiarly tenacious memory, I can close my hand over the ligneous twig-tip that held suspended this lovely green sea-urchin and then all I have to do is to clamber up as far as the solid wall of leaves to reach the neighbouring pines. Further on it is all sand, birch trees, heather and bramble-bushes laden with berries. Just let me go there, I shall not lose myself. Shut the door of my bedroom. I need nobody to guide me on my walk. All that I needed were these three chestnuts, packed tight in a single half-split-open husk. Au revoir, au revoir, I may be a little late for dinner.

Jean Marais has given me a landscape, painted in oils on a small panel. In the foreground, on the bark of a great branching tree, he has inscribed my name. Beyond this tree, the fields spread out and lose themselves in the distant sea near Arcachon, and on its azure blue I am lying.

The stage vies with the screen for the allegiance of this tall, stern-visaged archangel, and the stage is fighting a losing battle. To visit me he has to fold the wings he has battered against the sets and burnt in the " sunlights ". He does not complain, he calls his angelic patience into play. But often he tries to make good his escape. Some-times he succeeds, by availing himself of a little entresol tunnel with a very low ceiling. Sitting with knees up to his chin and elbows to his sides, stiff all over and happy, bent over a panel no bigger than a cigar box, he painted for me a splendid section of immensity. After which he came to give it me, embraced me, did not jar my crippled legs, did not upset my working-table, or send my spec-

tacles flying. He shoved his forehead—his "Beast's" forehead—his tawny mane of hair and his puckered nostrils,
between my ear and my shoulder, without in the least bit
crushing me, expressing in a single caress affection and
strength. Meanwhile at the back of my room Moulouk,
who owns allegiance to Jean Marais alone, who ages
when he is away and grows young under a look from his
master, turned away his head and refused to say good-
day to me.

Last week I became a receiver of stolen fruit. "A lady
of my quarter" brought it me, speaking in a whisper but
bubbling over with the story. A slightly wrinkled apple
clung tenaciously to a bare twig in her hand. "It's a
Japanese apple," the story-teller murmured. "It comes
from the gardens at the foot of the Eiffel Tower. Some-
body stole it for Madame Colette, just when the gardener
was lighting his pipe." I gave myself up to an incontinent
dream that the Tower Gardens, hitherto unexplored, were
really a paradise of exotic trees given over to mango,
chcrimoya, or pineapple—perhaps, who can tell!—to the
gigantic fruit of the jacquier.

For hardly had I got the apple to myself when it began
to exhale a half quince, half apple odour which I can only
qualify as Circean, enchanted and enchanting, and so
potent that even the atmosphere in the next room—more
often than not so redolent of fried onions—was cleansed
by it. In a matter of minutes the stairwell, Mecca to their
too assiduous lordships the tom cats, smelt of nothing but
the strongest apples and quince mitigated by lemon juice,
magnified twenty thousandfold, all three of them. Losing

all sense of proportion, the fragrance continued on its way down to the ground floor, where it woke up the lady of the book shop who, two fingers to her dreamy forehead, took herself to task for having allowed her preserves to overcook.

When night fell I invited the stolen apple to sleep close beside me, in the embrasure of the window, for all that midnight and the waning moon might quadruple its propensities, and though my dearest friend from his adjoining room might try his best to dissuade me by crying aloud, calling down countless maledictions on Japan, apple-trees, the dangers of toxic exhalations, and pilferers from public gardens. But since he is well mannered enough never to raise his voice when driven to cry aloud, I did not hear him, and trustfully embarked on a wave of sleep almost immediately fraught with dreams and delusions such as had never before assailed me on my divan-raft.

Even then the last word was still left in dispute between myself and the origin of evil. Since the weather was clement for so late in the season and I was able to sleep "in the garden", I had only to make a long arm to take the apple in my hand and cast it forth. I then noticed through the balustrades of my window, for the garden below was already whitening with the dew at dawn, that a long cat had sprung out from the spindlewood hedge and was chasing after the apple. But no sooner had he caught up with it than he retched violently and at once began covering it over with earth, according it thus the fate it doubtless deserved as a fugitive from some dubious Eden. Then he made off with a cat's measured step, supposedly satisfied that he had exorcised the malignant spell by the potent means of ashes, vomit and oblivion.

I have long since discarded the habit of examining an envelope before opening it, or scrutinising the hand-writing before perusing it. This habit persists only in the case of solitary persons, of those deprived of letter-writing friends. Too soon I took to massacring the envelopes, sometimes to the detriment of their contents. André Lecerf would tell me that herein lay a revealing feature of my character, but not, I fear, a very flattering one.

Why do I not make use of a paper-cutter, so much more convenient and more elegant? Ah, there's the rub! Why, among my total collection of paper-cutters, can I never find one to serve me faithfully? In the good old days I used to buy them ten or twelve at a time, of white wood, at station bookstalls. Thereafter they would disappear, all ten or twelve of them. The point of my pencil insists on breaking and flies up into my face. The pull or push-bell has become a stage accessory, a wire without a voice. My watch, as I have said, is cardiac. The evening paper simply melts away, disappears. All these are family misfortunes, and are hereditary; my father could only control the mad antics of *Le Temps* by sitting on it. What's more, the human paperweight was hardly adequate. What use do people find for a piece of india-rubber? Or for a ruler? The various chattels designed to make work easier have never stood me in good stead; but my form of spite, which is simply to do without them, has theirs beaten. I almost persuade myself that I am now in the course of achieving a measure of independence. And high time too!

The times of postal deliveries are exciting moments

indeed in a writer's life! Mangled the envelopes, lacerated the letters from strangers—oh, if only they wrote more briefly!—an unavowed appetite, the hunger for the society of one's fellows which makes one ask for more, plays havoc with their missives, and at the same time calls forth an "Ouf!" or "Is that all?" What is left of my interest in graphological studies leaves me grumbling and offended at the sight of certain handwriting. If every script paints a portrait, I object to each single written page bearing the speaking likeness of a disagreeable grimace.

Between the ages of six and nine, I wrote quickly and badly, as did all children who were taught only the slanting hand, called "English", which involved keeping the shoulders straight in line and the right index finger humped. About my thirteenth year, to my great good fortune, a lively, exacting young woman was promoted to the post of teacher in my village, who said, as she bent over my copy books, "Your handwriting is vile. Why?"

I was not expecting the final monosyllable and could think of nothing to say.

"Yes, why? Your writing is inexcusable. I give you a week in which to improve it. That's ample time. Take to using a Flamant No. 2. nib, which has a broad point. That will help you to form your letters slowly and clearly, and more upright. Has it never struck you that to be illegible is an act of grave discourtesy? I will not tolerate such an offence against myself."

The results of a wigging such as that were not slow in taking effect. Fifty years later I tried out a similar gambit on Claude Chauvière, whose handwriting positively repelled the reader. Flowing to the extent of being formless (a feature not, alas! without significance), negligent of loops and lines, omitting any couplings, her script was like a streaming banner struggling to free itself; to decipher it caused me as much annoyance as discomfort, so I treated Claude like a badly brought-up child.

Being both proud and quick-tempered, she went red and pale in turns. "Madame, I shall spare you the sight of my distasteful writing and the company of a person of no education! "

At that I called her a noodle, a word she drank in as the highest compliment, and her face suddenly dissolved in tears and laughter. Now I am very happy to come upon her and her careless hand once again, in the margins and the interlinings of that gale of exaltation and perplexity of soul which I have in proof and to which she gave the title *Manuscript found in a Monastery*.

The magnificent, harmonious handwriting of Germaine Beaumont brings cheer to eye and mind. In it can be seen and read all the vigorous merits of that great writer of fiction, and even one extra for good measure: I mean a sort of noble disdain, to which her talent, and the independence that she has won for herself, give her the right.

My own writing is not ugly, though I say it who shouldn't. It is like myself, a little stocky, the upstrokes full and rounded, and legible. I may as well pay myself a small compliment every now and again.

It is by no means easy to rid ourselves of the idea that the time of a postal delivery—especially the first morning delivery—is a time of hope, surprise, and reward. There is animosity in our love of the bundle of scribbled envelopes when still fastened down, then opened, then thrown away. We stop loving it as soon as it holds no more secrets, no more confidences, no more endearments, as soon as it becomes prolix, or degraded by consorting with prospectuses, advertisements for patent medicines, book catalogues and cards from galleries.

Our closest friends, when far removed from us, are the only ones who write us letters with a maximum of reserve and a minimum of news about themselves, remaining silent about their own troubles and concerned entirely with ours—let me particularise and say "with me" and my arthritis: they have discovered an osteopath who . . . a radiologist whom they . . . They quote the case of a miraculous cure, a thermal spring whose . . .

This has the immediate effect of bringing out the worst in my character, since I had anticipated reading an account of their journey, the events of their stay, the exact number of teeth cut by their small daughter, the exact height of the floods in their district—in short, their news. Have none of my friends, my dearest friend included, the least idea of what interests me?

I console myself with the remainder of my post—the letters written to me by strangers. Other than having the good luck to happen upon the peculiarly French grace of writing good letters, I may yet come upon something to astonish me. For people ask me for things which I had never supposed to be at all in my line, for instance "a trustworthy person who could look after a lady of advanced years". And again ". . . if it is not an impertinence, a decent man, grocers' assistant type, who would accept comfortable post in a town of middling importance. I take the liberty of asking you this, Madame Colette, since everyone knows that you are renowned for your knowledge of the world."

Certainly, Madame! Perhaps not exactly to include the life of a grocer's assistant; but "everyone knows"—I like that "everyone" which gives me self-confidence—that a request for advice about the ailment of a pet does not frighten me, and that I do not throw into the waste-paper basket the story of the caged canaries, set free for reasons of economy, that became crossed with house sparrows and, two years later, are still producing offspring with a small yellow feather showing here and there in their plumage, and with the suggestion of a trill in their throats. I do not tear up the account of a domestic tabby who by dint of love and patience finally induced a handsome, suspicious wild cat, step by step, quivering with exhaustion, to enter the house in the woods. Nor do I throw away the drawings of children. If I were to follow my own inclinations, I would throw away nothing. I do my best to follow my own inclinations as little as possible and to husband my harsh words for anything evil that may come my way in search of strength and encouragement, for the momentary itch that goes by the name of vocation, for the proliferating novel, the literature that loses its way, and for bibliophily in its lazy and primitive form: "Madame, I am leaving my copy with you, and tomorrow I shall return to pick it up enriched by a dedication from yourself." You find the formula somewhat summary? I am not the author of it, I would have you know.

Not all the young bibliomaniacs are quite so . . . succinct. Are they mistaken in taking such liberties? Possibly, since once my initial fit of spleen against the hard, businesslike methods of youth is over, we sign, we respond! However cross they make us, we never feel we

are entirely free or quit of them. A single start of refusal
brings me up sharp before the most legitimate claim they
have on us—the claim on what they call our experience.
They need advice and criticism. They want, like my little
Yniold, not only "to go and say something to some-
body", but to listen with attentive ear to a voice that
will speak to them of themselves.

Children and young people, you who make bold to
write to me and in the very first lines tell me of your
"timidity", have you never envisaged the possibility of
my timidity being greater than your own? I seek protection, I remain silent, I fear you. I try, but without either
naming you or betraying your confidence, to laugh you
out of this crazy business of writing to an old woman as
if she had no option but to perform a crazy act herself—
answer you. Since I cannot do less, I read you, and with
scrupulous care. But I have a well-founded suspicion that
those who are worst afflicted with the itch to write are
not the predestined favourites of literature. Yet to tell
them as much . . . I feel that I have neither the right
nor the inclination to do so!

Let us, if you will bear with me, read over together
some of the shorter letters, which have to my ear an im-
perturbable note of complacency and fruitless childishness
about them. In the first one I catch an overtone of
Marguerite Moreno and her businesslike method of
answering letters, with something of her gentle raillery.

*"Madame Colette, I am much inconvenienced by the
death of Madame Moreno, since it has deprived me of
the chance of meeting her. This lady had been very kind,
she had promised to receive me and to give me favourable*

notices in the papers. For I have the gift of comic writing, and people of my acquaintance tell me that my essays and light verse are striking. One day when I telephoned Mme Moreno, I told her that it would be advisable not to put off publishing them too long since I am sixty-nine years old; but she told me that, on the contrary my age would be an additional attraction. Seeing that she has just died, I take the liberty of addressing myself to you, etc., etc. . . ."

"Madame Colette, I wonder if you remember me! When you were once staying at X, in 1904 it was, I was the little girl of seven who used to run errands. Since that time, I have married and we have suffered many misfortunes. Things are beginning to look up a bit, but we are still wanting for a number of little things. So I thought of you to write to, and if you know anyone who would let us have for nothing a motor-car that is due to be scrapped. My husband is very clever with his hands and he would be sure to know how to make something of it. Thanking you in advance, dear Madame Colette, etc., etc. . . ."

Another one? Let us take one more, in my opinion the most unexpected of the lot.

"Madame, I should like to put some of your writings into verse, among them La Maison de Claudine. Spontaneously I make you this offer, to superimpose on your rhythm my own strictly poetic versification.

If, as I hope, you like this idea, perhaps you would

also like to write the preface? I should find your advice useful on a number of points (publisher, typeface, method of sale, and so on) . . . I enclose a few samples, which I consider representative of my work."

Believe it or not, these things do happen, just like that.

In what spirit should letters of this kind be read? Is there anything to be found in them other than calm self-assurance, with above all an astounding ignorance of real life and, in contradistinction, the secret cult of the self and the crying need for publicity?

Would not you fall in love, as I do myself, with those who advise me for my good? Not all of them wish me well, but to one who lacks self-confidence, their assurance is like a slap on the back.

"Madame Colette, reading is our greatest pleasure; but we do not conceal from you the fact that we find your stories of days gone by a little fatiguing, we should prefer something more of our own day. We do not scruple to write to you, for what we have to say may be of some service to you, etc., etc. . . ."

"Madame Colette, my sister and I enjoyed reading your last book. Do, please, give us some more stories about your childhood, they are much the most amusing. As to your talks on the wireless, you ought not to read them out as you do; you should talk naturally, as though you were having a conversation with yourself, etc., etc. . . ."

" Your ' Souvenirs ' are a bit colourless, a bit lacking in go. What is required is more emotion, more tenderness, in your dialogues with your dearest friend. On the one hand too lifeless, on the other too literary, and marred by insincerity as well. Surely there were better and more important things to say. Take it from a fellow-author who has been prevented by ill health from continuing in his profession, etc., etc. . . ."

Which of them to believe? If only I had twenty or thirty years more to live, I should end by reaping some advantage from all this disinterested advice, contradictory as so much of it is.

My object in quoting it is not to offend but to disclose by what methods a reader gets into touch with an author, to the point of fulfilling some imperative need. I believe there is no effective way of escaping his commandeering method. I also believe, after being thoroughly trained for nearly half a century to his arbitrary requirements, to the mad lack of restraint that guides the pens of lonely women, men with obsessions, and those monomaniacs who persist in asking questions, that I prefer their indiscretion to their silence.

" Madame,

" I send you my life's work; it consists of my impressions and opinions of the books I have read. I have left a blank page between the title and the text, and would ask you to be so kind as to write a preface on this. I shall call for the manuscript in a week's time. Believe me . . . etc., etc. . . .

" P.S. Please make the preface as long as possible."

May I never see God if I am lying, as we say where I come from! The weighty manuscript had been sent by registered post and at the cost of 146 francs to the sender.

"Madame,
"I am thirteen and a half years old. All my life I have been obsessed by a craving to write. People have always told me that I have plenty of talent. But I have hesitated. And now I think it is too late to take such a serious step. My parents tell me that I must continue with my studies, but I have little interest in them. Would you oblige me, Madame, by giving me your opinion . . . etc., etc. . . ."

The underlining of "all my life" and "always" is mine. As I read them I thought of the little boy-acrobat who rode his bicycle round and round the mosaic pavement at Chartres making dizzy figures of eight, with his hands off the handle-bars. I asked his bearded grandfather who was watching over him how old the child might be.

"Four and a half."

"Four and a half! And he rides like that!"

"Oh!" said the proud grand-parent, "he learnt when he was quite small."

I admire child gymnasts, but I am a little afraid of child writers. To start with, there are too many of them. Then who in the world would not be afraid of a child's vigour and ease of movement through the impenetrable? He lacks only the vocabulary to be our equal when the passion to write comes upon him. I could give the name, at any rate the pseudonym she has chosen to write under, of more than one girl of fifteen whose literary baggage already comprises a slim volume of poems, two plays, three if not more novels, and *Memoirs* (*sic*). There is the same facility among boys. Of course I feel no pressing hurry to form an opinion on so many youthful works, confided to me as they are without my consent. But I still retain my faculty for astonishment, even if it should only be for youthful writers' attempts to exploit their own novelty. Sometimes, it is true, they conceal their identity, but they never forget to state their age. *"Madame, I am thirteen, fourteen, fifteen years old . . ."* Do their parents, tutors and schoolteachers call them "little fiends, exclusively addicted to violent sports"? Certain it is that some of them are deceiving themselves, certain that some are being deceived. Certainly there is, in the almost child-like urgency and frankness of their efforts to reach us, something more than the mere itch to show off, some-thing that comes very close to practice in perfecting the use of a weapon *"Madame, I am so young!"* Almost I find in this a note which cannot be the cry of helplessness alone, and then I reproach myself for my suspicious nature. But the devil will out. *"Madame, do you not feel tempted to know how young I really am? Look at this . . ."* and out slips a photograph from the letter. What meaning should one attach to the sending of photo-graphs—if a girl, hair in ringlets and the briefest of skirts; if a boy, in bathing-dress and the briefest of briefs? Well they know, these inspired children, that youth is always a weapon, and one deadlier than ever if it goes hand in hand with beauty.

Fate has decreed, where writing is concerned, that I should be incapable either of holding myself back or of giving instruction. What have I to teach, unless it be self-doubt, to those who since early youth have become secretly infatuated by self-love rather than by self-torture?

O you chorus of cynical child-writers. Children indeed you are, but what pain it is to know you cynical already, willing to sell yourselves to anyone who offers you leisure enough, bread enough, warmth enough, even solicitude enough—objects of barter all—just as it is difficult not to give you another thought! The whole problem seems solved for me when I hold to my vow never to listen to the echo which prolongs certain phrases: *"Madame, I am fifteen. All my life the imperative urge to write . . .".* From the brown paper parcel tied with string and containing sheets already crumpled and faded from having tried their luck elsewhere, there erupts, flutters, cascades—I cannot stop it—such an intoxicating odour of lies, heady despair, bumptious arrogance, craftily selected truth—an odour, did I say? No, a menace!

" It seems a pity to eat them," said Marcelle Blot.

" You're not compelled to, Marcelle."

All among my collection of paper-weights, tight-stuffed with curlicues, burnt sugar twists, flowers and small insects, Marcelle arranged her round, impeccably red tomatoes, with never a crease or a rib on them, the last tomatoes from her Saint-Cloud garden, and with a sigh murmured " Yes, it is compulsory. Because they are good."

There is about la Grande Marcelle, friend of artists—and my friend—a faint but pungent smell of tarragon, chervil and parsley which she had arranged into a bunch for me round a centrepiece of celery, white as ivory, and sprigs of purple-flowering thyme. Whatever emerges from her hands always has a suggestion of the skills of weaver, braider, florist, and decorator. She dictates the fashion in women's hats. And then, of a sudden, she refuses to make any more hats. Because of the hats? No, because of the women. She retires to Saint-Cloud, and goes into retreat. She is so essentially unsociable! Yet it was none other but she who invented the art of delicately plaiting reeds and raffia into the shape of leaves and making belts and sandals of them. I have seen her contrive a bridal wreath by imaginatively stringing white pearls of mistletoe berries on the spikes of a branch of thorns. She arrived from Saint-Cloud to pay me a visit, graced with the tricolour of a healthy peasant woman, blue eyes, white teeth, red cheeks.

"So you're not working at the moment, Marcelle?"

"Oh yes I am," she said. "I've constructed something of such beauty that I waste all my time in admiring it. In my garden I have four large privet bushes. I'm overrun with privets, as it happens, and since I could see no future for them as privet bushes, I wanted to be rid of them. I've often wondered how they could best be improved, and now I know. I hollowed out with the clippers the entire centre of each clump, taking care to leave quite a thick outer covering, and I removed every leaf from these branches. Those I had snipped off I interwove in and out of the ones I had left, till they made a basket, or rather a cage—the sort of work I am good at—making the most of a few little apertures here and there in the close-knit weave. Through these I fitted transverse canes across the inside, some to serve as perches and others on which to hang food and drink pans. Do you see the idea of my out-of-door cages? I have strengthened the weave on the side of the prevailing wind, and made it thicker still over the top, woven in the shape of a dome."

" And what do the birds say to that, Marcelle? "

She raised her hands in admiration. " The birds? They have talked so much about it that they've got practically nothing more to say. I'd hardly finished the first cage before they knew what it was for. If you could have heard the commotion among them! And their committee meetings, and the contradictory views expressed! I spend my time with them. I've seen three kinds of tit, bullfinches, chaffinches, and others I don't know the name of. My cat laughs behind his paw at me. He must be thinking I don't know the first thing about making a trap. The fact is . . ."

" But what about the birds themselves? Haven't they thought it might be a trap? "

Marcelle's azure blue eyes quizzed me for an instant. " No," she said. " They know who I am. They're already popping in and out through the small windows. The chaffinch goes in with its head down, cramped up like a parakeet. And just imagine, the others fly in and out at full tilt, the very opposite of birds who dislike being caged. It's overwhelming. They tell me that they'll be fighting for possession of my cages when spring comes round."

Marcelle thoughtfully closed down the lid of the basket in which she had brought me the latest adornments of her kitchen garden, before saying with a note of determination in her voice, " So much the worse, in that case. From now on I shall have to invent something to stop them fighting."

She tied her foulard under her chin and made to leave the room, but I called her back.

"Marcelle, Marcelle! Haven't you brought me back my little black velvet hat?"

She poked her beautiful rustic face round the half-open door.

"Did you ever! No, I have not! I've not had the time. My clients the privets were more pressed for time than you! For you hardly ever go out, and they sleep out of doors every night."

GRASSE, 1948

O^N each successive day following the appearance of the first fully ripened fig of the second crop, you can count on any number up to a dozen "secondary figs" being ripe and ready to fall into your hand, soft, with inflexed necks, bearing the pheasant's eye mark at their base and on their sides the parallel stripes that crackle their tender skins of mauve and grey. For the first few days you'll not be able to eat your fill. There's little to be said for your appetite if you can't polish off six, ten, or even a dozen figs with the chill of night still upon them; they readily split apart and are as red inside as a pomegranate. They are not as yet runny with their full measure of honey-sweet stickiness, and are so much the easier to put in the mouth.

But the figs multiply with the rapidly increasing rate of maturity. Before the week is out the huge fig tree, the young tree further down, and the contorted tree will all be overwhelmed with ripe fruit, pendent from the neck like the stocking nests of the Haitian cacique bird. There is no end to them. Every single one deserves to be picked and placed on a wicker tray. Time is of the essence, for by now it is easy to see that in their turn the grapes are insistent on being cut, that the tomatoes have reached the peak of their red lacquer lavishness, and all that remain on the peach trees are the fluffy little pellets destined to become the hard ammunition for children to pelt each other with.

After which the trees will bear no further crop but apples, in abundance down in the hollow of the valleys round Grasse and in the orchards of Solliés-Pont. Here and there one of the splendid expatriate Normandy pippins falls into the torrent bed of the Gapeau and bobs along to the astonishment of its now diminished stream.

I might very well have believed the factory for the slow processing of floral essences to be sound asleep within its extensive gardens, had not my arrival coincided with that of a dray drawn by a stout-limbed percheron and loaded with lengthy thick-wicker baskets, scrupulously veiled with heavy cloth. Nine hundred kilos of jasmine blossom were discharged from this rustic equipage. My wheel-chair became firmly stuck in their way.

Only four hours previously had they left the fields and they were still perfectly fresh. They were on their way to be consumed and they drew me along in their wake. An atmosphere that could have been cut with a knife existed beneath the ventilated ceilings, yet parted slowly before the silent footfall of the men employed in the service of perfume.

Nine hundred kilos of jasmine blossom lay in a still white litter where they had been summarily dumped on the polished flagstone floor, not far distant from another bed, of withering tube-roses that breathed out the odour of mortal decay yet still retained their flesh-coloured pallor. From these inestimable stacks arose an aura of consenting torpor, almost the desire to be quit of life; there I willingly would have remained, physically, mentally, optimistically exhausted, under the watchful eye of a young lady who had devoted her energies that morning to pushing my wheel-chair. She was a delicious child and I nicknamed her my little fairy horse. When I enquired in some trepidation whether I were not too heavy, she tossed her head up and down in a negative response: nothing is too heavy for a little fairy horse.

The factory owner wished to guide me to the successive fates that awaited in sealed vats the spoils garnered from the various harvests of Grasse: no eye would ever look upon them again as flowers.

The integrity of an industry such as his is an unrivalled marvel. From jasmine is extracted the scent of jasmine, and from iris bulbs the scent of iris. " If you were staying a little longer at Grasse," Maurice Maubert said to me, " I would show you the huge multicoloured mattresses of freshly picked carnations that embalm the air with essence of cloves."

When, on taking my leave of him, I asked at what stage in the proceedings, by what stress of cunning, the scent of jasmine reappeared in the extract of jasmine, he slipped into my hands a packet of that compound known as " *le concret* ", resembling a cake of dark, sticky chocolate, thanks to which, though I had barely touched it, I not long after established the fact that boiled eggs smell of jasmine, that fish salad tastes of jasmine, that baked aubergine and crème caramel follow suit. The man responsible for such an excess of perfumed delights offered no excuse for it, quite the contrary: he filled my cup with hot coffee vaguely enraptured by jasmine, saying " What better proof could I have given you that this concentrated essence of jasmine is irrepressible? "

Toward six in the evening the scent of jasmine begins to bar the roads as effectively as a rope stretched taut across them. All night long and until first light the flowers will make their invisible presence increasingly potent. All the same, as we pass by on nights the blue of wood ash in the moon's absence we can distinguish the little starry blossoms, white against the dark foliage. Between dawn and sunrise there is time enough for a picking, with nimble fingers that pluck only the corollas and leave behind the tiny sepals. The jasmine bushes are trussed into loose sheaves, both to facilitate the picking and to prevent the flowers from coming into contact with the light soil in which tuberose and sweet onions flourish side by side, and also to spare them the weight of so much as an ant, a grain of sand, or a ladybird!

On evenings when a heat haze reminds us that August is nearing its end, my crippled condition earns me a run in the car. The region round Grasse—which has no summer rainfall—secretes a wealth of subterranean streams. Gushing springs abound, the smallest *mas* has its miniature cascade; each village is supplied with a constant flow of water from the three all but ice-cold jets of a full-bodied stone urn in the *placette*, and often enough this water is beaded with tiny bubbles; at all costs I have to borrow a cup, or drink from the pitcher attached to the fountain-head, as I was wont to do in the past when travelling through Aix-en-Provence. A spring is an eternal miracle.

A property up for sale, where the carriage ways are open to certain visitors, is a babble of bubbling brooks, a simmering of freshets in the shade; with a flourish of crystalline muscles, a solid arm of water gushes up from a gash in the ground. On the tenantless terrace, in the area surrounding a single-pedestalled fountain, time, moisture, birds and winged seeds between them have contributed to the formation of a vast vegetal sponge, where each blade sheds its pearly tear, as at the ancient fountain at Salon.

Whether they break surface or remain beneath it, the waters of Grasse, in the unbroken silence of the pure night air, create an elusive mist in which the jasmine fragrance is entangled and held captive. Nothing stirs before the peep of dawn. As the last stars fade from the heavens and a reddish brown bar rises along the horizon, we are but three—my dearest friend, a striped cat and myself—who infringe the laws of sleep, perched on the heights above the gradation of cultivated terraces. Before ten in the morning there will not be a breath of air to ruffle the leaves of the crinkled, misshapen mulberry, or those of the young plane trees. It was the same at Saint-Tropez, where we used to wait under the huddled wistaria for the moment when the wind from the west and the sun, in conjugation, awoke the sea, the cicadas, the morning glory, and the purslane of four differing colours. In those days, with the confidence of my fifty years, I would stir the sleeping waters to frighten the shy reptilia by dipping my foot in the pools, pick the mauve statice in the salty marsh and at that incomparable hour I would be saddened by the thought that after the first bathe I should have to retire within my shuttered house and work at *Break of Day*. I no longer possess that house, and it is a far hark back to my fiftieth birthday. What is left to me is my avidity. Of all my forces it alone has not humbled itself to time.

I am shown none but the most beautiful things. The kind attentions of my friends, never entirely devoid of humour, ensure that I am taken out for a drive of fifteen miles or so along the whole length of the Croisette, at the very time when among the concourse of bathers the nude figures of a man and a woman are on the point of clambering out of the water on to a float, at the precise moment when one man among a host of others in search of refreshment is staking his claim for a place at the pedestal table for himself and his fruit juice, where one bare back may be heard saying to the bare back beside it in a tone of defiance " But I tell you I've gone a far darker colour than you ". I find the spectacle so strange that I insist, as at a merry-go-round, on having another turn.

Out at sea a boat is towing its pair of water-skis, for all the world like a silvery insect at the end of a line. In their coupled state, and lent enchantment by the distance, their pairing is the only one down here that evokes the idea of love. As for the rest . . . I do not believe I have ever seen a crowd less concerned with love, or so stripped to the buff, as this Cannes Vintage of 1948. They look just about as voluptuous as a keg of sardines, packed in their serried ranks. Let it be said, however, that here the weather is fine, whereas everywhere else it is raining. " Just one turn more? " I am granted it, driving along at a snail's pace between the sea and the dressmakers', the sea and the jewellers', the sea and the sandal-sellers, the vendors of brassières and fruit juices, the sea and hotels, cars, flowerstalls, sun-bathers and walnut-stained women. One yellow hotel has exceeded all reasonable proportions, making a mock of architectural harmony. An orchestra strives to make its feeble strains audible in the open air. I observe women who, in the guise of bathing costumes, wear creased or uncreased shorts of poor quality flowered fabrics and gorgerins like the hollows of one's hands. Such is their promenading attire of an afternoon; the hem above the thighs greasy and dirtied by oil. The men, in the security of a brief and highly revealing slip, give a far better account of themselves. No matter, there are far too many of them, men and women alike. "Would you care to take another turn? "—" No thanks! " I find it hard to tell whether all this varied display of human flesh is turning me into a vegetarian, or whether I am shockingly jealous of those who apparently derive pleasure from their own agility, the briny, and going naked. I go back gladly to the slopes of Grasse, though this means that I must be parted from the sea. It lies beyond the line of little hills—over there, look!—between those two little breasts rising from this land that breathes so easily. It's not so very far away; you'd almost think that by standing on tiptoe . . . Let us resign ourselves: the sea is not visible from here. You won't console me by referring jokingly to the Mediterranean as being hardly worth calling a sea. There is little doubt, when the mood is on it, this sea knows only too well how to bring havoc to the Côte d'Azur.

When at Hyères, though from quite a distance, we could see its hard lapis blue and its wind-rows of sand.

From where we are now I am taken sometimes in the morning to La Garoupe and dumped down there on the wave-splashed spit of the shore. Below the balustrade the foaming sea joins in the frolics of the naked children; to my now useless feet the feel of the sand is sometimes cool, sometimes warm. At Antibes the evening before last, all along the sea-wall where I was being promenaded in my chair, I saw the sea far better for it being a moonlit night, and for the fact that my turning-point happened to be at the spot where a restaurateur of genius, by placing his tables exactly in the centre of the arc formed by the rampart, has provided his summer clients with an ideal view. On one side are the port and quayside, on the other, in due course and when their hour has struck, appear the light of the moon, the flares of the fishing smacks, and the phosphorescent back of a breaking wave. That night we all felt that nothing could go wrong and everything we could wish for was ours. The patron, brown as a berry and dressed in white tight-fitting clothes from collar to espadrilles, was wreathed in smiles as he came and went with silent tread, chatting freely in anticipation of a long July night devoted to good food and drink.

Between our tables in the foreground and the distant backcloth there passed, some stopping and others not, a succession of those disconcerting touring cars that are to be seen eating up the miles on all roads, noiseless as often as not, yet whose very discretion renders them the more dangerous since, gleaming from the final authoritative flick of the polisher, they seem to rise from an oil-bath only to plunge back into it the very next moment.

The white-clad proprieter felt no apprehension as he watched them approach. He had the knack of applying an

American, Venezuelan, Scandinavian, or Swiss name to every dress and every face behind its tanned mask that drew up in front of his premises. Sure of himself, certain of his minions keenly employed in cooking and gossiping in the recesses of his kingdom, he would disappear only to reappear in a twinkling, arms laden, to set before his guests from Chile or Colombia a long dish of raw vegetables, white fish piled high, a firm-fleshed *rascasse*, and, the pride of the evening, a luscious langouste ready dressed in its rose red carapace.

Few and far between, along the Côte, are the wayside inns constrained—like the chronometer at Marseilles which struck the hour for you every forty-five minutes— to 'fit' their season into two-and-a-half months and to keep alive their fame and fortune within that limit of time. The finical tourist—certain of that ilk do still exist —known to the natives of Provence as *l'estrangier,* can tot them up on the fingers of one hand. He makes a bee-line for them, and emerges properly stung. Yet he returns to them again and again. He is a devotee of the mysteries of the French cuisine, for all that he may well ruin his palate by preliminary libations of alcohol. I watched him at work the other evening in one of those enchanting spots to be found in the Midi where everything in the garden is lovely: trees properly tended, plants and shrubs well watered, maidservants with plump rounded arms which, the Lord be praised, are kept too busy ever to grow thin, where mint and basil vie with lemon-scented verbena in an atmosphere already fragrant with rose-geranium, suggestive of Morocco.

By half past nine, my four table-companions and I were feeling pleasantly replete after dining off small red-fleshed melons, white-fleshed fish, *courges gratinées*, peaches, our glasses still holding the glint of a young wine—how difficult nowadays to come by this *tendron du pays!*—when our eyes were arrested by the arrival of the invaders, people who never think of dining before ten and who must have a drink before they eat.

It was up to the hard-working staff to satisfy their every whim. Into the hands of each was put an identical, heavily moulded glass embossed with tortuous scrolls, over which passed a multicoloured cloud-burst of pastis, cocktails, and champagne. In a twinkling the bright fire of the drinks was dimmed by the clink of cubic bonbons of ice.

Showing a certain reluctance to be seated, one or two clinging couples remained on their feet and began to go through the vague motions of a dance. Yelping females intrigued in particular for the embrace of an American film-star, a man of dubious age, long since gone to seed and slap-happy in his cups.

Another time, and in another place, I came to a halt beside an inn that lay just off a main road and sparkled like an elongated island edged with lights and flowers behind its fringe of parked cars. Enthroned in state at the entrance sat she whose presence ensured the prosperity of the house, *la patronne,* its organiser and its guarantor. Vast in bulk, she made no bones about it, knowing full well that in her noble and strenuous calling there is no authority without fulness of figure. Her impartial smile provoked no jealousies, yet behind it lurked a hint of irony. Her speech was concise, clipped, with a detectable disdain: her " Fish? Meat? Both? ", a typical example. " What have you got in the way of meat? " asked an impertinent fellow, assuming, as he hoped, something of the air of an habitué. Sizing him up, she administered a single word snub: "All." The whipper-snapper, disappointed, shifted his ground. "I'd rather have fish. What fish have you got?" "All," the good lady repeated. How my heart warmed to her, how infinitely superior she was to the man who was trying to find something "difficult" on her menu! He chose *truite au bleu* followed by a *ris de veau*. The lady of the house, merciful after her fashion, saw to it that a touch of authentic thick cream was added to the sauce of the sweetbreads. Not but what, the meddlesome diner was not deterred from taking a squint to his right at my piping hot, velvety fish soup, and to his left at a fourfold crêpe, oozing with a bubbly cheese fondant, a speciality of the house.

There is a time and a place for everything. Here we are not assailed by any such twinge of conscience as, in Paris, may reduce us to reprobates when faced by a display of exorbitantly priced delicacies, for here we are proffered in profusion, by hands rich in cunning and traditional skills, the fruits, fish and game of Provence, brought in direct from the kitchen garden or still alive from the farmyard, landed from the sea or from fresh water tanks, or even poached from the neighbouring pine tracts. Heavens! how readily we revert to a state of savage euphoria, eager to set off in pursuit of the black pig in the forests of Tahiti as to sample that imaginary dish which in my part of the country both symbolises and ridicules the extreme of luxury, the dish known as "*fersues de caquesiau*", or, in plain words, "midges' livers". We fly from one extreme to the other: either the shell-fish bristling with legs and claws and coral-trimmings, or else

273

a snack by the road side, a *casse croute marseillais,* soaked in good oil and garlic.

We have only to transplant ourselves, by a turn of the wheel over the dial of France, and we are no longer recognisable, so easily do we become amenable to nature's bounty. Beneath the fig-tree, under the sky-blue plumbago, let yourself go and take your ease in the midst of pimento, sea-urchin, and a well-stocked salad-bowl, with *loup-de-mer* at a thousand francs each and out-of-season game *sur canapé,* let yourself go, openly and in the sight of all! Nothing that we enjoy eating need cause us shame. Nothing is too beautiful or too good to put the finishing touch—just once in a while, what say you?—to the natural lavishness that surrounds us, even though we have to be ready to renounce it all once the time comes for returning to the long, dietary discomfort that has for so long been our portion for three out of the four seasons.

There is always the return journey to be made. We have to leave that which we love and deserves our love, that which touches our heart no less than that which makes us laugh, as for instance the basset hound who could work up an appetite only to the sound and fury of his own pretended ferociousness; no longer can we look forward to a pattering of feet and a morning visit, no longer listen to the prattle of the diminutive artiste who, at the age of eight, displayed both on stage and screen the skill and aplomb of an old stager.

The troublesome question of my return to Paris became the subject of a friendly discussion in my presence. "No, not by train. Anything rather than the train for her. The

heat! The car's out of the question.—Why so?—Takes
too long. Not comfortable enough.—Right. Then it
means by air.—Oh, I don't much like the thought of her
going by air . . . —But what, after all, would she like
best?—She's not said anything."

She's not said a word. She's not heard, she was reading. She was trying not to laugh. My dearest friend
glanced in my direction—what had I got to say? He
weighed me up. How best pack an object that one
moment agrees to everything, and the next reacts in the
strongest possible terms! Where can a basket be found
to take this great cat on a journey a thousand miles long?
But the cat made up its own mind, and the object gave
herself the pleasure of cutting short the debate and
choosing to go by air. It is pleasant on occasion to assume
the prerogative of a foreman of the jury and decide the
issue by a casting vote.

My wheel-chair out on the tarmac, then the hot air
bath while waiting for the take-off, the frail of newspapers, a pinch of absorbent cotton-wool to caulk the ears,
the neat little lunch-basket and the flagon of wine, all of
them prime necessities when travelling Air-France, for
I become bored in a plane. Nothing up there is to my
liking except the speed. " See, we still have a strip of the
sea to cross! Do look, that ribbon of a road down there,
surely that's the very route we took last week! " A fig
for the route, and for the unexpected cloud we pierce
straight through as though it were a cocoon!

I confess my inaptitude. Once before, on the Toulouse-
Fez-Toulouse circuit, I realised that riding on high is not
for me. My flights of fancy do not rise above ground level.
" Look down there, do you know that we are passing

right over your native heath? " And do you believe, companion mine, that I am going to recognise my native heath in this flying mist with its criss-crossing roads, its chequerboard of fields cloven by a streak of water you tell me is the Yonne? Not a hope! One thing is certain. Even if I do happen to draw my inspiration from the malicious sense of fun that lies at the ever impenitent heart of septuagenarians, even if I do have to reckon with my impotence and at the same time with the spirit of curiosity engendered by it, I never wish to travel by air again unless it is a question of saving precious hours. Whilst I am being borne along by it I forget the aircraft, for it possesses the magic power of eliminating distances. Thus all we have contact with is the point of departure and the distant goal which looms up out of nowhere before our eyes. My flights of fancy remain on ground level. But you, winged monster, you withhold them from me, for you alone can make the descent! It is the descent and not the sudden uprush into the wilderness of clouds that I find enchanting. Four hours, it takes you but four hours to muster a miniature France beneath your wings, crushing her mountains, obliterating her towns. Finally I achieve the greatest miracle of all: my red and white room, the bed on which I navigate my own course, the stage moonlight of my blue lantern: all that, and I did not know it, is but four hours from Nice.

MARGUERITE MORENO

OUR first meeting—1894 or '95?—took place before lunch at the house of Catulle Mendès. The sun was streaming into the room and at that mid-day hour its light gave a vivid outline to the long silhouetted figure of a slight young woman who was leaning forward under the weight of the load she was carrying; this turned out to be a fine, heavy child of between eighteen months and two years old. Fair as summer, he turned to look at me with his grave dark eyes, inherited from his mother.

This splendid child, whose birth had all but caused the death of so frail a mother, this child of light himself died of meningitis before he was three, after battling against death with a strength already far beyond his years. There are few of us left now who remember his short life. And I believe that Moreno—the lovely, austere name chosen by Marguerite Moreno—hardly ever spoke of him except to those of her own age who, like myself, had caught a glimpse of this son of too early promise during his brief existence.

In the home of Catulle Mendès I failed to pay proper attention either to the excellent coffee prepared with his own hands, or to the anti-Semitic couplet, always to hand, which enhanced his reputation as a wit. I had neither eyes nor ears for anything but the tall young woman.

Her own wit, the easy and sparkling delivery of her words, the timbre of her voice which rejoiced the ear of the listener, the unredeemed pallor of her complexion, a head of magnificent chestnut hair with here and there a glint of gold! I can still see the warm look in her unwavering, lively eyes that scorned any coquettish appeal. Everything about her humiliated and enchanted the exiled country lass that I was at the time. From the first moment of this encounter I admired and adored Marguerite Moreno. The astonishing thing is that she returned my affection. We were young enough, having both recently come of age, for our friendship to develop into the sort of schoolgirl crush which young ladies at boarding schools find so intoxicating. Throughout the period that Mendès contributed theatrical notices to *Le Journal*, he would frequently take us both to the critic's box. I squeezed myself in between his crumpled shirt-front and Moreno's lovely swanlike neck. One night he took us to a music hall.

"You're going to see the strangest little creature," Marguerite said to me. "Any producer worth his salt ought to grab hold of her and rescue her from herself and her idiotic songs. Even from her stage-name, which is quite ridiculous. She's gifted with the most attractive ugliness, and she looks as if she invented her own dance numbers."

At that time Polaire was twirling and spinning on the boards of the Scala, like a midge caught in a sunbeam. She had not yet had her auburn hair cut short—auburn, mind you, not black. Her stage costume, the perfectly cut dress of a period "smasher", did credit to the taste and talent of Madame Landolff who, as a costumière, has

278

had no equal. A full, short, nondescript skirt concealed, when not in motion, its embroidered underside ablaze with concentric circles of all the colours of a rainbow. The least twitch made by the midget singer—during the reprise she danced with eyes shut and arms stiff like a woman falling asleep—would unfurl about her, around legs in a froth of black lace, the seven reverberant colours. Her hair, swept up and back and twisted into a clown's topknot, displayed two exquisite ears, which later in her career were hidden by her short hairstyle.

Madame Landolff delighted in designing dresses for her, all of which seemed deserving of a better fate than a music-hall turn. I well remember one of white lace, like rigid spindrift against that brown statuette. I can see another, a miracle of rustling silk resembling paper, in dark and ever-changing shades of green, slashed with a hundred small cuts that opened upon an acid pink foundation during the dance; a mat terra cotta dress closely matching her skin, which appeared to be naked, decked with a few mauve feathers.

"What did I tell you?" said Moreno. "She looks like nobody else. Perhaps she is a wraith after all."

For at that time Moreno herself was unaware whose compelling hand it was that would drag the dancing and singing, rainbow-encircled Polaire away to the legitimate theatre.

I am forever losing only to discover afresh my very earliest memories of Marguerite Moreno, for the lives we both led tended to scatter and then reassemble them. She travelled far and wide, I never stirred. We both got married, became unmarried, married again. She dwelt in the pure regions of poetry, and tried her hand at

279

imparting higher education to the Argentians; I played in pantomime at the Apollo and elsewhere. After lengthy silences, which caused me to fear the worst, an exchange of letters would put us back where we were, at the heart of an unbroken friendship. On leaving the Argentine, she returned to the stage in one of those deplorable plays by Bataille that were saved only by their cast—Bady, Yvonne de Bray, Huguenet.

She staged her return at the Vaudeville, in *La Phalène*.

During my pregnancy I used to hoist my burdened body up to her dressing-room where, of an evening, she would lavish on me in short flashes the colour, flavour, adventures and disillusionments of her sojourn in the Argentine. "Yes, yes, *mon vieux*, the very first night, a butterfly the size of a vulture, with a luminous nose, flapped all over my room making as much din as a threshing-machine! Didn't you hear my cries for help from here?" She knew how highly I prized a description depicted in the strongest colours, the delight I took in the enlargement of the thing described, and we would "mon vieux" each other like children at a village school.

Today I find it surprising that at the very time when she attained the full glory of womanhood, when thanks to the Argentinian climate she returned with healthier cheeks and a fuller bust (in the title rôle of *The Green God* she showed off her superb long legs), she should have dropped her charming and romantic first name. Her public called her "Moreno". Her friends and ardent admirers—she always had them in abundance—referred to her as "Moreno", a dusky name that beautifully suited her matchless pallor with its suggestive hidalgo look. When she was acclaimed a star celebrity, when the vast array of cinema-goers became infatuated with her trenchant yet restrained gift for playing comedy, as a delicate act of gratitude the crowds restored to her her lovely christian name. In all public places it was hurled at her. "Marguerite . . . there's Marguerite!" More intimidated than she wished to let it appear, she would flutter her eyelashes when struck by this flower.

After Marcel Schwob, who was madly in love with her, she was married for a time to Jean Daragon, the actor, on whom a false beard could confer the elegant virility of *The Ironmaster* by Georges Ohnet, or the poetic hirsuteness of Richepin's *The Tramp*. Ill health kept Daragon out of the First War, and no woman ever excelled Moreno in lightening the protective yoke as she watched over this man of fragile health camouflaged as a bruiser in the pink of condition. So skilful was her gentle raillery that he never detected the anxiety or the pity behind her smiling mask. But she was unable to prevent him from dying even though she took him with her to Nice, where she worked in a hospital for the wounded. If only I had kept every one of the letters she wrote to me at that time!

"I carry on with my duties among my legless ones, who are gay, and my armless ones, who are sad. It doesn't take long before my legless ones are drawing, writing, making small toys, propelling themselves from place to place as best they can, and getting up to every sort of nonsense. Whereas my armless ones grow melancholy: because for a man it must be the greatest humiliation, perhaps the worst of all, never again to be able to undo his own trouser buttons without a helping hand."

For long months of the long war we both remained

faithful to Paris, living as near neighbours. She lived on the ground floor of a modern house in Rue Jean-de-Bologne and I in a Swiss chalet in Rue Cortambert. Annie de Pène had a cottage, with steps running up to it, at the very end of the countrified Herrent blind-alley. Musidora had recently done up one of those bachelor establishments, in a wedge-shaped gore in Rue Decamps, a single room, with hot water, central heating, and bathroom "with every convenience", that put to shame anything our tottering houses in old Passy had to offer. On nights when the sky was peopled with Zeppelins, she would sleep at Rue Cortambert on a small iron bed, and do the shopping and cooking in the day time. I acted as char and did the washing. We made up a fine female squad! We used to tie the hand-washed sheets round a stout copper faucet and wring them out by twisting them tight, while Marguerite Moreno, a cigarette between her lips, would sprinkle our domestic chores with the beneficent dew of news, true or false, anecdotes, and prognostications. Annie de Pène knew of a certain carriage gateway beneath which a man from the country sold chickens, tossing them over to her with an "Up she goes, little lady! Now chuck me my four francs five sous!"

It was the hardest thing in the world for us to break up for the night. From those black times dates Moreno's inspiring influence on Annie de Pène, on her daughter Germaine Beaumont, and on Musidora. We drank in the consolation of lovely words, sinuous verse, the distant scene, all magically evoked. In the shadow of Moreno followed Jean Daragon, bulky and breathing with difficulty. My little garden brought forth its usual offerings and, after a watering, exhaled its garden smells. My daughter was enjoying life in the unravaged Limousin; the finest Paris peaches cost five sous apiece.

All the members of our phalanstery of the XVIth arrondissement owed a debt of gratitude to Moreno, for there she sowed the good seed of laughter, inimitably, miraculously, the laughter of crises, the nervous, un-restrained laughter of war-time, self-assertive insolence in face of looming danger, the cut and thrust of wordplay as intoxicating as drafts of wine. On windless nights the belch of the howitzers, each distinct, reached us from the east. This deep-seated, close-sounding concussion had the effect of silencing conversation, and was transmitted through the distorted regions of the air to reach as far as our deserted but keenly alert quarters. It happened one night that Moreno, doubtless at a loss for verbal quips, became engrossed in the rhythm of the cannonade, snap-ping her fingers and clicking her heels as it rose and fell, and improvising on the spot a mock-Spanish dance; with a twist of her hips and a roll of her eyes she restored laughter to our midst, banishing all thought of danger by a display of healthy impertinence with the temerity of a heroine. Pierre Fresnay can surely not have forgotten a post-war occasion at Marseilles, when we, Marguerite, he and I, were leaving the theatre about midnight after playing in *Chéri!* Moreno was brilliant in her improvisa-tions as she sniffed the aniseed-laden air of the Cannebière and instructed Fresnay in the joyous adventures of nomadic life. She left him doubled up with laughter, com-pletely dazzled by her arresting glance and the wide range of her fanciful imagination.

I can still see the gasping tip of her cigarette that was hardly ever stubbed out—"Marguerite, you're smoking

too much "—her honest appetite that never boggled at
the foie gras and black pudding of the snack-bars—
" Marguerite, you'll make yourself ill! " Her own special
gifts, and among them I would choose the sudden serious-
ness and fullest over-tone accorded to the measure of the
alexandrine, and the healing magic to charm all creatures,
for I benefited from them for more than fifty years, but
intermittently, alas! One cannot always have the good
fortune to play Léa in *Chéri* when Madame Moreno has
consented to play the part of Charlotte Peloux! In
Brussels, as elsewhere, I learned many a lesson from her
genuinely roving accomplishments. She would watch me
with detachment as I arranged a writing-table, put three
flowers into a vase, or set out on a plate a bunch of fresh
but insipid large grapes. Already up in her room she had
half-unpacked her valise, hung up her scotch cape, and
chucked a packet of cigarettes and the day's paper on the
table. On going into it I would exclaim " Marguerite
Moreno's room, I can tell by the smell of it." For a lingering personal fragrance, to which my keen sense of smell
has always been highly susceptible, denoted her presence.
Nothing whatever to do with body odour, it was not
axillary—" I'm drier than tinder," she was in the habit
of saying—nor did it derive from any perfumed essence
or lotion.

The particular place on her neck below the ear, where
I would give her a kiss of greeting, was embalmed with
the invariable, captivating scent of her skin, as well as
that of tobacco smoke. All you many men who have at
some time or other been violently in love with Marguerite,
you at least can never have failed to note, never have

forgotten the scent exhaled by her glorious, creamy skin, with a hint of amber beneath its white texture!

An hotel bedroom, by no means the best, a valise or two, a book, two volumes of verse, a manuscript, a cape, *the* cape—a reversible tartan—that she would lend to anyone in need of it (it once saved my dearest friend and me from a downpour of hail that lashed our open carriage), from this meagre assortment of props she was capable of creating comic effects by sheer force of will. On the stage, a gold or silver shoe might occasionally peep out from beneath the hem of her skirt; the foot it shod, worthy of the fairest raiment and itself beyond compare, was designed for freedom and, naked, to tread the coolness of flagstones, a foot such as that of M'Barka, the bare-foot dancing-girl of the Pasha of Marrakesh.

When touring the provinces Moreno and I were sometimes able to keep together. Pierre Moreno used to play Patron, the boxing instructor, in *Chéri*. Every now and again he would work off his homesickness by singing songs in his native Gascon dialect, well suited to his delightful tenor voice. All three of us loved Brussels, the gilt of its Grande Place, the busy gaiety of its inhabitants, the beer, the coffee, the buttered slices of tasty Belgian bread; while sitting outside that huge restaurant, you must know it, *Les Trois* . . . whatever it was, we would bathe in the stream of passers-by and enjoy our bohemian idleness to the full.

Moreno did not put aside much money from her earnings at that time. Later on the cinema woke up to the fact that it was worth their while to offer her a fortune. She accepted with disillusioned serenity. She owned certain properties, among them an exceptionally blue " Blue

Spring ", an ancient castle, as well as patrimony and land more than sufficient to satisfy her needs. Who could have imagined that the first few months of 1948 would be the last of her life! According to the demands made on her by cinema, theatre, and late-night cabaret, she pitched her tent first in an hotel in the Batignolles district before moving to one in the Avenue de l'Opéra. Knowing that I had for some time been unable to stir from my room, she would conquer any feelings of fatigue, walk a little way along the Avenue de l'Opéra, take for fun one of the little passages that honeycomb the Palais Royal, climb up the flight and a half to where I lay, and appear decked out in her usual array; cigarette, felt hat pulled down over one eye, and coat the colour of dusk and rain. Oh, how grateful I was to her for being always her own true self, ready to set off again and again, fagged out but untiring! How I loved her perpetual motion which, truth to tell, never parted me from her, loved her for her regularity in writing to me when far away, her zest for work which seemed to keep her young! I would make the pretence of putting her through a severe cross-examination.

"Marguerite, I demand nothing but the truth. Where have you come from? "

" From Courbevoie. I'm filming."

" What is the film? "

" Less than nothing, as you might suppose. And I had a matinée at the A.B.C."

"Are you hungry? Thirsty? "

" I had lunch in the taxi. But rest assured, tonight I'll have a bite of foie gras and champagne. Always supposing I have the time. You see, I have two performances at the A.B.C. and I've promised to go back to Courbevoie."

"When?"

"In . . . in ten minutes. After that, as you know, I'm giving a poetry reading at Tonton's at midnight.".

"How many more nights have you got to put in at Tonton's?"

Her lovely hand flew to my shoulder and, with a gentle look, she stared me straight in the face.

"That, Macolette, is something I never wish to come to an end! Cabaret, as I have come to know, is something unique. Just think of it, I'm in the process of teaching them Verlaine. *They* gulped down Baudelaire like an untried drink. If only you could see them! For the most part, they have come there for the champagne, and the hell of it. I wrung their withers with Hugo and Delavigne all right, that was relatively easy work. But to lead them to the water of Baudelaire and Verlaine! With the slightest encouragement I'll win them over to Mallarmé! There I sit surrounded by their heat and their smell, their knees make room—but not always—for mine, by making a long arm I get a light off one of them, I fish for a cigarette in the cases held out to me. You can picture the scene! You hear them bawling, then watch them gradually grow silent till you feel they are listening. It's like the courts of heaven, with the crowd pressing in upon the speaker."

She lowered her eyes with pride, showing a reserve in which I have many a time found, a purely personal discovery, a look approaching sensuality. Now that she will never again stand beside the divan-bed, never again be the life and soul of Tonton's overheated cabaret, why should I conceal from my reader one trait among a hundred others in my attempted portrait of Marguerite? This lowering of the eyelids, which was her way of breaking in on a phrase, of hiding a part of her thought, was one of the rare movements, lasting but a moment, that to my mind brought to Moreno's broad, austere, pale features a significant flash of sensual pleasure.

After giving a defiant laugh, and making me laugh with her, she asked what time it was, hurriedly drew her coat round her, hurriedly made for the door after bending her tall figure over my raft that I might kiss Marguerite's fragrance, under her ear. But she remembered before leaving the room to point on her own body to the seat of some discomfiture " Bitch of a leg, and now this sciatica! "

Perhaps her object was to prevent me in my half-helpless state from envying her lovely slender feet, still capable of going up and down the staircase of the Palais Royal unaided.

She liked to see me alone, when no one else was there. She liked to see Madame Brisson alone, or one or other of her daughters. She liked to see Jeanne Roze without me, and Pierre Blanchar when no third person was present. More than I could name, and I don't believe I knew them all, were those with whom Marguerite Moreno loved to hobnob tête-à-tête. All of us, without exception, showed ourselves jealous of the moments that she spared for each one of us. What we had to have was Marguerite Moreno between our window and our fireplace, the famous felt hat, for so it became, pulled down over one eye, her well-worn vanity bag, her cigarettes, her untiring voice. I was sorry when she gave up wearing

her hair in the style that became so long the hallmark of
every rôle she played, the neat well-groomed cut of a man-
about-town, exactly fitting the shape of her head. At her
wrist jangled a wide-linked gold bracelet. What more can
I recollect of her who showed contempt for all outward
finery? A ring? Probably. But one's eye rested not on the
ring but on the hand, a hand needlessly elongated and
exaggerated in its refinement in the portrait that now
hangs in the Luxembourg. I can forgive the artist,
Granier, in favour of the speaking likeness: there, at its
frankest, with every dissembled thought removed, there
is the face of Marguerite Moreno between the age of
twenty and twenty-five.

She suffered considerably, I believe, and with barely
a word of complaint, from the life of the film-studios.
It is a cruel life for sensitive minds and bodies, in that it
brings face to face beings who were particularly intended
never to confront one another—a form of brutality from
which life in the wings of a theatre has been up till now
exempt. During the hours in the studio when she was not
on the set, Marguerite, respected by all, withdrew herself
to the best of her ability behind a screen of newspapers,
feigning drowsiness or a desire for rest. Her perfect manners, which made it impossible for her to snub or show
the least sign of impatience, did not come to her effort-
lessly, I am convinced. Many were the times when I tried
to question her about those working days which began
at dawn in an outer suburb, the endless rehearsals during
which the player extracts from the part, like pus from a
gathering, some short phrase that has to be tested for
sound over and over again, until its sterling worth is
proved by its ring and practice has made it indiscernibly

perfect. I still remain wilfully ignorant of the silver screen and its various techniques, a fact that proves me a person not only of a certain age but, as they say, of another age altogether.

Marguerite would tell me little or nothing in reply; shaking her head, she would gently say "You simply cannot imagine what the life of a film actor or actress is like. Impossible, I tell you. I have accepted it, I have no cause either for reproach or explanation. Macolette, drop the subject."

I have already spoken of her various abodes, of her gift for imposing her personality on them however common-place they were to start with. It would seem that pure chance guided her choice. Rue Jean-de-Bologne, Rue Saint-Louis-en-l'Ile, Rue Notre-Dame-des-Champs, Boulevard du Montparnasse. But the moment she was in them, they became worthy of her presence. Whether she really cared for them I cannot be sure, it was I who became attached to them. Never shall I forget her kindness to me when she was lodging in Place Pereire, at a time when I stood in great need of moral support and could go for it to none but Marguerite. I would climb her stairs and ring the bell at the half-landing. In her room I remember a rough Spanish chest, a round table, the single place laid on it encroached on by a number of books, the books themselves forced into retreat by a strong cheese, a foie gras or some form of sausage meat, all from the Lot. The sun entered from the right quarter. The plum tart came from the near-by confectioner's. "Help yourself, Maco-lette.—I'm not hungry.—If you're feeling peckish, help yourself. Food is good for you in the state you're in. Sit down. I'm going to tell you the story of my life and of my miracles."

I wonder who is the present tenant of that low-ceilinged lodging from which has departed, if not the sunbeam, at least the presence that bestowed on it meaning and life! Marguerite Moreno left it as she left all the others, neither on sudden impulse nor from dislike. She particularly liked, I think, her last Paris domicile—I do not count hotels—Boulevard du Montparnasse, within easy distance of the blazing Rotonde, the warm glow of the many-coloured brasseries, the combination of deference and familiarity that escorted and vociferously saluted Marguerite Moreno along the wide sidewalks of the avenue.

Previously she had frequented the grey cement of some sort of new-style barracks, and about 1900—with Marcel Schwob—the period wood-panelling and frigid elegance of a house on the Ile Saint-Louis. The creamy white and narrow bourgeois respectability of Rue d'Argenteuil held no terrors for her. A few months before the end she was cracking up to me the genial good-nature and coun-trified fun of a family pension near the Batignolles. She also cracked them up to Pierre Moreno, who began to worry, came up to town from Touzac and found her in one of those hotels whose secret belongs to Paris and which are never without an antimacassared drawing room or a large, lavishly dismal garden. By dint of per-suasion and authority he succeeded in winning her away from this romantic background and establishing her in more up-to-date comfort. But she complained about it to me and, despite all Pierre Moreno's solicitude, her kindly hosts were not prevented from shedding copious and heart-felt tears at her departure. " I should have liked to stay on there a little longer to please them," she confided to me. "They were so nice." How I adored the occasional weakness of one who gave every outward appearance of being able to measure up to both the dangers of living alone and those of a life *à deux* with the same unwavering eye.

I had the pleasure of applauding Moreno in *La Folle de Chaillot*. A sharp attack of arthritis made me fear up to the last moment that I should have to stay at home. But I was sustained by the good wishes of my friends and overcame my reluctance. Jouvet gave me his stage box, my dearest friend his arm, and a lady unknown to me her unexpected and providential shoulder, at the very moment when I was about to collapse in the foyer. I attached considerable importance to that evening performance. Before long Paris was to show even more regard and enthusiasm than myself. I found at the Athénée exactly what I had anticipated: virtuosity in the acting, Giraudoux in, an ebullient mood, and in myself a certain lack of warmth. I had no great liking for the text. I was therefore not open to criticism when I surrendered myself to the delights of Bérard's décor and to my irrepressible admiration for Jouvet, to whom all must be forgiven in recognition of his inventiveness and tyrannical despotism. Finally I had eyes only—I am coming to the point—for Marguerite Moreno, totally absorbed in creating before our eyes the part of La Folle. Such a store of apparent naturalness, so perfectly simulated a disregard for the audience, the control of a commanding voice in allotting to each salient word in a clever sentence its due share of sonority and rhythm, the audacious sallies of a dolled-up warhorse, in short the orchestration of the rôle by an incomparable artiste had in it the power to overwhelm us, and overwhelm us it did.

From the shadows of the stage-box I subjected Marguerite as indiscreetly as you please to the full force of my faculties, with an eye as critical as that of a dresser or stage manager.

I was soon reassured. Under the coating of black and white chalk, beneath the tinsel frippery of her clothes, a great artiste was observing us, a keen-eared musician was profiting by our silence just as much as by our applause. Once my fears were allayed, my pride assuaged, I was able that evening—it was, I think, the fifth performance —to forecast a long and triumphant run for Moreno, and prosperity for the Athénée.

That I might taste and enjoy to the full one dazzling pleasure only, I denied myself for once all interest in the writing, and I would not have exchanged my lack of warmth on that evening for no matter what brand of enthusiasm.

Moreno's inspiration in her part did not begin to wane till after several hundred performances. I have never much cared for the way the public have of judging a stage performance as they would a track event, and applying the term " exhausting " to the eighteen hundred lines or so that devolve upon La Folle. Passing serenely through both moments of anxiety and ovation, Moreno pursued her triumphant way once and often twice a day at the Athénée, yet still found time to visit me.

" But you don't even look tired! " I said in admiration.

" I am tired all the same," she said. " All those stairs to climb up and down! The dryness in the air that's so harmful to one's throat, the lengthy periods of standing about on the set . . ."

I interrupted her with a gesture she understood.

"Oh yes, I see, the exacting nature of my part! Macolette, bear in mind that if I don't look tired it's because I'm not very tired. What I have to do comes quite easily to me. La Folle is a very long part, an eccentric part requiring no great subtlety. It carries no mysterious psychological overtones, so it doesn't take a lot out of me. Would you like to know what I really think? No one has a better claim than you to be privy to it. It's my idea that anybody could play the part, no matter who. Only . . ."

She broke off to open her bag and go through the ritual of muttering: "My key—I've lost my key! Oh no, there it is! I've left my money on the mantelpiece. . . . And now what have I done with Pierre's letter!"

"Only," she resumed, "nobody realises it. On reflection, I think it would be best if nobody but us two ever did know it."

And now here I am giving it away, I, the faithless trustee of this strange confession that bears the stamp of excessive modesty and mystery-weaving fantasy, crying it aloud; but it no longer carries its confidential tone, its accompanying look. She left it with me one day just as she was making off under the wing of her felt hat—chestnut was it, or beige that day, or possibly aubergine!

I did not go a second time to hear *La Folle de Chaillot*. Moreno used to come occasionally to give me news of it, never failing to laugh at herself.

"Still going from strength to strength, Marguerite?"

294

Penny Carey

"Still going strong. Between performances they bring along children for me to bless."

There would follow some anecdote or other that took her back, that took us both back into her past. Any resemblance she might have had to her mother—whose malevolent, well-preserved good looks I remember—assumed on her own lips the mordant quality of an inspired replica. When made up as an elderly woman in a comic film, she would suddenly remind me of her mother (as in *Les Jeux sont faits*) so forcibly, so majestically, as to be disconcerting. When she played the White Ghost in *La dernière Nuit de Don Juan*, one saw for the last time, between the folds of her tightly drawn veil, one saw the dazzle of beauty fall on features that for so long had disdained it.

I keep on looking all about me for Marguerite Moreno. While she was alive we could do without each other for long periods at a time. A telephone call or an exchange of letters would give me back across the space that separated us the tone of her voice and all its clarity. My colleagues, her friends and admirers have given me a bitter-sweet pleasure by printing in the papers an ever increasing number of likenesses hitherto unknown to me. I have been provided with all save her living presence.

Shortly before her death she had invited a grand-niece to stay with her. She had been incapable of hiding her astonishment, her deep feelings, at the sight of a human flower full of health and intelligence. This I deduce from her last letters, in which I find an affectionate constraint, a feeling of watchful pride, even to the extent of discovering something quite new to her, the freedom to welcome by name the idea of the future, at the suggestion

295

of a radiantly beautiful child. Yet in all this persisted a reticence, blurred by a sort of timidity in speaking of the future, of a state of permanency, in admitting the possibility of her life easing off as a result. Only after hesitation would she have sacrificed the poetic and wandering use to which she had put the autumn of her days. Her letters, which are the letters of an artist expert in the choice of words, might cherish the idea of further spiritual adventures, but surely, for her, the most enthralling project would have been to renounce the adventurous! A little prudence on her part, a less glacial March, and Marguerite Moreno would still be with us. Or else, some hundred miles from here, she might have preferred to be free of the life-long fetters of her art in the enjoyment of her own wondrous blue spring, her vines and cultivated lands, and enhanced family circle! "This year," she wrote to me, "you are going to find a new creature when you come to stay with me, so much has everything changed since your first visit! This year you are at last coming to live in my lovely countryside . . ."

At this point, I don't doubt, she paused in her writing to let her eyes linger on her estate, on the jewelled blues that the darting black-backed fish set flashing in her spring waters, to let her ears listen for the cry of a very small child. Yet this time, too, she did not dare to write "home" in place of "countryside".

XI

H Y S S O P, my dear Sir, it must be hyssop, this already shrivelled twig that still keeps its clinging scent and is almost as delicate as snow crystals. But I do not guarantee this. Just because Mermod's, the Swiss publishing firm, have issued a little book of mine, in which I speak of a few plants in the most familiar terms either informatively or to their detriment, it hardly deserves to be compared by you to *La Botanique des Dames*, an excellent work where you will see pictures of elegant ladies of the manor hunting for mushrooms in patent leather dancing-shoes and full flying flounces, and butterflies dying in agony under white-gloved fingers!

Yes, I incline to the view that it is hyssop. Starting from pure camphor, its scent runs the whole gamut of two or three chaste perfumes suggestive of capsicum, such as lavender and rosemary, before it ends up as—why, in heaven's name!—as hyssop. *Hysopo et mundabor!* Would you like me to sing to you over the telephone a good part of the mass in latin? I could. You would never believe your ears, my dear Sir with the good sense not to give your name, so you must take my word for it, that the little sweet-smelling herb is hyssop: myself, I take it for one of those presents that fly out from a letter, roll out of a

297

cabbage leaf or pill-box, in other words, one at which I should never dream of turning up my nose.

Before yours came today I had already received, from H. E. Brahim el Glaoui, a bottle from Marrakesh filled with some grey antimony, spangled and delicate, which goes by the name of kohl, koheul, or mokoheul—I cannot be sure which is the right name for it. What does the spelling matter, now that I am well supplied with cosmetic which can act as a surgical dressing, which prevents the eyes from reddening, allows one to face up to a strong light, sun or electric, and dust-laden air into the bargain: in short, the antimony they use throughout the orient to slip in between the eyelids of newborn babes!

For a great many years I religiously went to buy my koheul at Bichara's, " Syrian Perfumer ", from a thin, slight, swart man whose handshake was always so dry and so gentle. He supplied all the very latest novelties, from clay for washing the hair to cakes of soap the shape of small cylinders that looked good enough to eat. I recollect that he never failed to touch wood when asking after my baby daughter, to protect her from the powers of evil. He spoke very low, in a tired voice, and coughed a discreet cough, which was to land him, discreetly enough, in the grave! A man with an aura of physical distinction about him, which gave his place of business an air of enchanted alchemy. He left a daughter who wrote poetry.

I am indebted to a lady from Oran, the wife of General C.—she had married a man of my father's year in the army, a young and dashing captain—for my daily habit of using antimony. A converted Jewess, the general's lady instructed me in many a nicety practised by inmates of the harem, among them the regular use of kohl. In her widowhood, she still affected some peculiarly African forms of adornment, such as hair-curlers of leather, ropes of blue pearls or necklaces of gazelle-droppings, and other magical fetishes, despite all of which she never missed going to mass on a Sunday. In Paris, where I once stayed with her for three weeks, I soon developed a liking for couscous and the plump sweetmeats of Oran.

All the same, I never dared to ask Sido, my mother, for leave to pay a second visit to Paris, or to tell her how one morning there I had happened upon the general's wife while she was busy supervising the household chores of a former batman turned house-boy. Perched high on a double ladder and wearing a blue apron, the lad was engaged in wiping the panes of a fan-light, to the accompaniment of a stream of advice from his Oranese mistress positioned at the foot of the ladder. "You short-arsed little runt," she cursed him roundly, "I can see from here the streaks and blurs you've left on the glass! What you want is a touch of encouragement, eh!" And with that she wantonly seized hold of him by the rump in so tight a grip that he whinnied with surprise and delight. Then he leapt down off the ladder and returned the compliment.

I was then at that uncompromising age when one denies to persons of advanced years the right to indulge in amorous love, when one takes exception to the slightest gesture which may give rise to love and disapproves most thoroughly should it find expression in unseemly high jinks. Far more than the playful prank played by Madame la Générale, it was the man's answering cackle that sent me indignantly back to the room I had just left. I was fifteen! The very age when one quivers with scandalised horror at the salacious behaviour of one's elders. At fifteen, love is on the brink of tears for a yes, for a no: it sees nothing to be amused at in the pinching of buttocks.

Like most dogs with big rounded heads—bull-dogs, bull-terriers, little Brabançon terriers, and boxers—her memory was acute. My elder brother's boxer bitch *knew* several songs, and Souci, my own French bull-dog bitch, an exceptionally large number of words: she was so quick in picking them up that for my own amusement I would give her a few faulty pronunciations. She adored fruit, with a marked preference for ripe raspberries and grapes, and to these, but solely for her own benefit, I gave the names of "raspbeeries" and "gripes". Sometimes, when this ritual had slipped my memory, I would say to her "Would you like a raspberry, or a grape? ", and she would then give me a puzzled look and say nothing. I would then correct myself: "A nice little raspbeery? A gripe? ", upon which Souci took heart at once and bounced forward full of overjoyed acquiescence. So it was until the day when she made the discovery that not only the vines but the raspberry canes as well bore their fruit within the reach of a full grown bull-dog; thereafter she dispensed with my help and my mispronounced vowels, and went out at seven in the morning to breakfast off raspbeeries and gripes.

I had bought her at the Tuileries Dog Show, where she had won First Prize for French bull-dogs, Class "7 kilos and under ", and I had paid nine thousand francs for her. Her brother, sold for his weight in gold, went off to

America. This transaction made such a hole in my pocket that I had to forego my new tailor-made costume and afternoon " ensemble " in order to enrich Souci's wardrobe with a scarlet morocco-leather harness. It is possible that when we went out together the threadbare state of my right elbow and my felt hat (the one the Comtesse de Noailles called my " old huntsman's cap ") between them gave me a rather moth-eaten look, but the bitch attracted every eye. In all our eleven years together, Souci and I never encountered a similar couple where so much envious admiration was bestowed on the bull-dog.

For some little time before Souci's day, three of us were to be seen taking our constitutional in the Bois de Boulogne : Belle Aude, a sheep dog from the Beauce, on her high black-and-flame-coloured paws, myself on my bicycle, and Pati, the miniature terrier from Brabant, tucked away in a strawberry basket tied on to my handlebars. On reaching the less frequented rides, I would put the impetuous little lady from Brabant down on the ground, where she invariably did her best to outpace the huge shepherdess from the Beauce. Both came to heel only when the weight and effect of my words of command were fully appreciated because given in the vernacular.

More than one passer-by would remain stationary with surprise for a good minute, on observing that the two bitches were able to distinguish between their right and their left without the slightest hesitation, and of taking up their position on the nearside of my machine.

The Last Cat knew the melody of one song only, a pleasing American number, delightfully sung by the Sophomores, or by the Revellers. Sometimes, when she was sleeping the venerable sleep of cats I would put on

301

the familiar record. She did not always completely wake up, but as she lay dozing a smile of dreamy connivance would blossom on her enchanting lips: "Yes, yes, I hear it. Don't wake me up altogether." I think the title of her song was "Blue Heaven". You may be sure that if and when I buy another gramophone, I intend to buy that record as well.

If ever I cease to sing the praises of the Last Cat, it will be when I no longer have anything to say about anything. Perhaps that day is not far off; but since it has not yet arrived, and since I have been able to tell only of what I know, I still have a word or two to say on this subject and on that, to prevent myself from falling back on my old loves: not that these bring a blush to my cheeks, or that I have any wish to run them down, but simply because there are more than enough of them. I have no longer any desire to look at myself in the mirror of the past with my hair in the style of a gentleman about town or, for that matter, adorned with a wreath of pompom roses.

The vogue for the chestnut poodle is clearly nearing its end, and that of the black cocker spaniel will not long survive it. Since the war, various breeds of sporting dog have acquired favour and high prices, principally the spaniel, mahogany red, or spotted black and white, or liver and white. You may come across them on the sidewalk, always on a lead, with that look of rational despair that befits a sporting dog up on a visit to Paris. They are certainly sagacious, as they wait, eyes down, in the banana-queue at the fruiterer's. Sagacious they may be, yet they are gifted with a singular aptitude for getting lost. " *Lost, between Rue de Miromesnil and the Gare de l'Est, setter with collar but no address . . . Lost, Breton*

302

spaniel answering to the name of Gamin . . . Lost, spaniel . . ." Who is to blame? On whom should my suspicion fall? Alas, poor spaniel! Like Madame de Sévigné, you find that to you the Paris pavement is a place of torment, where the pads of your paws dry up and crack, accustomed as they are to roam the marshlands and hidden ditches where the veronica speedwell grows! "Take the dog with you, you'll exercise him in the course of your shopping!" And then all of a sudden there is no dog, no lead, only the net-bag full of lettuces, Toulouse sausages, and never quite ripe enough bananas, that, and a poor lady deprived of her spaniel. *"Lost, Market Lane Albert-Ier . . . Lost, Saint-Honoré Market . . ."* Perhaps to the sensitive, chamois-leather nostrils of the spaniel there came, somewhere between the stall of rotting oranges and the gypseous cheese stall, a whiff of Rambouillet from the water-cress crate, of spring water, the scent of a young rabbit or a bird, the smell that puts wings on a spaniel's paws and brings madness to his highly trained narrow mind. *"Lost . . . Large reward offered . . ."*

Spurned by fashion, what will now become of the prolific cocker, with his eight-pup litters, black as Erebus? His masters may love him, as often as not, for his own sake, for his incurable sentimentality. His two main worries are an atavistic nostalgia for the chase and any chance remark he has half overheard, to which ever after he attaches an unkind intention. He dwells on these continually and sheds secret tears. We do our best to console him for the sake of his beautiful sad eyes. "Come here, my precious darling, and let me pin back your lovely long ears so that they won't get soaked in your food!" At least he will never join the ranks of the forgotten schnautzer with his gendarme's mustachios, or the bedlington with his frizzy lamb's wool, who always reminds me, because of the bump on his nose, of the late Duchess Sforza, *née* Antokolski! But that is impertinence enough with regard to the high and mighty persistent breeds, and Madame Steinbock-Fermor will tell you better than I what points to look for in a sleek bedlington.

The market for chestnut poodles is getting easier. Trading in jet-black poodles shows signs of recovery. The run on snow-white poodles is at a standstill. Little demand for curly-haired poodles. It is worth noting that certain poodle-fanciers remain faithful to the chestnut, to wit Mlle Hilda Gélis-Didot and Francis Carco. M. Watermann still keeps to the jet-black breed. I purposely forgot that one. I omit any mention of those clipped like topiary, their sensitive bare backs exposed to the nip of rheumatics and their bearded heads resembling Victor Hugo, or Bébé Bérard.

The vogue for the boxer is at its height. No canine character better deserves it, the bull-dog excepted. The female has all the virtues, friendliness and mother-love, and is so courageous in a fight that one fears for her life. I speak from personal experience of one called Gertrude, given us as a companion, short in the leg, fat as a sausage because overfed, whose bright eyes spangled with grains of gold dust earned her the nickname of "The lass with the golden eyes". She knew how to hate as well as to love, and would bare her teeth behind a curled back black lip to rivals of every race. But to each member of our family, hers by adoption, she meted out an impartial affection amounting almost to an intoxicated vocal display, for boxers sing and do everything but speak, and in this the cats were not excluded. O all you female boxers in your black masks creased with silky wrinkles! Here's a toast in your honour, and I don't mind saying that I am ready even now to be overcome with emotion when you go past me, leaving a trace of your short-haired racial odour, of warm ponies and clean-smelling breath! Your unforgettable way, entering body and soul into the family circle, there to sit and dream as you gaze at the fire, listening to the sound of voices, to thoughts, the last bang of the door closing, the overhead step on the ceiling!

Here, I think, is an *amende honorable* paid to the dog world. I have never boggled over them, but long experience has taught me that we are far too prone to excite the lyrical expression of a communicative dog. Three words in the special doggy tone of voice, a single pat, and a dog, quite unable to control his nerves, will break into his own language. "Get along with you," my mother would scold, "it will soon lead to tears." Handsome she was all the same, a sphinx with precious few secrets, as she sat there among us.

Her name was Gertrude. She used to sit on her creased haunches, like a naked woman, and dream as she stared into the fire. The life of an excitable dog is passing short.

That child, now, crying down there in the Garden, his mouth squarely open . . . He's been crying for some time. He puts me in mind of a Belgian child, who regularly started to cry at meal-times. Four to five years old, with lanky silken locks the colour of butter. In his relations with his weak-minded monther he always made use

305

of the persistence which is the heritage of certain children, persistence on a scale to bring to the parent's face a sort of hunted look in which may be read the fleeting desire to see the death—to bring it about even!—of the child who is crying so shrilly. On one occasion this Belgian child, whose name was Jules, started to cry on sitting down at table and never left off. His soft-hearted mother did not send him packing, did not shut him up in the cellar or in the broom-cupboard.

He continued to bellow, with long-drawn, full-throated yells, while his mother, white as a sheet, said the first thing that came into her head. "Come, come, my pet . . . Jules, be quiet! A big boy like you, getting on for five! You won't get any whipped cream! If you don't shut up at once, Sir, you'll not go to mass—no, I mean the circus. My God, how miserable you make me feel! Why couldn't I have had a child who was dumb! Jules, I beg of you . . . Jules! obey your mother!"

Suddenly the child stopped short in the very midst of a bellow, whereupon the mother's face took on renewed colour and hope. She proceeded to give him crême Chantilly, gâteau de Savoie, dried plums, all of which he gobbled up. Next she treated him like a mother's little darling "was he feeling unhappy then!", and wiped his eyes and mouth. At once Jules started bellowing again, louder and more incurably than ever. His mother stared at him, trembling before the mystery. "But why," she ventured to ask, "why are you crying again?"

He dried up for long enough to answer with composure, "I had not finished crying."

I have never understood it, never tolerated, never made vain use of this outpouring, this crying scandal, this square-mouthed grimace as in the act of being sick. With a sort of horror I view the quaking chin, the convulsive twitch at the corners of the lips, all the apparent signs of a cold in the head magnified twenty thousand times, the blackmail which is all that an access of sobbing amounts to. At the root of this horror of mine is the indignation shown by Sido at the wanton tears of children. Later in my life, I came across a feeling similar to my own in the ugly, providential old English paragon who looked after my daughter for seven years, and who used to say to her when only two and a half "Cry! Are you not ashamed to cry in front of me and in front of your mama? You should no more cry in front of anyone than do your business with the door open!"

In our intimate talks together Miss Draper would make profession of her faith. "Crying is a bad habit, that and no more. My baby doesn't cry when she falls down or has to go up to bed." The catalogue of her infant charge's virtues was interrupted only for the purpose of outlining for the same child a whole series of well deserved punishments. In times of juvenile rebellion and crisis, it was a never-failing satisfaction to me to mark on my daughter's rosy-cheeked face the battle waged with tears, the lip bitten in proud restraint, the struggle, begun so early, for self-control.

Once upon a time, however . . . On one special occasion I had to take my daughter up from La Corrèze to Paris and Miss Draper could hardly be said to have entrusted her to me with good grace. Bel-Gazou was five at the time, and with her fresh complexion and boy's

307

knickers she enjoyed in Paris the success that was her due. For three full weeks, between the circus and the cinema, she never gave the least sign that to be parted from her Nursie-dear was an infliction. It is true that I saw her fetch one or two yawns and occasionally pull a long face, but I put all this down to her Paris diet. Also the suspicion that it might have something to do with the frivolous habits of her paternal grandmother, who wanted to teach Bel-Gazou the tango along with some other social amusements.

We set off on the return journey, the child and I, back to the Limousin fields speckled with cows, and small country houses perched on the tip-top of the little hills. On the train I introduced some subject of conversation which my daughter sifted for the purpose of acceptance or rejection in her usual calm if rather distant manner. As we approached Varetz I pointed out to her, in the setting of the landscape she knew so well, all the wonders she seemed to have forgotten, the osier-beds, the farmsteads, the winding Vézère, haunt of kingfishers. We had no carriage to meet us at the station, but the little toy-train would be putting us down not far from home. I looked out of the window before we drew up and caught sight on the platform of the tall, military figure of Miss Draper.

"Darling! Bel-Gazou! Look, there's 'Miss' waiting for us on the station! Now mind you say how d'you do to her nicely."

There was no question of her saying how d'you do nicely! I had beside me a small creature who had just burst into a flood of tears that were rolling down her velvet cheeks without wetting them. So shaken with

308

emotion was she that she never dreamed of getting down from the train and could only sob " Nursie-dear, ooh-ooh-ooh! Nursie-dear! Nursie! "

There and then I learnt that a very small child can weep for joy in just the same way as a lovesick maid. As for Miss Draper! Never have I seen a gendarme at a country station weep so unashamedly, in full view of his half-section.

Before a moment was out, as we were crossing over the line, my daughter and her nurse were back in their usual state of estimable dissembling. My daughter was painting a vivid description of Paris, with an air of complete disdain for Le Long-Pré nestling among its flowers below her. Stiffly Nursie-dear was thrusting behind her all the seductive pleasures she had never experienced: " If you love Paris so much, you would do better to stay there. For my part, I've found it most peaceful here without you to plague the life out of me! "

The child down there in the Garden is still crying, but intermittently, now that his mother is gone. The enclosure being relatively free from dangers, children can be left there by themselves to learn about life, early and on their own, according to the codes of language and activity established during the last war. The crying ceases each time that the turning-out of a mud-pie (in the proportions of 50 per cent moist earth to 50 per cent droppings of various denominations) makes a call on the child's fingers. After that he starts whimpering again, but without real conviction. Another small boy now comes out from the shelter of the arcades, advances right up to the wire-netting round the lawn, lifts his head and shouts, as

309

though summoning the pigeons, "Nah then, yer two muckers! 'Ave I ter come and take you by the . . ."

His shouts at once arouse a pretty little fair-haired girl, and a big curly-haired boy, who still stumbles as he walks. The trio move off. They are old acquaintances of mine, about whom I know almost all there is to be known, as you are now about to hear. Jojo, the eldest, is seven; he has reached the stage of his first year at school. A Paris street-urchin like so many others. Distinguishing marks: none.. For cheek is not a distinguishing mark.

His sister, la Carrée, is four and a half. She is a pretty child, well filled-out, always with a cold hanging about her.

Their mother is a tired woman. Distinguishing marks: none. Tiredness is not a distinguishing mark in mothers with three children.

The Last, a boy of twenty-nine months.

Jojo, on coming home from school, hurls off his satchel with the authentic heave of the shoulders of an old salt.

"I've made it. I'm taken on."

His Mother: "Taken on? Taken on where? "

"Choir-boy. At Saint-Eustache."

"Since when? "

"I start—Sunday."

"You a choir-boy! I never heard such a thing! You're joking! "

"Joking! I'll say I'm joking! There's money in it— d'you get that! It pays. The pal who put me on to the fiddle has five hundred francs in his money-box already. Talk of a job! You fiddle a bit here, you fiddle a bit there. You say the mass. You fiddle a bit on that. I'm on to something, I tell you! "

310

"All the same, Jojo, you're not telling me that sort of thing can be fixed without the parents' consent! You're still under age—you can't go making your own agreements with curés! Even supposing your father . . . (*There follow many superfluous words that seem to have nothing to do with either Jojo, la Carrée, or the Last.*)

The following Sunday Jojo has a long lie abed, waiting his turn at the foot-bath.

His Mother (*with, for once, superior irony*): "Well, I thought you were going to mass?"

Jojo: "I've chucked it."

"Because why?"

"Because of the time, first. It's too early. And because of the métro. With the price they charge you for fares, I'd be lucky not to be out of pocket. I've given it a miss."

"And how about your tooth?"

"Still in. It moves a bit but it's still in. Look!"

"It's gone on for long enough. Tomorrow I'm taking you to the dentist."

"And what'll that cost you?"

"About two hundred, I don't doubt."

"Bit steep! (*Thinks*) M'man, will you pay me over the two hundred if I bring you the tooth tomorrow?"

"First bring me the tooth, then we'll see."

Jojo (*in the afternoon*). "There you are! (*He puts the small incisor into his mother's hand and then holds out his own.*) My two hundred?"

"Your two hundred! Two hundred francs to a child of your age? Two hundred francs, when a person such as me finds it hard enough to earn as much? I never heard such a thing!" (*Jojo howls. Interchange of loud cries.*

311

Jojo gets fifty francs. Appeasement. Momentary childish-ness.)

Jojo (in good humour): " Hi, la Carrée! What d'you say to a game of marbles? "

Voice of la Carrée: " No! It's raining in the garden."

Jojo: " We'll play on the landing. We'll make the pot in the hole left by the missing tile."

(Silence. Enter la Carrée with blood on her mouth. She is crying, but making no fuss about it.)

Jojo (interested): " What ever's the matter with you? "

La Carrée: " The bit of string cut me. I wanted to pull out a tooth with a bit of string."

Jojo: " Never knew you had one loose. Which tooth is it? "

La Carrée: " No, it's not loose. I wanted to touch fifty francs."

(Explosion of cries in the next room. Maternal cries, and cries from the Last.)

His Mother: " Now what's up with him? What's wrong with him? What a curse it is to have a child like that! Just take a look at him! His mouth all cut to pieces! To go and slash himself like that when he's only twenty-nine months old! What are children coming to these days, I ask you! "

La Carrée (aside to Jojo): " Don't let on. He's been trying to get a tooth out with the tin-opener. He wanted to touch fifty francs! "

Since December we have gone back to being ten at the Académie Goncourt. Lucien Descaves, however, a brisk octogenarian, is kept at home by his great age, a friend

become fragile now and light as a vine-shoot. I have
always enjoyed the Goncourt Lunches, even in the days
of abstentions, frictions, and cleavages, when no more
than five or six places would be laid. If there were not that
little lift at Drouant's, I should certainly be rather cut
off from my enjoyment; but then I could rely on the
clasped hands of three or four men prepared to haul me
up to the salon adorned by the flaky portrait of Edmond
de Goncourt, and there I would settle down content. For
we are a mixed company, fervent in our agreement to
differ and wholly rebellious to the idea of unanimity.
Dorgelès never misses an opportunity of going pop like
a chestnut roasting on a brazier. Carco gets a fit of the
sulks every now and again, when he relapses into silence
and deprives us of the delightful timbre of his voice,
that of a trained singer (the finest voice of any on the
radio!). Larguier has the mischievous humour, and mane,
of a playful lion, and roars in alexandrines. As for Billy?
Billy knows everything that I do not know: that surely
must make him the fountain-head of knowledge!

It is no good my posing as an old buck, for I still
thoroughly enjoy the intensely feminine pleasure of being
the only woman at the Goncourt Lunches, where I sit
surrounded by a veritable Areopagus of men—five, six
eight, nine of them. And real men, worthy of the name—
age does not enter into it—with all the faults and attractions of the male sex. Descaves has to be seen to be
believed when he bangs on the table the size of a wheat-
field, which destroys all confidence and intimacy, or when
he submits the wines to the test of his nostrils or his
tongue, or criticises the cooking; Rosny-jeune too, highly
qualified to be present was a good sight, ruddy-cheeked

as an apple in autumn, his memory and hearing as sound as ever for all his eighty-seven years! I perceive, and derive comfort from the solicitude they do their best to conceal. They have the air, one and all, of remembering the woman I was once. From time to time our dashing last-elect, Gérard Bauer, inscribes a " paper " to me in words affectionate as a love-letter! I should like, as I glance at the round table, to put on record that Arnoux botanises like an angel gardener, and that Carco expounds on the radio his novel method of writing history. But at our meetings one person, and one person only, is sub-jected to our praise or dispraise, the candidate: we do battle solely on behalf of outsiders. And I behave like the others, as I sit among my male colleagues who bear the outward signs of hard work, and often enough of weari-ness and ripe old age, and who, good men and true that they are, lose their tempers, raise their voices, blaspheme. Like any other human beings, they quarrel among them-selves, but, thank heavens, they enjoy their food! Not one among them has lost his zest for writing or his admiration for authors. What else is there, other than this love and devotion, to sustain us, year by year, along the hard high road of the literature we have to read? For read we do. We read a hundred to a hundred and twenty books. We read novels of four hundred up to eight hundred pages long. Once the time has come, we demolish, we scatter to the four winds, the solid brick wall that has lined my room. " Fortunately," say some of my friends in a flippant and knowing tone of voice, " you don't need to know their full contents, you can pick and choose at will." No, that we cannot, even supposing we were so minded. I tell you once again, we read. A strange assembly indeed, that out of ten members numbers ten conscientious readers! Scrupulous, fallible, capable of making allowances for the still immature writer, of doing justice to youthful promise and living to regret it the following year! Does anyone imagine us to be reclining on a bed of roses when the bell rings for the last hour of the competitions? Our perplexities are summed up in a few faintly humorous lines for the evening papers: " With the help of the traditional oysters and the renowned *Blanc de Blanc*, all ten members of the Académie Goncourt are to be found gathered together at this time . . ." But no, no, things were not as gay as that when the time for the white wine and the casting of votes came along. Unanimous on Salacrou, but I could have wished for Anouilh too. Cheers for Hériat, but Miomandre has been too long forgotten. And then, why not Robert Kemp?

For me to feel happy, the Ten would have to be increased to twenty—at least.

This evening my room has the appearance of a robbers' cave: it is one of the days on which a jeweller neighbour of mine amuses himself, and amuses me still more, in pouring out over my table the contents of the velvet-lined case in which he carries round his latest treasures. Before my eyes is a gold clip, studded with sapphires. I can see a snail-shell embossed with turquoises in which has been reset a vivid though half-concealed little watch hardly bigger than a freckle. A heavy bracelet, most delicately wrought for its weight, has contrived to slip out to go and have a drink at my half-filled tumbler, as might a tame grass-snake. It is watched by the green eye of a

315

chrysolite, a massive chrysolite ringed with brilliants, all that could be wished for to load a slender little finger and put the finishing touch to the mauve varnish of a convex nail.

Unguarded, an aquamarine pendant strays under my magic blue to replenish its own blue waters but these have been impounded with the thinnest network of tiny diamonds and enchained with gold. Thus it will have to wait, pendent, till it finds the more favourable shadows of the cleft between two breasts. Now where on earth has that heart-shaped tourmaline disappeared to? A moment since it was playing about with its all but wine-coloured pinks and reds between two turquoises. "Perhaps in the waste-paper-basket," my jeweller neighbour suggests, being a man of dry humour. The walls of my room are splashed with the dazzling glories of a Persian fairy tale as they catch the flashing sparkles from the unfathomable facets of the cut stones. That opaque contribution to the feast of colour—the turquoises—does something to assuage my own particular disorder. My friend and neighbour, the jeweller, assures me that the contemplation of precious stones brings relief to arthritic pains, that the majority of the gems snatched from the bowels of the earth are of beneficent effect. "Beneficent! What about the opal?" —"The opal too."—"But think of its reputation! Think of the well-attested instances when it has brought bad luck!" My neighbour shrugs his shoulders. "There have always existed clumsy folk who can't hammer in a nail without crushing their finger. They will always be with us. Take a particular look at this setting for a ring. I rather think it is my own invention. 'Knitted gold', it is called. Do you like it?"

Its mesh is certainly fine enough to merit the name "knitted"—or "netted", as we used to say in my part of the country—each link atwinkle so that it appears sprinkled with a fine sand of diamonds: definitely, I like "knitted gold". What else is there that I like? This fat chalcedony tortoise, smoky and star-spangled as the night sky over Paris? No, I don't much care for it. It reminds me of an idiotic craze for inlaying the shells of baby tortoises while still alive. That dainty flowering spray of beryls? I don't care for that either. It is too showy for my taste. Let me have, rather, that bracelet of knotted pliant cord, distinctive, oriental, a symbol of wealth and respectability. I praise it unreservedly, I try it on. And since, the Lord be praised, I can admire without coveting, possess all without acquiring, I savour a pleasure which itself is many-faceted, one which stems from a thoroughly Parisian art, the fruit of inventiveness and patience, requiring manual dexterity in a high degree . . . When I dub my neighbour artisan, he blushes with the pride of a man rewarded.

By improving my acquaintance with him, I am able to increase my familiarity with an expansive taste in which I have never indulged. I learn any number of names. I finger the lovely yellow metal, cold at first but quickly warming to the touch, the abettor of so many crimes and wars. More than once, anticipating its eventual recipient, have I held in my hands some gorgeous plaything long promised and awaited with feverish impatience. In the hollow of my hand I have held a precious stone, naked as a slave without a master. I might well have believed it to be a live ember I was smothering, so curiously did its darting red and yellow fires glow within it. But my

317

neighbour shrugged his shoulders. "Pfui . . . that's a mere nothing. Even its name, a fanciful one at that, is of little account. There is not a single orange-coloured stone that is of value. If ever we break away from rubies, emeralds, and sapphires, or struggle to free ourselves from diamonds, we come back for all that to the diamond, the emerald, and the ruby. Or else we have to fall back on these other stones!"

These other stones I find charming, with names suggestive of liquid and transparent essences: the peridot, in which the bronze green always shows true, the vari-coloured tourmaline, the easily accessible ruby spinel, the blue-green aquamarine, ever true to its name; and there is little danger of my forgetting you, my facetious chrysoberyl, green in the morning and turning red at night, such are the pleasing dissonances wrought in you by my blue lantern!

"Well, in that case, why do you not fall back on these other stones?"

But the master of the velvet-lined case showed little else but resignation as far as they were concerned.

"Pretty enough in their way," said he. "Amusing. I quite like using them as paving stones on cigarette-cases, as plaques on belts, as anything on a large scale. Up till now they have mistakenly been put to finicking uses. It would take more than our entire stock of ingenuity to give them what they lack . . ."

"And what may that be? My dear friend, you are on the verge of falling victim to the kind of snobbery that consists in reproaching them for their lack of hardness, popularity, rarity, consistency . . ."

318

He put a stop to my words by raising his hand, before he delivered a disconcerting monosyllable. "No," he said. "The real truth is that they lack the genuine look."

My evening visitors never fail me. Yesterday it was the small grey and green parrot with Maria Lydis. Last week I had that nice little woman, Madame Margat, and her female chameleon. Yes, my dear Miomandre, a female chameleon, just think of it! I doubt her long surviving her tiny mate, killed by our climate. She used to sleep in his arms, and he hugged her tight all the night long. Once bereft of her husband, she no longer wanted to go on living. After a few days she consented to eat a little, but her lustreless skin hung loose. The nice lady who brought her along to me set down her cage on my bench-table, beneath the blue lantern, and slowly, slowly, as if drawn by a magnet, the chameleon started to climb towards the source of light and heat. Once she had reached the roof of the cage, she again became quite motionless. We are always adepts at placing the right barrier, be it roof or wall, between an animal and liberty. Clinging tight by hands and tail to some leafy branches, the chameleon gradually assumed over the surface of her skin the varied harmony of their greens; meanwhile she kept flashing one or other of her eyes towards the lamp, so that they resembled a Directoire lorgnette in miniature.

I watch, I ask questions. I know so little about chameleons. But I had the presence of mind to refer Mme Margat to Francis de Miomandre, and that was something to the good. It was also good to learn from

319

Mme Margat that the small, lovely creature sometimes climbs to the top of a bottle and there reclines her chin on the cork. That in the evening she returns to her solitary abode among the leaves. That she sometimes instals herself in the fruit basket and puts her arm round a banana. That she licks the moist inside of a pear-peeling.

I do not always possess the courage and good sense to turn away from my door those whom I call my "evening visitors", be they birds, cats or dogs. They leave a wake behind them, the mark of creatures with whom I have exchanged credentials. I delight in nothing but their presence, and their departure drives me on to a growing sense of destitution, to a decision to forego the touch and sight of them, the coat, the paw, the deep-set eyes, the smile. My evening visitors normally make my time their own: they keep burning within me the persistent element of a flame, and of a dialogue. The Carcos' poodle (chestnut) deigns to endure boredom here from time to time. The poodle (chestnut) of Hilda Gélis-Didot is next in turn, but derives the same cold comfort. His name is Unic: he vents his impatience in huge sighs, looks at the time, deposits at the feet of his mistress a glove, a leash, a bag—all of them objects of a highly suggestive character. If Hilda pays no attention to them, Unic gives up, makes a melancholy meal off a detective story, or a sandal, or the small hearth brush. What a change is here from the worldly cheer of a parrot! Anatole-of-the-entresol sings, mimics to the best of his ability the bark of a watch-dog, the mewing of a cat, the human voice. And I would advise any burglar to keep away from his curved beak which can cut clean through a cutlet bone.

Yesterday evening the other parrot, the one belonging

to Mariette Lydis, took a strong dislike to his transport waggon when he had to reinstate himself in it. The bird is hardly bigger than a quail and dumb except for a very low cry. Back in his prison again, he took to demanding his immediate release by striking, time after time, three hard blows with his beak against the wooden side in perfect ryhthm: tock-tock-tock . . . tock-tock-tock. There is not a country in the world where prisoners and captives do not talk to each other in the language of tapping. But where had he learnt to count up to three, and even to three times three times three?

In this way there has been built up between animals and myself an understanding which has at times enriched and at others darkened my life. Each of my friends contributes something to it. From America I am sent cuttings from the illustrated papers in which I see that a bluish-grey cat is the model for baby linen de luxe and hats made to her size, that a dozen branches of the New York subway have been immobilised one after the other to allow the rescue of a fine tom-cat that had fallen into the cavity of a ventilation-shaft, that another tom-cat is able to open various locks and latches by a series of combined movements. But "Mimile" Blanchar is just as cunning without her picture ever having appeared in the papers. News from Bordeaux: a fine boxer bitch has just presented to the world a litter of eleven pups! (Madame Colette, what are we to do? They are all quite enchanting, but my bitch will soon be worn out. What advice can you give me?" Answered: "Buy good-milker-nanny-goat.")

News from elsewhere: "Madame Colette, I have at your disposal a pretty little sea-horse." I remember the proposals of Père Raux: "Wouldn't you care for a lovely lion-cub of four months? She sleeps on my bed." No, I do not want a pretty little sea-horse. Not even a tender octopus with great dreamy eyes, like the one that used to snuggle down caressingly into the hollowed hands of its keeper and friend at the Oceanographical Museum in Monaco. Above all, not an ape unjustly punished for its sins by looking like a sad little man!

A lonely little female chameleon; a Polish nightingale; a couple of parrots; a gentle, jovial boxer, Zorro Piguet, the colour of pig-skin, heavy as a tight-packed valise; the tiny pekingese, whose short life was entirely given over to the passionate worship of Germaine Fraysse; Crockie de Polignac, the golden basset-hound subject to nervous pregnancies—it is a short list, the list of my evening visitors. The Eden permitted us has nothing of a Noah's Ark about it.

The only living animal left to me that I can call my own is the fire. It is my guest, and the work of my hands. I know all about covering a fire, succouring a fire. I know the art of surrounding a fire in the open air with a circular trench, so that it may burn up well without "marking" the stubble and setting the ricks ablaze. I am well aware of its dislike of even numbers, that three logs burn better than two and seven than four, and that like every other animal it likes having its belly scratched from underneath.

Between it and me lies an old question which it takes me most of my time to resolve since it burns on my hearth for three-quarters of the year, there in my bedroom which has adopted its colours, red and white, and its presence. I burn it ceaselessly. Ceaselessly, but with a certain thriftiness. I pile it up, but with the air of doling out beggarly alms. I show it that I am a native of a distant province, where everyone learns not to waste wood and bread. I give it its quota of splinters, twigs and dried leaves, and I intend always to have the last word with it— that stand-by of trainers acquired through long dealings with animals. It repays me, by hurling itself upon the least of my offerings; it makes much of me, encourages me in my by now automatic incantations to it: the business of incantation loses nothing by it.

The hearth at which I solemnise my fire worship is of ancient construction and required, I don't mind betting, no more than the hand of a simple mason to build it. Within the precincts of the Palais-Royal we do have here and there some door-furniture and wainscot-panelling of artistic merit, along with a few fine fire-places. The marble has been stripped away from my own and replaced by a sort of pink and beige galantine. No matter, it has kept its intrinsic nature and its appetite for heat, together with that allegiance of permanent fixtures devised to share intimately in the life of man and his rudimentary needs.

Anyone who is given to meditating in front of a fire, during the hours when the shades of night beyond the window panes guarantee him safe protection, need no longer fear being joined at the fireside by the dog and the wolf of twilight—the shudder and the sudden start. Only novices in the art are liable at that time to be assailed so powerfully by age, fright, evil, or a guilty conscience. Let me run through my little incantation.

A fire affords such genial company
To the chill prisoner, the drear night long!
Close by my side there sits a good fairy
Who drinks, or smokes, or sings an ancient song . . .

Whose lines are those? I might almost go so far as to say they are my own, since once upon a time a competition for reading aloud was held in my canton for those of us who, when twelve or thirteen, were made to read with meaning and expression from both verse and prose. A certain well-intentioned man, having heard in our chief town that no child in the district had any conception how to read other than in a monotonous drone, was roused to indignation and, after pointing out the dire peril into which the ignorance prevailing in the department of Yonne could not fail to plunge the whole of France, founded an elocution prize. A red and gold volume, and a diploma, confirmed that at the age of twelve-and-a-half Gabrielle-Sidonie Colette knew how to read, and consoled me for having slurred my words while reading, so that I said "who drink sore smokes", and inadvertently altered the prose of Madame de Sévigné.

A fire affords such genial company
To the chill prisoner . . .

Perhaps these second-rate verses really are mine. Mine as is the fire, as is everything that surrounds me at night.

Poetry does not necessarily have to be beautiful to stick in the depths of our memory, there to occupy most mischievously the place doomed to invasion by certain melodies which, however blameworthy, can never be expunged.

" A fire affords . . ."

Reading at night is a fickle ally. More reliable than a book is the setting I have arranged in honour of the minutes and the hours. I am not always equal to my bouts of insomnia, but I usually succeed in getting even with them by the application of a sort of mental restorative, which drives away fear of the unwonted from my mind and my surroundings. It is not later than three in the morning, nothing at roof-level is yet beginning to pale. By reason of there being a lamp on every pillar, I could count the number of arches along the Palais-Royal from my bed. The inhabitants of this house are so quiet that I never hear a soul at night; but the clatter of my tongs into the grate would ruin the fitful rest of even someone sleeping two doors away. Now, if I am lying here motionless tonight, there is good reason for it, for I can feel stirring within me—apart from the twisting pain, as if under the heavy screw of a wine-press—a far less constant turnscrew than pain, an insurrection of the spirit which in the course of my long life I have often rejected, later outwitted, only to accept it in the end, for writing leads only to writing. I am still going to write; I say this in all humility. For me there is no other destiny. But when does writing have an end? What is the warning sign? A trembling of the hand? I used to think that it was the same with the completed book as with other finished ploys, you down tools and raise the joyful cry " Finished! ", then you clap your hands only to find pouring from them grains of sand you believed to be precious. That is the moment when, in the figures inscribed by those grains of sand, you may read the words " To be continued . . ."

*This book was designed by William B. Taylor
for Heron Books, London*

Printed in Switzerland